What ▮▮▮▮▮▮▮▮▮▮▮▮▮ astoni▮▮▮ ▮▮ ▮▮▮▮▮▮▮ that her blouse was wide open, every button undone. She clutched it feebly to her - which merely served to show up the enticing curves of her bubbies and their swollen nipples, which now strained against the delicate cotton of her garment. 'It gets rather hot in here,' she explained feebly.

I slipped my hand inside her blouse and felt her breast lifting itself toward me in her eagerness. She moved to press herself against me and I took both bubbies into my hands. She collapsed into my embrace and pulled my lips urgently to hers . . .

Also by Faye Rossignol

A Victorian Lover Of Women
Ffrench Pleasures
The Ffrench House
Lord Hornington's Academy Of Love
Pearl Of The Desert
Pearl Of The Harem
Sweet Fanny
Sweet Fanny's Diary
The Girls Of Lazy Daisy's

Smiler's Memoirs Part II

Nude Rising

Faye Rossignol

HEADLINE

First published in Great Britain in 1993
by HEADLINE BOOK PUBLISHING PLC

10 9 8 7 6 5 4 3 2 1

ISBN 0 7472 4209 7

Printed and bound in Great Britain by
HarperCollins Manufacturing, Glasgow

HEADLINE BOOK PUBLISHING PLC
Headline House
79 Great Titchfield Street
London W1P 7FN

Nude Rising

After my father discovered Kitty Bossom's charming little sexual fantasy in my possession, which was in the September of 1897, when I was young and twenty, he told me never to darken his door again. True, I had copied it in my own fair hand from Kitty's original, so he had every justification for thinking it was my own composition. And I could hardly tell him who the real author was, partly because my honour as a gentleman prevented it and partly because Kitty, or Kitten, as I called her, was the sweetest young whore at Lazy Daisy's and I was her macquerau – two facts he would have experienced the greatest difficulty in assimilating.

Thus it was that I moved into my own set of chambers off Headrow, in the centre of Leeds, for good – or, at least, for a good time. I had begun renting the place some weeks earlier, after the betting coup that turned me from an idle scrounger, living at home, into an idle young buck of independent means who was only going through the motions of living at home. It was a most convenient place to bring girls – like Rachel Cohen, the daughter of my father's partner, who lived next door (or next to the door I was never to darken again) and her French maid, Nannette.

It was Rachel who, in a roundabout way, persuaded me to go to Lazy Daisy's, where I first discovered the fine and secret pleasures of the female body. One hot afternoon in the July of that same year, she sported her breasts at me from her sickroom window. My first impulse was to make my way to her that very night, as soon as darkness fell. But then I realized that, though my tool was great, my experience was lamentably small. It was, therefore, out of duty to Rachel and my desire not to disappoint her that I undertook a course of instruction from the delightful young fillies at Lazy Daisy's, then the most famous sporting house in Yorkshire. (Its very foundations now lie buried under the northern 'ring road' of Leeds, alas.)

The pleasure of stretching my naked self upon the soft, curvaceous body of an infinitely willing young girl, of easing her thighs apart, and slipping Iron Jack up into the hot, juicy receptacle that is set a-purpose between her thighs for his unique satisfaction . . . that pleasure, I say, was so shattering, so utterly overwhelming that even now I am amazed I survived those earliest weeks of my lust, to say nothing of the heart-stopping ecstasy that attends its satisfaction. At once I became haunted by a cunny-conspiracy. I sought to spend my purse and my strength in the pursuit and possession of cunny. I dreamed cunny. I breathed cunny. I could not look at a woman, young or old, fair or plain, without imagining those delirious folds of flesh in the fork of her thighs and the spicy arbour they guarded. I still cannot to this very day. It seems I have lived out my life within the confines of one universal cunny.

And it all began at Lazy Daisy's.

It was Kitten and Rachel between them who (again in a roundabout sort of way) helped impose some order upon my obsession. Kitten was the daughter of Sir Charles Bossom of Heatherington Hall, the most offensive prude in all the world. He caught her *in flagrante* with one of the footmen and told her never to darken *his* doors again. In point of fact, the servant had done nothing more serious than finger her a bit and slip his tool up and down her furrow on that one unfortunate occasion when they were nabbed, but her father would have made no distinction in any case. His parting words to his daughter were that she'd no doubt find congenial companions 'at Lazy Daisy's.' It was by sheer good fortune that I was the first fellow to take her upstairs and initiate her into The Game.

We sparked beautifully from the beginning and within a couple of weeks I was her macquerau, which meant that I could sleep every Sunday night with her and look after her during that one week each month when The Cardinal made work offensive. Her father's words were truer than he could ever had guessed. Lazy Daisy's was frequented by judges, bishops, industrial magnates, aldermen, army officers, and members of the nobility. Most of them showed an almost pathetic eagerness to talk with the girls – not just about the most obvious topic of interest, but about anything under the sun. There were no women in their everyday social circle with whom they could converse in such relaxed terms. My darling Kitten, who had been slowly dying of boredom in her stuffy, bourgeois home, absolutely bloomed in this new environment; indeed, she so adored the social aspects of her new trade that she became the most dedicated whore I ever met – a woman to whom no other way of life was even thinkable.

As part of that dedication she persuaded me – her macquerau – to sample the other girls of that glorious establishment, one after the other, and write a report on each. Lord, what a chore! What a sacrifice to ask of a fresh young fellow like me! But I bit the bullet, girded my loins, framed myself to it – as we say in Yorkshire – and screwed all twenty-six of them in the line of duty. Kitten claimed she learned a lot from my reports but I'm afraid it taught me nothing – beyond the discovery that the wellsprings of desire are inexhaustible and that there is no such thing as a bad lay.

I said that Rachel, the amateur, helped me, too. Her unique contribution was to impose a system on those delightful tests, which might otherwise have been no more than twenty-six dizzy bouts of joyful anarchy. During the course of several glorious encounters in my bachelor set she helped me devise, by means of ardent trial and careful revision, the perfect routine for an hour-long screw – a routine that will infallibly reveal a woman's finest talents and her weakest skills in the old four-leg frolic.

I shall probably find cause to mention it again before long.

It is a curious element in human nature that a forbidden pleasure, snatched in the very teeth of discovery, is ten times more acute than the same pleasure when enjoyed under licence in some secure and private place. Why else does marriage pall so swiftly? Why else are nine out of ten of a whore's customers married men, many not two years spliced?

Some lassitude of that sort settled upon me soon after the new year came round. It was nothing very terrible. I mean, it kindled within me no thoughts of the bottle, nor of suicide, nor even of reform; yet I could not deny that some of the zest had gone out of my independent, gay-dog, bachelor life. And thus it was that one bitterly raw January evening, around six o'clock when all the mills were emptying out their day shift, I found myself wandering in a try-anything-once sort of spirit near the canal between Hunslett and the city centre, which was then a notorious haunt of the lowest kind of common prostitute.

Why that particular night? And what strange power guided my feet to the precise stretch where *she* had taken up her pitch – *she* being Clementine, or Clemmy, or Calamity – the girl who was to become my next obsession and to fill almost all my days until spring was well advanced? It is hard at times not to believe that I was not put into this world for a particular purpose.

Actually, it was not Clementine but her mother who had chosen that especially noisome stretch of the canal bank; the girl herself was too drunk to make any sort of choice at all; merely to stay upright demanded all her concentration. I was attracted to them at once – from a distance, that is – because an older woman with a young girl usually turns out to be a mother training her daughter to The Game. Therefore the daughter is usually fresh, juicy, and, medically speaking, clean.

I cursed my luck as I watched first one gentleman, then a second, forestall me. However, I began to *doubt* my luck when I saw with what speed they backed away. And when I in my turn drew close, I very nearly turned and followed them. Even now I find it hard to explain why I did not.

Mother and daughter were both drunk, though the older woman could hold her liquor much better than the younger. She was coherent enough to inform me that her daughter was a virgin and that it would cost me five pounds – and that she, the mother, insisted on being present in a neighbouring room with a connecting door open; she probably thought this showed what a concerned and caring mother she was. The daughter meanwhile hugged her lamppost, hummed a formless little tune, giggled, and by the look in her eyes, tried to decide which one of me was going to be first.

A filthier and more ragged young specimen I think I never saw. Her long, fair (or once-fair) hair was matted and bedraggled. She had rubbed a wet rag of some kind over her face, but that only served to show up the grime along the borders of her hair – and all of her neck – where the cloth had spared her skin the shock of water. She had good teeth but her gums were crimson and weeping blood. Her breath was corruption itself, as if all the drains in town had been thrown open at once. I simply could not believe it was my own voice that said, 'I'll buy her from you for thirty pounds.' [*It would be worth almost £1,500 in modern currency! – FR*]

Nor could the mother. Her daughter continued to 'sing' and sway.

'What'ya gonna do with her?' she asked. Her accent, slurred though it was by drink, was not that of the common

6

poor, who would have said something more like: 'Wha's tha gwin to do wi'er, then?'

'Fatten her and serve her up for dinner,' I said. 'What do you care?' I began counting out her fee.

I doubt she had seen even one crisp, white fiver in her life before that evening – let alone six of them. She snatched the bundle from me the moment I finished, and in the next moment she was gone – leaving me to stare in dismay at what I was now sure was the costliest mistake of my life: a filthy, ragged, drunken young female who could hardly stand, and who certainly could not walk – a female whose breath and body reeked fit to choke me. I had not even the chance to ask if my prize had a name.

Fortunately – if that is quite the word for it – she fetched up most of her guts on the way from the towpath up to the street, which made the cab ride a little less hazardous than it might otherwise have been. She was sober enough to walk the last few paces between Headrow and the door of my set; she had also passed from giggly to tearful and kept throwing her arms about me and calling me her salvation.

The moment we were inside I held her at arm's length and shook her gently but firmly. 'Listen . . . what's-your-name,' I said. 'What do they call you?'

'Cul . . . Col . . . Clamty,' she mumbled.

'Calamity!' I said morosely. 'The parson must have known a thing or two about you. Listen, Calamity. You're going to have the most thorough scrubbing you've ever had in your life – which is probably not saying much. And as for those clothes, I don't think I could even ask the dustmen to remove them. Get them off now and we'll burn them while the vermin are still in them. Come on – you undress yourself while I run your bath. I want to find everything off by the time I get back.'

I set the geyser as hot as flesh could bear it and left the water running while I returned to the sitting room. She was curled up, fast asleep, in front of the fire. I had deliberately not turned up the gaslamps, in case some few shreds of modesty remained to her, and I have to confess that, in that dim light, with only the glow of the firelight upon her face, there was a decided hint of gamine charm about her – or would have been to one who had not seen her earlier.

There was nothing for it, however, but to undress her where she lay and to cast her rags directly into the fire as each was peeled. But first I took the precaution of removing my own clothes – for fear of contamination, of course – and then I shook liberal doses of Keating's Powder into the carpet all around her, creating a *cordon sanitaire* across which her livestock would venture to their death.

It was an almost hopeless task to undress her in any orthodox fashion for her tatters were held about her by a finger-defying mixture of patent safety pins and agricultural twine. In the end I took Kitten's embroidery scissors and simply cut the material from her, from knee to neck. When her skirts fell apart, the stench that arose was of Hull fish market on a hot summer's day with the ice plant out of action; and to make matters worse she was in the height of her courses, with the blood oozing from her crevice and settling in a noisome patch in her dress. Her thighs were caked with congealed blood.

'Thirty quid!' was all I could say to myself. 'Thirty fucking quid!'

I had no idea whether or not it was safe for a girl to bath in hot water in that condition; but I did know that when Kitten had her week off from Lazy Daisy's, it did not prevent her from taking a daily dip – so I decided to chance it. True, the notion of bathing in one's own dilute blood was not appetizing, but when I thought of what other pollutants the water might contain before Calamity's bath was done, the objection receded into insignificance.

I had bathed Kitten several times – and Rachel and Nannette. When a girl has no more than a couple of days' wear-and-tear to remove it is a highly pleasurable experience and can progress quite seamlessly into the most delightful frolic, climaxing in the proper fashion. Of those gratifying occasions not even the memory lingered as I helped Calamity totter and hobble along to the bathroom. Behind us her clothes roared as the flames consumed them and the lice popped like roasting chestnuts.

The bath was already three-quarters full; by the time I manoeuvred her into it, the water was gurgling merrily down the overflow. Within moments of her entry it was discoloured to a thin gruel and there were *things* bobbing on the surface – some of their own volition. I decided to leave the geyser running so as to introduce at least some fresh water, though I feared that for the next twenty minutes at least it would be fighting a losing battle.

It must have been the most pleasurable sensation she had experienced in years. She let out a great sigh of contentment and raised her arms toward the heavens, closing her eyes and smiling like the glowing-with-health woman in the liver-salts advertisement. It was the first moment I saw some small possibilities in her. True, they were only of a physical kind but one has to start somewhere. Her breasts were most alluring – not large but firm and beautifully rounded, with large, dark nipples. The slope of her shoulders was delightfully feminine, a perfect counterpoint to her elegant neck. And the tilt of her firm chin . . . the nice delineation of her smile . . . oh yes, I thought, if this skin would ever come clean and her gums could be healed, all might not be lost.

Her breath, however, made it impossible to stay near her for long. I dashed out to the kitchen and got one of those strong 'imps' of liquorice, which toping husbands suck in the forlorn hope that their wives will never guess they've been drinking. I returned just in time to prevent her from drowning, for she had slipped under the water and was fighting not to breathe it in.

The experience both sobered her and brought her wide awake again. She squinted at me and asked me who I was. Like her mother she was no simple working lass.

'I'm a doctor,' I told her. 'You've been in a little accident but fortunately you've broken no bones. Pop this pill into your mouth and you'll soon be right as rain.'

She peered over the edge of the bath and saw that I was naked, too. She looked at me and frowned. 'Doctor?'

'*That* was the accident,' I explained.

Of course it made no sense to her but at least it shut her up. 'Now I'm going to wash you clean and then examine you,' I said, taking up a sponge and soaping it vigorously.

'Starting with your face. Eyes tight shut.'

It took ten laborious minutes to get the grime out of her skin, just around her head and face. I used all four corners of the flannel, twisting it into the little cones of cloth, to clean out her ears – and there was still employment for a (real) doctor and a proper ear-syringe. I almost gave up on her hair. In a workhouse they'd simply have cut it short and sold it, for it was breathtakingly long and reached down to the small of her back. But a lot of perseverance on my part – and a lot of complaining on hers – had it floating around her like the drowned Ophelia's in the Millais painting. I don't think she had ever seen it so free and languid; and if there was a single moment when her perception of herself began to change, that was it. She ran her hands through it again and again and then stared up at me, quite at a loss for words.

By then the rest of her skin had soaked so long that the grime almost fell off it. I got her to stand up – which she was quite capable of doing by then – while I soaped her long, luscious legs in the most clinical manner possible. Unfortunately Iron Jack let me down by lifting his head like a retriever and banging away at the side of the bath. I had to kneel in a most unnatural – and excruciating – position to hide my distress from her.

It was even more sublime – I mean worse – when the only place I had not washed was in among the folds of that delightful furrow between her thighs. 'Now this,' I said, swallowing heavily, 'is the most important part of my examination. Please do not be alarmed.' And I slipped my fingers down over her belly, on among the silken strands of her bush, and so into that divine cleft at last.

There are artists who can draw hands with their eyes shut . . . pianists who can play any tune after a single hearing . . . everyone has at least one skill literally at his fingertips. Mine is the most intimate knowledge of the folds and rilles of the female quim, from the little *coquille* that hides shyly at the front, beneath that Mound where venery's hunter loves to rest his head, to the soft, wrinkled button of love's alternative grotto. To my fingers they are the Braille of Venus, those secret pleats, those exquisite creases. I read them and am at once in touch with the force that drives the universe. I could have explored happily among Calamity's darling tucks for as long as she'd let me; but I stopped the moment my exploring finger slipped into that most secret den of all and came up hard against the very last thing I expected to find down there – the membrane of an intact maidenhead!

Virgo intacta!

I had to feel it several times before I could induce myself to believe it. This drunken, verminous girl from the canal bank had somehow come through heaven knows what ordeals of poverty and deprivation with her virginity unscathed! It was probably the first time such a thing had happened in a hundred years. It might even be the first time such a thing had *ever* happened. Usually the sort of girl who 'descends' (her word for it, not mine) to selling herself down along the canal had been screwed by her brothers almost from infancy, and later by her father and whatever 'uncles' may take his place when he is resting at Her Majesty's pleasure.

Of course, it entirely changed my attitude to Calamity. I had already put all thought from me of enjoying her that night, and possibly for several nights to come. Now I realized it was not for me to decide when to exercise those 'rights' at all. If we were to enter into any kind of liaison, it would not be because I had paid her mother thirty pounds but because Calamity herself now decided it.

In strictly logical terms, of course, my scruples were absurd. But virginity, especially in a woman, is one of those magical-mystical states that transcends all logic. To have behaved otherwise would have been to descend (my word for it – and I hope yours) to the level of a brutish beast.

But at least I was not entirely without hope in the matter, for while my finger explored those landscapes where he is most at home, Calamity lay at her ease in the bath, eyes closed, a light, dreamy smile playing about her (mercifully closed) lips, and little sighs of happiness distending her nostrils.

'Come on,' I said at last. 'Let's dry you off and see if you can hold down a little broth. You don't look as if you've eaten for a week.'

She was like a child, willing to be led into almost anything as long as it was suggested in a pleasant enough manner. Rubbing her down with the towel produced the biggest surprise of all, for the skin came off her in great rolls – like you get on a breadknife if you try to slice a loaf hot from the oven. I'll swear she lost a good half-inch in girth, so much old skin fell off her at the pluck of my towel.

And everything was now a wonder to her. It must have been like lifting a veil or pulling rubber plugs out of her ears. Her nerve endings were now able to feel things for the first time in months, perhaps even years. Every touch was exquisitely ticklish – and erotically arousing, too, though whether she was sexually aware of herself I had my doubts. But her nipples swelled, her pupils grew large, and her breathing was mildly disordered.

It was a beginning, at least.

She snored contentedly in my bed, wearing a pair of my pyjamas, while I sat beside her, gazing at her scrubbed and polished little face and pondering the mysteries of virginity. I confess I was rather surprised that my response, on finding that Calamity was still, incredibly, a virgin, was to leave her untouched. I ought to have jumped over the moon – or right on top of *her*, at least. Wasn't she the very thing I had been seeking? My easy copulations with the likes of Kitten, Rachel, and Nannette had obviously failed to satisfy *something* within me – otherwise why had I gone down to the canal banks that night? It must have been in search of something they were failing to provide – but why seek it there, among that swinish herd of females?

Well, the only reason I can think of for consorting with swine is to discover the pearl that someone may have been foolish enough to cast before them! And hadn't I done just that? Hadn't I bought her, too, in a fair and unforced transaction with her mother? So why did I now feel I had to treat my discovery, my purchase, as if she were a free agent? Why did I feel I must now court and seduce her as one who owed me nothing? It was baffling.

Or was I being altogether too pious by half? I had spent

a blissful summer poking about three dozen fabulous young fillies; hardly a night had passed but my dear old spermspouter had shot his sweet benedictions high into the belly of one or other of them. However, apart from Rachel and Nannette – and Kitten, after I became her macquerau – all of them had wanted money before they'd open up the gates of paradise and let me in; and, no matter how good a value they gave once the coins were jingling in their grasp, it remains a fact that the fun of poking a girl who has no choice but to lie on her back and let you pump away is as nothing compared to the thrill of the chase and the final, *willing* submission of a spirited filly. Perhaps that was the missing element I sought that night – a girl who would more likely say no than yes. If so, I was the biggest fool on earth to go seeking her down by the canal. So perhaps my uncharacteristic respect of Calamity's virginity was a way of endowing her with that exciting power nonetheless?

Such, at least, were my thoughts that first night of all. How fatuous they seem now! And how fatuous they were to seem within a mere twenty-four-hours – but I shall come to that anon.

I left her sleeping and settled to a rather uncomfortable night on a chaise longue designed for a far more active pursuit than sleep.

'What in heaven's name is *that*!' were the words that awakened me the following morning.

I opened one bleary eye and saw with dismay that the clock was gone ten; with even greater dismay my other bleary eye discovered that Kitten had come somewhat early to my chambers – in fact, a whole day early by the Cardinal's calendar.

'Why am I sleeping out here?' I asked huskily, sitting up for the first cough of the day.

'Because there's some . . . *thing* in your bed,' she replied with distaste. 'It looks human and it appears to be female, but it stinks like an ancient midden.'

I remembered then. 'I thought you weren't coming until tomorrow,' I protested.

'Obviously,' she answered sharply.

'She's a virgin,' I told her. 'That's why I'm sleeping out here.'

'Are you ill?' Kitten asked, full of concern. She sat down and felt my brow; finding it cool merely deepened the mystery. 'Well, there must be *some* explanation,' she said thoughtfully.

I responded with the first thing that came into my head: 'I had the most wonderful idea last night. You'll be amused, I know. I was sitting here, thinking of you – an educated, accomplished girl out of the very top drawer of society – and how superb you have become at your chosen profession – and in so short a time . . .'

She interrupted: 'My heart sinks at every fresh compliment, Smiler, but do go on.'

'And I just got to wondering – suppose one took a girl from the very opposite end of the social ladder – a girl who could hardly sink lower – eh? Do you imagine one could teach her so that, in two or three months, say, no one could tell her and you apart?'

Kitten's head sank between her shoulderblades.

'Smiler!' she murmured with affectionate weariness. 'You are a most incurable romantic!' She nodded toward my bedroom door. 'Does it have a name?'

'Calamity. Or something like that.'

Kitten began to laugh. 'Something *very* like that, I'm sure!'

Our conversation was interrupted by the girl herself, who appeared in my bedroom doorway, pale and drooping. 'Gonna be sick,' she murmured.

She almost fell against me as I rushed to catch her. I got her bent over the lavatory bowl just in time for her first heave. Nothing came up, however. Not on that nor on any subsequent heave. I hugged her from behind, pressing hard into her abdomen to take the strain off her muscles. Iron Jack, of course, went stiff as a crowbar but I kept him penned back between my thighs; Kitten, standing behind me, saw what was happening and, crouching down at my tail, teased him without mercy, giggling the while.

But I didn't mind. Calamity was all woman – with her slender waist and the gorgeous swelling of her hips and the pneumatic roundness of her young bottom, she was going to be a prize worth pursuing.

Eventually she stood up straight, wiped a few flecks of spittle off her lips, and smiled at the pair of us. 'That's better,' she said. 'Got any gin?'

I stood up, too, and rearranged Iron Jack among the folds of my dressing gown, which I was now able to tie around me. 'Can she borrow some of your togs?' I asked Kitten.

I'll be damned if she may,' was her generous reply.

'Just so we can go out and buy her some of her own.'

'What did she arrive in?'

'I burned it all. It was . . .' I bit my tongue off.

'Full of livestock!' she said. 'And you want me to lend you some of my things! How can you!'

We argued in that vein for some time, getting pettier and pettier with each exchange – about who had paid for them in the first place . . . her money . . . my money . . . what a superb (or deplorable) steward I had proved. In the end she simply put her foot down and told me that either Calamity went or she did. By then I was too hurt to see sense, and being stubborn by nature anyway, told her she could go anywhere she liked – and take everything with her.

She must have begun to regret her impetuousness even then (I know I did), for her parting words were actually a promise to return after a cooling off. 'I'll give you three months, Smiler,' she said. 'I'll bet you can't turn that blowsabella into a high-class *fille de joie* in three months.'

'Who'll be the judge?' I sneered.

'The madame of the high-class maison that accepts her, of course.' She smiled sweetly and was gone.

I did not ask where she was going – nor did I need to. Lieutenant the Hon. Wellesley O'Toole de North–Tooley to his friends – had been badgering her for weeks to let him set her up in a little apartment, quite near my parents' home in Park Villas.

Perhaps all she wanted was a change of partner.

I went out and got the barest minimum of clothing for Calamity, intending to take her into the city and buy her a full wardrobe – with especial emphasis, of course, on the most sensual and lascivious underclothes in the whole of Leeds. Girls have no idea what treasures they possess until a man starts embellishing them. Then they cotton on soon enough!

However, I returned with my rather spartan collection of housemaid's clothing only to find her turning my place upside down. Bottles, it seemed, were the only things that interested her. Every bottle I possessed – from liquid paraffin to lamp oil – had been unstoppered and opened, and no doubt sampled, too, before being set to one side in mounting anger. By the time I arrived she was in a high old fury. 'Where's t' fookin' gin?' she yelled at me.

I slapped her hard across the face and told her she'd get another slap, just as hard, every time she swore. She had no idea what I meant. Every other word was fookin' this and fookin' that with her. She learned fast, though. Half a dozen more slaps, none quite as hard as the first, expunged the word from her vocabulary for several hours. But how to treat her craving for gin . . . I had no idea.

I recalled a wedding service I attended, at which I got a severe attack of hiccups. I tried everything – holding my breath, breathing extra fast and deep . . . I even went out to the graveyard tap and drank upside down – all to no avail. When I returned to my pew my Uncle Tommy (who is, in fact, only a year or two my senior) accused me of feigning the attack. He held out a sovereign and whispered that it was mine – *if* I could produce one genuine hiccup to his satisfaction. Of course, it cured me completely; the harder I tried, the more impossible it became.

I could not see a direct application of this technique to poor Calamity's craving but I did the best I could. I told her that if she could describe her craving for gin so vividly that I began to feel the same way myself, I'd go out and buy a bottle between the pair of us.

First she refused and just sat there in a sulk. Then she made a feeble attempt at it, and gave up again. But then something in her imagination caught alight and she said, 'It's like a 'uge, dry desert filling thy belly, or a dry ocean, with great waves of dryness lapping up into thy throat. It's like the biggest ache tha ever knew. A wanting that bad it stops tha thinking on aught else . . .'

After a few more of these heartfelt descriptions I was ready to yield and go out and buy her some mother's ruin. But, to my amazement, she appeared to have forgotten why she was performing this trick. The performance itself had taken her over. She was drunk again, but drunk on the power of her own words. It was only the (genuine) dryness of her throat that halted her at least – with the immortal words, 'Could uz 'ave a drink o' watter?'

She remembered her original purpose then and burst out laughing. Partly, of course, she laughed at how far her enthusiasm had carried her from her original purpose; but partly it was to express an unexpected sense of friendship with me – that I had been astute enough to point her along this path, wind her up, and let her go. It was the first, hesitant beginnings of a sense of trust between us – something that (thank heavens) undermined the inevitable teacher-pupil or benefactor-beggar relationship, which was all we had to start with.

'Calamity,' I said, 'you know what you need even more than gin?'

She shook her head but was willing to be told it.

'Some medicine to heal your gums. They're appalling! Surely they give you a lot of pain, too?'

She shrugged stoically.

'I know a good dentist,' I went on – carefully avoiding the name of tooth-puller, which was the only one she probably knew. 'Shall I ask him to come here and take a look at you?'

She nodded, and touched my hand aimlessly. I don't think she knew how to say a thank-you.

I raised the hand she had touched and gently brushed her on the cheek. 'You're actually a very pretty girl,' I told her. 'If you had good gums and carried yourself better, you'd be quite beautiful.'

She eyed me with the deepest suspicion. 'What dost'a want o' me?' she asked.

I laughed. 'A silk purse,' I said.

'Ah, well,' she replied, taking my words literally, 'I can sew as good as any.'

We ate a plate of porridge and, when I was sure she'd be able to keep it down, we went out to buy her some more clothes – but not the voluptuous set I had in mind at first, just ordinary, pretty clothes to take her along the first few steps to self-appreciation. As we happened to pass my dentist friend on the way back, we popped in to see if he could take a look at her there and then. I expected him to be appalled the moment Calamity opened her mouth, but all he said was, 'Oh, yes! This'll clear up quite quickly. Nothing chronic here – it's all fairly recent. You haven't eaten much lately, have you, Miss?'

Calamity simply shook her head and stared at him. 'Lately' was just a fog to her – also no one had called her Miss in a long time, if ever.

He gave her a bottle of alum dissolved in some liquid, which he said she was to swill around her gums and spit out every hour during the day. 'That should clear it up inside a week. Come back then and we'll see if there's any local ulceration.' To me he confided that her teeth were 'bloody marvellous.' He thought she must have been rather well fed in her childhood; if she'd fallen on hard times (which he surmised from the fact that *I* was her squire!), it had been fairly recently – three or four months at most.

She was so happy with the new medicine that half the bottle had gone by evening; when I sniffed it I discovered that the liquid part of it was a dilution of absolute alcohol – then, of course, her eagerness was explained. After that I doled it out – which she took in good part.

I had a meal sent in to us from the restaurant round the corner – roast capon in good giblet gravy, followed by spotted dick and custard. Although her breath was greatly sweetened and her dress respectable, her table manners would have got us thrown out of any eating house in town. I showed her how to wield a knife and fork and she copied me. Soon there was a strangely puzzled look in her eyes.

'Dost ever 'ave that feeling thou's done it all before, Smiler?' she asked, turning the eating irons over and over.

'I've dreamed of yon things – I'll swear it.'

For her sake we drank an Entre-deux-mers with the meal, too sweet for my taste but an excellent wine for absolute beginners. She gulped it like water at first but was quick to learn to savour each sip. She was what actors call 'a good study' – that is, she learned with amazing speed. Several times she said she felt she'd done all these things before, perhaps in another life. I did not press her for details of her past life because, like a good barrister, I knew how dangerous it can be to ask questions when you have no inkling what answer you're going to be given.

After supper (and the washing up – a process that fascinated her) we played Beggar-my-neighbour. She said she had never seen playing cards before, and I believe she spoke the truth, but she learned their values within a few hands, and was soon beating me to the count each time. So she was pretty nifty at sums, too. The enigma of Calamity Whatever-her-name-was grew more intriguing by the hour. And yet, in a curious way, I did not want to clear it up; I found myself precisely poised between wanting to know *everything* about her and wanting her to retain every shred of her mystery still – so that I would know nothing beyond what I actually observed and experienced.

Again we slept in perfect chastity – or at least we set out to do so. She took my bed and I made up a mattress on the floor beside it, so that we could continue to talk as long as we wished. I left two long candles burning and tried to start several conversations but she answered in the barest monosyllables, with a great deal of sighing and throat-clearing in between. Then her quilt slid down on top of me

23

and, in putting it back, I realized that her bed was shaking like a jelly.

I was intrigued, of course, for I thought she was diddling herself – which would also explain the sighs and the grunted replies. 'What are you doing?' I asked in an encouragingly naughty tone.

To my horror she burst into tears and told me she couldn't help it.

I assured her it was nothing to be ashamed of – in fact, most girls did it, once they learned the art of it.

'What?' she asked in horror.

'It's true, honestly,' I assured her.

'The art of *what*?' she asked. 'Where's the *art* in lying in bed, shivering to death for want of a sup of gin?'

Then, of course, it was my turn for sighing and throat-clearing.

After a longish silence she asked, 'What didst'a think I meant, then?'

I floundered. 'Oh, nothing really.'

But she persisted in her questioning and so forced me to a decision I might not otherwise have dared take for several more nights. I confess that lust and impatience played their part, yet my chief motive was this:

I had observed several times that day how her craving for gin could be pushed aside by any intense preoccupation of her mind; I wondered if the same might also be true of her senses. Could one powerful craving be supplanted by another? A craving for Iron Jack would be most congenial to my own purpose, too, of course, but little did I know what a Pandora's Box I was about to open!

'It'll be much easier if I show you,' I said. 'May I get into bed with you? You needn't be afraid.'

She laughed. ''Tis thy bed, maister Smiler. I don't know why tha didn't get in from t'first go.'

That plunge into the bewitching, vixeny warmth of her sheets was one of the most exciting moments of my life. I was still too afraid of the infection in her gums to risk kissing her on the mouth but I ran my lips in a gentle caress along her cheek and asked her if she found it nice.

'Mmmmm!' was all she replied.

I widened the exploration to include her ear and breathed out gently upon it. She gave out a little squeak of delight. I started to run my tongue around its folds and ridges and her responses deepened to a moan. Iron Jack was by now on fire and hammering away at my navel. I pressed him hard against her hip, where she must have felt him throbbing away, though she said not a word and made no movement, either to encourage him or to withdraw herself from his ardent pressure.

And so, inch by inch over the next half hour, I waged a campaign of thrills upon her passionate, virgin body. I caressed her neck with my lips . . . with the tips of my fingers . . . with the gentlest raking of my nails; shivers ran through her once again, but as different as could be from the shivers of alcoholic craving. I explored the fine twists and turns of her collarbones, especially the darling dimples, which some call 'salt cellars,' at the base of her neck; the shivers were reinforced by low moans of happiness.

More and more daring were the sweeps of my exploring fingers – down . . . down over the soft flesh at the tops of her breasts – always stopping just short of her nipples, which drove her to a frenzy. Softer and more languorous grew my caresses, while her whimpers of pleasure became almost continuous. At length, when she realized that the buttons of her pyjama jacket were inhibiting my movements, she ran a skilful finger up the division and neatly popped each one. And in case I missed her point, she took my hands and pressed them hard against her breasts.

Ah, breasts – what adorable things they are! Bubbies, bosoms, dairies . . . call them what you will, those two swellings, firm and soft, warm and full – a little larger than an easy handful, perhaps, and yet beautifully formed – they are surely the finest playthings ever devised, and infinitely pleasurable to man and woman alike. There are so many things one can *do* with them – some of which I now revealed to dear young Calamity, first as she lay on her side with her back spooned into me, then as I lay on my back with her lying face-up, half across me, and finally, turning her over so that she lay upon me, face to face.

All this while, though I had cupped her gorgeous breasts and caressed them in the palms of my hands, I had carefully *not* favoured her actual nipples with any special attention. Now, when she lay on top of me, tormented with desires she had never felt before in all her life, scourged by lusts she could not possibly understand – now was the moment to introduce her to the sweet, sharp pleasures that lay dormant still within her nipples, ready to tingle her half to death. I slipped down the bed until her breasts hung like ripe fruit over my face and at once began to tease her nipples with my lips, my tongue . . . my teeth. They were already engorged with her erotic desire; now they swelled until I feared the skin of them would burst open.

She gasped and, letting out a cry as of a girl in the ultimate throes of her ecstasy, collapsed upon me, almost smothering my breath. *An easeful death!* I thought as I toyed with the notion of letting myself be stifled by those delectable bubbies of hers. She did not lift herself away until she felt me begin to fight for breath.

'How dost'a always *know*, Smiler?' she asked in an awed kind of murmur.

'Know what?' I asked between grateful gulps of air.

'What I want thee to do next.'

'Has no man ever done these things with you before?' I asked.

'Eay, I don't know,' she replied. 'I don't know a lot of what's gone on lately. I've bin reight down in't bottom o' a jug o' gin most days – and neights.'

I wriggled in my pyjamas until Iron Jack leaped free and beat the air between her parted thighs. I spread my own beneath her, got my knees outside hers, and pulled them together, clenching tight on my hot, throbbing plaything.

She gave a little squeal of surprise and exclaimed, 'What's that?'

'You've never felt such a thing before? Never seen what men have down there?'

She wriggled a hand down between us and grasped the old fellow firmly. 'Nay!' she murmured. 'What can it be?'

'Can't you guess? What have you got down there?'

'Nought like that!' she exclaimed fervently.

'You're wrong,' I told her. 'You've got something almost identical to that.'

'I never 'ave!' she asserted stoutly, and began untying her pyjama cord to prove it to me.

'You have,' I repeated. 'You're just not thinking of it the right way round. We've both got a tube of flesh down there. The only difference is that mine sticks out while yours . . .?'

She giggled. 'So it does and all!' she gasped.

'I wonder why?' I said innocently – before her quick brain leaped to the same point.

She collapsed on me again and beat my shoulder tenderly with her clenched fist. 'Th'art doing it again!' she accused. 'All this while I've had a feeling down there – like being hungry, like wanting to piss and not being able to, like – don't laugh, now – but it were like wanting to breathe through that hole. Here! Shall us see if they fit?'

'Later,' I murmured, finding her nipples once again with the sides of my thumbnails. 'There's lots more fun we can have before we get to that.'

She wriggled her nakedness happily against mine and did not argue.

Over the next heaven-knows-how-long we did all that lusty boy and lissome girl can do short of entering into that ultimate embrace. We writhed like oiled serpents, over, under, and around each other, twining our limbs in ways that would have challenged Leonardo himself to record. Our hands, lips, tongues explored every passionate inch of each other's flesh – until at last (by what sequence of embraces and caresses I could not even begin to describe)

I found myself with my face poised above her divine fork, ready to plunge into her forest and there enjoy a feast for the gods, the ambrosia and nectar that pour in such prodigious floods from the quim of an excited young girl.

As she felt the first dainty flicker of my tongue among the delicate whorls of fur on her Venus mound she drew her thighs up and flung them wide apart, reaching her cornucopia of joys toward me – those engorged, pouting lips begging for more. By the light of our two candles I saw the ardent little jewel of her clitoris, glistening coyly among the folds of her labia. One of the secrets of pleasuring this most delectable organelle is to begin by laying one's tongue flat against it with no more than moderate pressure and then holding it still – or what you fondly believe to be still. In fact (as you may see for yourself if you peer into your open mouth in a looking glass) the human tongue is never still. It heaves, it writhes, it subtly alters its length and width and thickness – and these gentle, impulsive movements are all the exquisitely tender flesh of the clitoris requires to start her swelling and throbbing with the delights and thrills of arousal. Later, when your love is twitching madly and thrashing up and down, held in the invincible grip of ecstasies too sweet to bear, you may begin a gentle, provocative massage that will detonate raptures within her so powerful they will seem like the kick of a mule.

In that way, I brought my luscious Calamity to the first great orgasm of her life. She almost knocked my teeth out with the violence of her spasms; you would have thought she was lying on some bare electrical cable, so frenzied were her convulsions. At last, her poor, pleasure-racked frame could bear no more and she slipped into merciful oblivion.

And while she lay there, dead to the world and fighting for breath, I slipped briefly from our bed and prepared a lamb's bung for use.

Young men today, who have probably never even seen a lamb's bung and who use only the rubber-condom type of sheath, can have no idea what delights they are missing. The bung is the skin of a blind gut, or appendix, in the belly of a lamb, which, by the kindness of Providence, is of a perfect size to accommodate the male wand in a state of rampant excitement. I used to get them by the gross, properly cured and dried, down at the abattoir. In that state they have neither flavour nor odour; when I first saw them I thought they were the dried up seed pods of some unknown plant – round, flat, creamy silver in colour, and about the size of a half-crown coin.

The best way to put one on is for the girl to soften it in her mouth and then use her lips and tongue to slip it over the knob of your spermspouter and tease it gently down around his shaft. It is as flimsy as a sausage skin and yet is many times more robust. It fits snugly on all but the very smallest of organs – and I have never heard of one large enough to burst it. Being a natural membrane, it has all the give and take of a man's own skin – so much so that I have many times brought myself up sharp in the middle of poking an eager amateur (naturally, I don't wear any sort of sheath with professionals), cursing myself for having forgotten to put on a bung – only to withdraw and find I had, after all, remembered! That's how fine they are – in every sense of the word.

On that night with Calamity I prepared the bung for use, as I said, but did not immediately put it on. Despite the depraved circumstances in which I had found her, I felt she was as innocent of carnal affairs as any girl half her age. What was more, she was as innocent of guilty feelings about it, too. So if I could enlighten her into the merrymaking ways of men and women – without introducing that dreadful sense of guilt which was almost universal in my young days – I considered I should be doing her the greatest favour possible.

When she regained her senses, therefore, she found me once again spooned in behind her, with Iron Jack as lusty as ever, lodged tight the full length of her cleft. She gave a little squeal of pleasure and clenched every muscle she possessed down there, quite involuntarily; it was a gentle squeeze but he answered with a bucking kick that sent her into further rhapsodies.

Then, with all the ponderous strength of a mighty locomotive starting up a long incline with a vast train behind it, I began to pump that piston of hard gristle up and down, up and down, the full length of her warm and juicy furrow. At the tail end of each stroke I withdrew him far enough to let his swollen head linger on the soft button of her bumhole, and then I slid him forward again until he burst out at her front, his one eye peering up at her Venus mound and bush.

At the start of many a stroke I tempted myself with the thought that it would take very little change of angle to deflect him up into that virgin shaft, there to revel in the caress of flesh that had never known the touch of manhood before. I could feel her willing me to do it, though it was more of an instinctual urge with her than a matter of conscious desire. How I resisted the temptation I cannot say, but I was determined she should understand what powerful forces were now at play between us. And so I held to my plan.

After many a long, luscious stroke I felt her hand steal down to her groin, where it lay in wait to ambush Iron Jack on his next appearance. She pounced the moment he nosed out, thrusting aside the exquisite flesh of her labia and thighs as he emerged. Left to himself, of course, he could not avoid parting company with the front winkle of her vertical smile, where it curved round and upward toward her belly. But that was where her darling little *coquille* peeped slyly out, begging for a little tender attention. The silent scream of frustration from that rabid little organelle – which can drive girls to excesses of which men can only dream – now drove my dear Calamity to press upward on my spermspouter, keeping him firmly in the banana curve of her chink until, like Esquimeaux lovers, he and her dear little Clitty could rub noses.

From their first moment of contact she was gripped in the throes of another mighty orgasm; but this time, because she could control it to some degree – by pressing harder or more gently beneath my old pal – she kept herself on the boil without exploding into unconsciousness. I need hardly tell any male reader of these memoirs how exquisite a sensation it is when the delicate fingers of a young girl not only press the tip of a man's tool tight into her crevice but vary their pressure in time with her own gurgles of ecstasy; and female readers may like to know that, in the entire range of amatory gymnastics, there is hardly anything more gratifying to their male partner than that.

And, to be sure, it was not many strokes more before my spermspouter was ejaculating, too – great gobbets of hot sticky into the cupped curve of her hand. She plucked it away, more in surprise than distaste, but I clamped it back and held it while she felt how my spending surged out, how Iron Jack kicked and throbbed with each ecstatic pulse, and how, over two to three dozens spasms, he went from violent tics, each of which send fresh gushes of sticky into her hand, to the minutest little flutters that hardly registered at all on the sexual earth-moving scale.

Gingerly I withdrew altogether and assisted her to sit up. She cupped both hands tight and held them toward the candlelight, staring in fascination at the limpid pool they now shared between them. 'What *is* it?' she asked in an awestruck whisper. 'It looks like collar starch.'

Out of the corner of her eye she caught sight of Iron Jack – who was certainly lacking in starch at that moment. She giggled. 'Is that what made yon thing so stiff?' She offered her hands towards him. 'Shall us try and squeeze it all back inside him again?'

'Do you really and truly know nothing at all of these matters, Calamity?' I asked her.

'Nay,' she said stoutly. 'How could I?'

'Well then let me tell you – that "starch" is what men put inside women to start the babbies growing.'

'Eay!' she exclaimed. 'But how?'

'You just saw how – or felt it. Imagine if Iron Jack here had been up inside you . . . where you suggested a while back. Imagine him throbbing hard and shooting out that "starch" the way you felt it coming into your hand. The little babbies you've got inside you, ready to grow – they're no bigger than the head of a pin, you know – if they felt *that* come knocking at their door, they'd soon quicken into growth, don't you think!'

'Ooh, heck!' She bit her lip like a naughty girl caught red-handed and looked for somewhere to hide the 'evidence' she held in her palms. Then, on a sudden inspiration, she clamped both hands to her bubbies and massaged it in like a skin cream!

The mere sight of it brought Iron Jack back to attention at once – those beauteous orbs, at once so soft and so firm, gleaming in the candlelight, soaked in *my* sticky . . . it was more provocation than I could bear. I bore her down upon her back, to which she offered no resistance, and straddled her, my knees wide enough apart to let my Lad – now hot and hard once more – rest between the two pale, quivering jellyfish of her bubbies.

In the next moment I gathered them up, pressing them hard against my gristle while, once again, I pumped him slowly but vigorously up and down between them. She understood at once and, clasping her hands behind her head, peered down to watch in happy fascination.

To ensure that she gained at least some sexual pleasure out of this new encounter I began to favour her nipples with gentle, teasing caresses with the sides of my thumbs. But she put up her own hands and made me stop. 'I'll just keek at thee,' she said, 'if it's all the same to you.'

A short while later a new glint of devilment shone in her eye and she craned her head forward to try and tickle my knob with little darts of her tongue, each time he came questing forward out of the warm haven between her breasts. Naturally, I thrust him onward to the utter limit at each plunge; and I began pumping him faster, too. She giggled like a girl only half her age and several times I felt the gentlest nips of her teeth as well.

These delightful exercises soon had the predictable effect. 'Watch!' I gasped as my exertions rose in a crescendo. 'Going . . . to spurt . . . again!'

She stared, open-mouthed in wonder, as the second great sperm-gush flew like fleshy little bullets from my one-eyed Polyphemus. Indeed, her lips were opened so wide that my second wad impacted hotly on her tongue.

The idea must have hit both of us simultaneously for as I moved up the bed, she moved down, and her mouth closed around Iron Jack – as warm and snug as ever a man could wish – at the very moment he throbbed with his next libation. Like a starving calf she sucked; I swear that if the automatic milking machine had not already been invented, I would have filed my patent the following morning. And just as that agricultural marvel gets a pint more from any cow than she will yield to a milkmaid's hand, so Calamity's mouth, working frantically on my old man, sucked more sticky out of him than ever he yielded to *my* milking hand (or that of any girl at Lazy Daisy's, either, come to think of it).

The moment I'd fired my last tiny libation she swallowed the lot and exclaimed, with a triumphant laugh, 'Now I s'l have thy bairn, Smiler.'

I was too exhausted to explain that it didn't work like that.

Being somewhat dehydrated by then, I rose and made us both a strong cup of beef tea – and was delighted to discover that it put the beef back into Iron Jack yet again. That is to say, now that he had some beef inside him, he longed once again to be back inside some beef! I am happy to add that it also revived Calamity's desire that the beef Iron Jack would hide in next should be hers!

I was determined to slip bareback into that beautiful, untouched vagina. Not that the wearing of a bung would make it any the less exquisite for me – indeed, the mere physical sensation would be identical in either case. But I was gripped by a much more primitive urge – that mine should be the first actual man-flesh to stir those sensitive membranes, to awaken them with its kiss, to thrill them with its dance. And that was why I had taken such care to tap off my excess *joie de vivre*, my superabundance of sticky, before attempting the critical and hazardous ascent into that virgin paradise.

First, however, I wanted to be sure that her juices were flowing again, so I laid her on her back, parted her thighs wide, and settled between them, my head at her spread-eagled form, ready to gorge my fill of that innocent beauty. I have gazed into the quims of thousands of females, of all ages and races, and I have never seen two identical. Calamity's was everything one would expect of a girl who had never yet lain with a man. The outer labia were fine and slender, with perfect curves – like two parentheses (). The hair of her muff was auburn, downy and sparse. The inner labia were pale, like mother of pearl; they began as two ridges, parallel to the outer lips, but as they parted around her holey-of-holeys they branched into many folds, all whorled and feathery. Kitten's quim had been like that once, but it had long since fleshed out and darkened, engorged with chronic sexual excitation from the hundreds of lecherous tools that had rutted away between them, hour after hour, day after day.

It is a curious paradox that I hardly ever poke a *fille de joie* without first gazing at her quim and trying to imagine the last half dozen cocks that thrust their way in and out of that hole – short fat ones; thin, wonky ones; slender columns with huge knobs . . . I've imagined them all, piledriving in and out between those indefatigable lips, which go on smiling the vertical Gioconda smile to one and all. I imagine them, too, swelling and kicking as they pump the essence of their rapture as high into her belly as they can thrust. I see them shrinking and falling out, dragging the gravy of their feast in their wake. And then the thought of shoving my own lustful spermspouter up into the remnant stickies of half a dozen other men merely doubles and redoubles the pleasure I derive from that same divine dance.

Yet it is as nothing to the much rarer pleasure of gazing into the vertical smile of a virgin, and kissing it, and playing up and down it with my tongue, and parting her membranes and feeling the proof that no other man had ever seen this particular mossyface before, nor kissed it, nor toyed with its sweet little *coquille* until it wept like a cataract.

I was just about to scuttle up the bed and mount her at full flood when, all of a sudden, it occurred to me that I should derive even more pleasure from the operation – and she would risk less pain – if I lay on my back and let her impale herself upon me. In that way she could burst her own maidenhead and at her own sweet pace, while I would be free to concentrate on the unique thrill of penetrating her immaculate vagina. The moment I laid my body upon hers, therefore, I cuddled her in my arms and slowly rolled over on my back, easing her on top of me. A little deft work with my thighs and knees was enough to fork her legs wide and get Iron Jack within inches of his quarry.

'What s'l us do now?' she asked. 'Eay, my heart's going pittapat! Feel for yourself!'

I could see its beat making her bubbies shiver. The temptation to fondle them, to run my hands over her glorious form, was almost irresistible, but I managed to restrain myself. I wanted every ounce of her attention, and every bit of mine, too, to be concentrated on those eight glorious inches of proud flesh at present throbbing importunately at the entrance to its natural home. 'See if you were right about what you guessed,' I told her. 'See if you were made to fit me.'

Once again she bit her lip like a naughty little girl and, with her eyes all aglow, she writhed her bottom and wriggled her hips until the hot hard head of my Lad was nudged tight against the veils of her innocence.

'He'll go no farther nor that,' she said, breaking into a giggle and jiggling up and down with impatience. Her juices were still gushing and her excitement was rising to another climax; I believe she could have got herself off on anything that night.

'Jiggle a bit harder,' I suggested. 'There must be a way.'

I could feel the membrane bending and was amazed it had held so long. Then Iron Jack gave a wild kick in his exhilaration, which brought him to the very front end of her hole, where the maidenhead is always weakest; and at precisely that moment she gave an extra-vigorous wriggle, which did the trick at last.

The parting of a maidenhead over the questing head of a rampant tool is one of the most delightful pleasures a man can experience. There was a great trade in false virginity in the last century, involving girls whose membranes owed more to the surgeon's skill than to chastity and pure living; the fact that these counterfeits were so widely discussed in the arcane literature of those times must mean that the gentlemen were not really deceived. They merely thought the sensation itself was worth the pretence and the extra cash. And I do not blame them.

If you imagine your tool, ardent, hard, swollen almost to bursting ... imagine it in that excited condition thrusting between a pair of tautly held curtains – of doll's-house size, of course – curtains of finest silk, liberally soaked in some delicate lubricating gel – and bursting through at last into the tight, juicy clench of a living vagina – and you have some faint inkling of the pleasure I felt on that never-to-be-forgotten night with Calamity in my bed.

The moment I felt those membranes parting around the feverish head of Iron Jack I was seized by a kind of panic, for I knew in my bones that she was going to thrust herself down to the very hilt of me at once. Quick as lightning I raised my knees, brought them together, and tensed the muscles of my thighs – all to keep her at bay, with no more than the outer vestibule of her untried hole clasped hotly round my Lad; I wanted to savour every sensational millimetre of that most wonderful voyage of discovery in all the world.

She grasped my purpose at once and leaned forward, resting her body tenderly on mine, and giving out a great sigh of contentment. And thus began the most exciting fifteen minutes of my life until that moment – for it took all of that time for me to complete my first penetration of that enchanted grotto where all beginnings are joyful and all ends are ecstatic. During that time the Court of Venus herself fell silent while the gods and goddesses, the nymphs and satyrs, looked on in amazement that two mortals could so outshine them at their favourite sport.

Every moment of that marathon penetration will live with me until I die. Each tiny advance, measured in the smallest fractions of an inch, was like a fanfare of sensations playing through every limb and vessel in my body. By some miracle the column of my tool had become as exquisitely sensitive as the trembling head of him would normally be, while the head itself grew so sensitive and tender that the slightest flutter would send him into paroxysms of rapturous sensuality. If I had suddenly grown a myriad of new nerve endings there, the ecstasy could not have been greater. And it was the same with her, my precious darling, too. Every muscle in her body was tense and vibrant as she concentrated on the thrills this wonderful new game was sending in great waves through every particle and fibre of her being.

And when at last, at long, long last, Iron Jack butted softly against the inner neck of her vagina, she let out a sigh that would melt a mountain as she collapsed upon me in a swoon of joy.

It was a further two hours before my spermspouter lived up to his name for the third time that night – an eternity during which we exhausted love's almanac and ourselves. We feasted on each other's bodies every minute of that while, making playthings of every pore, every hair, every wrinkle. The rarest sensations, known to none but a handful of lovers since the dawn of time, were ours to enjoy in abundance. I never saw a girl so utterly transformed in so short a time. Until that night she had not known of the very existence of that delectable cavity behind her veils of innocence; in two short hours it became the entire focus of her being. She began to live and breathe for the passions which brewed in that lustful cauldron of the erotic appetite.

She woke me again at two that night, having got Iron Jack stiff while I slept; I emerged from the depths of my slumber just as she – trembling, wide awake, and all juiced-up again – was sliding herself down on him. The urgency of her craving set me alight and we gave old Eros another good hour of worship before exhaustion (and twenty aching, empty squirts) sent me to sleep in a haggard stupor.

Six hours later she was at me again, panting with desire, shivering as if I'd been gone a whole month, and writhing her body all over mine between our come-stained, sweat-stained, blood-stained sheets. I had a fleeting memory of moralistic engravings with titles like 'The Drunkard's End' – showing similar scenes of sordid debauchery. But that was after *weeks* on the bottle; we had achieved an equal squalor in the space of one night!

I made a manful effort; I must award myself marks for that. I tore myself from the bed, ran the bath for her, whipped the sheets out from under her protesting body, stuffed them in the laundry basket, plumped up the feather mattress, and spread fresh linen. By then she was in the bath – singing! I lit the fire, cooked a hearty breakfast, and took my own bath as soon as we had eaten. I dried myself and shaved, feeling on top of the world and fully resolved to start on her education in earnest – her education as a lady, I mean, not as a lady of pleasure. But when I returned to the bedroom to dress, there she was, naked between the sheets, her eyes gleaming with an invitation that Saint Anthony himself was lucky to have avoided (otherwise he'd have been plain mister). And just in case I was made of sterner (or, by now, more wilting) stuff than any saint, she threw off the sheets and showed me her divine young form from head to toe. Her nipples were swollen and burnished where she had been stroking them; her sweet little Clittie was all fired up and glistening between her parted labia; her bosom heaved, the pounding of her heartbeat shook her entire frame; and there was in her face a mute petition I would have been a monster to deny.

We did not surface from that engagement until gone noon. From somewhere I summoned the morale to insist we rise from the bed, get dressed, and go out to luncheon. We ate three lamb chops each, with great relish, in the chop house behind the variety theatre. We took a brief constitutional to the bottom of Headrow and back, and then returned to my chambers – where it took five minutes for me to convince her I was serious in my intention of putting some education into that clever but quite empty head of hers.

By that evening it was beginning to dawn on me what a dreadful thing I had done. I had cured Calamity of her addiction for booze – and her brief addiction to its substitute, the alcoholic mouthwash my dentist had prescribed – but only by introducing her to the most fearsome addiction of all: the pleasures of the old four-legged frolic, the knee-trembler, the dive in the dark, the shot between wind and water. I have known some desperately randy girls in my time but never one to equal Calamity in her need to feel hard bone in her *filet mignon*.

At school we had a filthy song about a woman of monstrous sexual appetites who, to satisfy herself, invents a tireless pleasuring machine. I remember little of it now but the chorus, which began:

Round and round went the fucking great wheel.
In and out went the prick of steel . . .

The joke behind the song was that in the end her own

invention gave her such a perpetual orgasm it killed her. Somewhere near the end were the lines:

This is a tale of the bitter bit:
There was no way of stopping it!

I can only guess that the poem must have been written by a man in the same position as I now found myself, and he must have fallen victim to despair, for if *his* voracious female was anything like my Calamity, she would have left that machine in a mangled, smoking heap.

And in precisely what position did I now find myself?

Well, several dozen, actually – both by day and by night – *every* day and *every* night. Whom the gods will destroy they first grant all their innermost desires; mine were certainly coming home to roost!

I cannot blame my dear Calamity. Her sexual needs were as huge as high Olympus and she satisfied them on the only tool available. I was powerless to resist her – and anyway it would have done no good for she would have out-smarted a fox-cobra-owl all rolled into one. She had the nimblest wits I ever encountered. Lord knows what her mother had done to keep her ignorant for her age; my dentist friend said that to judge by her teeth she was barely sixteen; I, judging by everything else, could easily have guessed she was a thousand. Or immortal. But, under my easy-going tutelage she fairly blossomed. In mathematics she could already add, subtract, multiply, and divide – and with lightning speed, too. She could not recall who had taught her and thought it likely she had 'always knowed it.'

I considered it would be useful for her to be able to work out the odds on various hands at cards – to improve her 'luck' at gambling. That was the first night she left me in peace. The following morning at breakfast she jotted down in her illiterate hand all the odds at poker – from 34-to-25 for a single pair right up to 640,739-to-1 for a royal flush. And every one of them was bang-on. I asked her how she did it. She said, 'I shut me eyes and the figures just . . . float in.'

If she was quick on the uptake in matters of regular education, she was ten times more so when it came to learning new erotic skills. She swiftly discovered, for instance, that – no matter what *I* might say – Iron Jack had a more primitive approach to the joys of copulation, and one that was far more in tune with her own insatiable tendency. I might be lying there, exhausted and at the end of my tether, but it made no difference to her. She was quite without mercy. Ignoring me she would begin to entice Iron Jack. She knew just how to flaunt her charms at him to make him twitch; and once *he* twitched, *I* was lost. She would coax him into a useful stiffness that left me racked with pain. She thought that was very amusing, for, of course, the sight of my pego, one moment like a candle too long in the sun, next minute standing to attention and throbbing in the air to the beat of my heart and the crack of her whiplash (or do I mean the whiplash of her crack!), was a wonderful proof of her power over me. I often thought that power was even more satisfying to her than the physical pleasure she took in the fornication that invariably followed.

By the middle of February I was convinced I would die of exhaustion before the month was out; by the end of February, however – hey presto! – I began to develop what, in athletics, is called 'second wind'. What could one call it in the world of amorous sports? Second Coming? Four-ball stamina? Whatever name you please, I suddenly found myself blessed with it. I stress it was not priapism, which is a state of permanent erection – and a most painful condition, too, especially for those who try the most obvious cure. I have (touch wood) never suffered from it but I have known three men who did and would not have traded places with them for all the girls in the Orient.

This was, on the contrary, a most delightful condition in which Iron Jack was ready for service, without pain, without even the slightest discomfort, as often as he was needed; and, with Calamity sharing my lodgings, he was needed at least a dozen times a day. Once, just for the heck of it, we tested him to discover his limits, twice every hour; we gave up at thirty, when he was still game for more.

After that we began to take such delight in each other's sexual gluttony that we might have gone on for years; indeed, we might, for all I know, be at it still – though, knowing me, and knowing her, I doubt it. However, my wager with Kitten was beginning to nag me. I still had a month to make good my boast that I could get Calamity taken in at a high-class house of pleasure and still I had not the first idea how to go about it.

To start with, I knew only one such house in all the world – Lazy Daisy's, right there in Lidgett Park, on the northern edge of Leeds. Somehow I felt in my bones that

Madame would never accept a girl who was so obviously rough and local – no matter how glorious her body might be nor how skilled she was at using it. But I went along to see her, anyway.

Madame was very frosty with me to start with, mostly because I had not patronized her establishment for several weeks. I put that right at once, of course, and took two new girls, Charlotte and Eleanor, for a ninety-minute romp in the French Boudoir. Charlotte, who was about twenty, was short and dark; her stocky chest supported two large, soft bubbies with flat, pink nipples as large as coffee-saucers; her waist was so tiny my hands almost met around it, but her hips were broad and her buttocks rotund and pneumatic. She raced out of her clothing and threw herself, panting, on the bed, spreading her soft, creamy thighs wide. Her quim glistened like two bright red peppers in the dark forest of her bush. As soon as I was naked I flung myself upon her and tucked Iron Jack firmly into her tail, pumping in and out like a ramrod. Her vagina, buried in all that opulent flesh was a delightfully firm, tight little sucker.

Soon, however, I turned my attention to Eleanor. The younger by some years, she was fair, tall, and willowy; her movements were lascivious and seductive to the most perfect degree; and when she stared up at me through her heavy-lidded eyes, letting her lips hang slackly open as if panting for a suck on my Lad, I forgot that her breasts were rather small, that her figure was distinctly immature and boyish, and that her buttocks were rather pinched and sharp – for she could fill a man's breast with the subtlest hints of promises and satisfactions. Later, when I got my pego well and truly drowned in the depths of her belly, I found she could make her vagina squeeze like the mouth of the best fellatrice I ever knew.

Iron Jack, with his new-found four-ball stamina, showed off dreadfully, I'm ashamed to say, passing from one to the other with complete abandon, as if promiscuity were his middle name. (Come to think of it, promiscuity *is* his middle name, but never mind.) He came twice into each of those gorgeous young fillies, ramming as hard and high into their bellies as he could. Naturally, he had little in the way of milt to fire into either, but he kicked and throbbed as if he were leaving a cupful each time. Both girls begged me to return another day and choose them again, and, who knows, they may even had meant it a little too.

That encounter brought me back to my senses, however. I saw at once that no matter how wonderful my association with Calamity might be, no matter how all-satisfying I might judge it at that moment, there were simply too many beddable girls in the world, amateuse and pro, for me to keep myself for her alone. Already, as I returned to Madame in her boudoir over the entrance hall, I was planning an agreeable further visit to this house of pleasure, there to renew my loving acquaintance with several of her delightful young ladies and those secret smiles they kept warm for all comers between their thighs.

When I told her of Calamity she at first showed the greatest interest. I was flattered for, obviously, my recommendation carried a certain weight with her. But the moment she heard that the poor girl spoke with a pronounced local dialect she lost all desire to meet her. Most of her girls were middle class; some – like Kitten – were actually gentry. But even so she had several with strong regional dialects – Welsh, Scottish, Irish, and West Country. Her clientele, she said, would not accept a local proletarian accent – or, rather, there were plenty of other houses where they could find it at half the price!

However, seeing my face fall, she took pity on me and gave me the name of some very high-class establishments in Paris. She let me into the secret that there was an informal ring of the very best houses in all the large cities of Europe; their madames would pass their best fillies on to each other when the girls grew tired of spreading the gentlemen's relish for the same three or four dozen pricks each week. Among these establishments was one called the *Maison ffrench*, which she assured me was founded and run by an English lady, Mrs ffrench, who was the daughter of an Anglican bishop, no less! Naturally, I swore I believed her, never for one moment thinking it could be true.

More to the immediate point she asked if Calamity would be willing to work in a maison de luxe at all? Had I bothered to canvass *her* opinion of the business yet? I thought Madame was working her way round to offering to put one or two gentlemen her way, just to see; but no such offer materialized – only a warning to be sure of the girl's cooperation before introducing her to Mrs ffrench or any other madame.

This last piece of advice occupied my mind the whole way home, for I had the gravest doubts that Calamity would even consider such a proposal – why should she? I wouldn't have done so in her situation. The problem occupied me to such an extent, that my feet automatically carried me toward my *old* home in Roundhay Park, even farther from the city centre than Lazy Daisy's. I came to my senses just in time – that is, just before I entered our road. I spun on my heels, and trotted south again with some haste. I fanned my face and blew out through pursed lips – as one often does after a narrow escape, even when there is no audience to amuse by the gesture.

But on that day I did have an audience – an audience of at least two, though I saw only one of them. He was Lieutenant the Honourable Wellesley O'Toole de North (Tooley to his friends) of the Duke of Leeds Light Infantry. He was also, for the moment, Kitten's languid, arrogant, military lover and keeper. Suddenly, from the shock and suspicion in his eyes, I realized that his love-nest must be very near; if looks could kill, his would not only have torn me limb from limb but cell from cell. However, he said nothing. He swept on by with lordly mien. And I, cunning as I suddenly was, took to my heels and ran.

'Swine!' he cried after me. 'Don't let me catch you again!'

And thus it came to me that this little accident offered the perfect chance to lead Calamity, step by step, into accepting her manifest destiny, which was to earn a fortune in a maison de luxe in Paris. I would force her to deceive me, for women are ten times more singleminded in deceit than ever they are in faithfulness.

I adore women. If they vanished from the world, I should

shrivel and die inside a week. Yet I cannot imagine why they were ever associated with purity, gentleness, self-sacrifice, kindness ... and all those finer human qualities. Their sensual appetites take my breath away. The ferocity and selfishness with which they pursue their own desires puts any man to shame. And as for kindness ... I'd sooner take my chance with a pack of lionesses, any day!

When Calamity saw that her demands on Iron Jack were sending me to an early grave, she couldn't get enough of him. But when he developed that happy four-ball stamina, so that there was no contest of wills for her to win, she began to lose interest and her demands became more moderate. Mind you, 'moderate' where she was concerned was a fairly relative term; it meant no more than half a dozen vigorous pokes a day – which, in turn, meant I was free for most afternoons.

It suited her, too, for her addictive nature had now enlarged itself to encompass the world of learning as well. The university just up the road would not have called it *learning*, mind, but she was certainly acquiring the sort of knowledge that would stand her in good stead down the years. She read every lady's magazine in the bookstall. She devoured four biographies or autobiographies a week, retaining only those bits she could reduce to gossip – which she never forgot. She scoured *Debrett*. Books on etiquette she gulped down in one. And last but by no means least, she pillaged and plundered every erotic book and magazine I could beg, borrow, or buy.

She was very two-faced about them, though. She loved tales of youngsters making their first sexual discoveries of each other's bodies, of rich middle-aged men befriending poor seamstresses, of nuns being seduced by priests and monks, of girls at school being rogered by the gardener, of cousins who used to sleep together as children continuing the habit into adolescence, of wealthy young masters and pretty young chambermaids... but let a coin change hands to ease the transaction and her scorn knew no bounds. She conceived a loathing of prostitution that was quite hysterical. Once or twice I gently reminded her how she came to be in my chambers in the first place and she grew so angry that I had to give up. To her, eroticism was a kind of religion.

She believed in Free Love and its endless indulgence; the prostitute, who did it merely for money was to her what Satan and the Antichrist are to the Christians. That did not, however, prevent her from reading stories of prostitution as avidly as the rest – just as many a bible-thumper will devour the seamier court reports, tut-tutting at every paragraph!

I ought at this point to introduce Miss Campbell, for, though I only discovered it much later, she was the one who was poisoning Calamity's mind against The Noblest and Most Ancient Profession. How they even understood each other I can't imagine – Calamity with her broad Leeds dialect and Miss Campbell with her even broader Outer Hebrides (or wherever it was). She shared chambers with a Miss Monteith, who travelled around the North selling moral undergarments for females, which meant that Miss Campbell was often alone.

When I first met her I thought no more than that she was a dreadful waste of a very pretty young girl. She had ash-blonde hair, bright blue eyes, bonny cheeks, and a lovely smile; she was slender as an aspen, with a bust that made men tense their arm muscles – to prevent their hands from doing what powerful instincts were trying to make them do. She made her living – and not a bad one, either – as what they then called a 'lady typewriter.' She typed theses and papers for the lecturers and professors at the university, which required a high degree of education and the ability to transform badly written squiggles into words like *phenolphthalein* and *metempsychosis*.

She was also a religious maniac – went to church every day – prayed loudly when alone in her chambers, which were just down the corridor from mine. I could occasionally hear her through our party wall, despite the sound-damping between us (of which I shall say more later). I would not have minded so much except that one of the souls she often prayed for was mine. She was engaged to be married. At least, she wore a diamond ring on the appropriate finger, though I never saw her suitor, nor were there daily letters such as parted lovers are supposed to write.

For months we had done no more than bow gravely to each other whenever we chanced to meet. But one day, shortly after Calamity moved in, I met Miss Campbell just inside our common front door. She was resting her arm from carrying a rather stout bundle of manuscript. Naturally, I offered to carry it upstairs and, naturally, she accepted. In all her girlish innocence, and utterly oblivious of the torture she wreaked on poor Iron Jack, she went ahead of me up our steep and narrow stairs.

The bustle was one of the most wonderful items of female clothing ever devised. How generations of strait-laced Victorian ladies were ever persuaded to wear anything so devastatingly erotic is one of life's grand mysteries. And the rather small bustle in fashion at the end of the old queen's reign was the most stimulating of all, for it was just large enough to let you imagine that the curves which swayed and danced and pranced and twinkled as she walked were *real*! Merely to see them was to imagine those two swelling moons backing into your groin, cool and pale, while the hot, wet, steamy trench beneath them closed around your ramrod . . . I was all in a muck-sweat by the time I deposited the heavy satchel at her doorway.

In thanking me she put her hand lightly on my arm. When she took it away she looked at it in some surprise, flexing her fingers and staring at me as if she saw something she had never noticed before.

'What?' I asked.

'Och, it's nothing,' she said, collecting herself. 'Until a moment ago I felt a gey pain in yon hand – from all the typing, ye ken. But it's gone the noo.'

She smiled and vanished into her virginal chambers.

I thought no more of the incident at the time.

To return to Calamity and her erotic reading. She would reserve it until the end of the afternoon – to the hour before my return. Then she would undress completely and take them to bed, where she would read them and diddle herself into a lascivious stupor. By the time I came home – and heaven help me if I were five minutes late! – she was sweating and trembling all over in her need to feel Iron Jack tucked gleefully into her tail and pumping glory through and through her.

Once or twice, in the beginning of this new phase in our life together, she asked me what I did when I went out. Her interest waned when I replied that I placed bets on horses (which was true) and that was how I really made my living (which, if you ignore the income on my investments, was also true). In fact, it took less than half an hour to place my bets. The rest of the time – every day – I went out to Roundhay Park and loitered about near the Tooley-Kitten love nest until I saw him coming up the street. Being a military man, he was fairly regular. Then I would saunter down toward him, looking for all the world as if I had just come from Kitten's boudoir. I don't know what arguments it caused between them (well, I do actually, because she told me later – and they were pretty searing; but I mean I didn't know at the time)(nor care), but it fairly rattled the languid oaf himself. After a day or two of this torment I tightened the screw by giving out little sighs of happy exhaustion as I passed him.

Then came the day when we didn't meet at all. I lingered around Kitten's house but of Tooley there was no sign. I felt sure I knew where he was – thoughts of revenge come so easily to military men. The following day I took refuge in the dark interior of my bootmaker's workshop, whose window was diagonally opposite my front door. And sure enough, just as I suspected (and hoped), Tooley came warily up the street, his eyes fastened on my sitting-room window – which, as he drew level with my bootmaker's, revealed a brief flash of Calamity's smiling face. He crossed the road at once and she opened the door the moment he knocked.

That smile and the thought of her racing heart as she flashed down the stairs wrenched my heart. I admit I had done all in my power to provoke this betrayal ... I admit it was for my own ultimate benefit ... and yet ... and yet ... she need not have smiled quite so broadly.

I remembered the end of Kitten's first working day at Lazy Daisy's. I had had the pleasure and privilege of initiating her to the traffic the previous day and, though itching to get stuck into her again, had nobly stayed away until gone midnight. I expected to see her coming down the stairs on the arm of some crapulous old toad whom it had been her grisly job to pleasure for the previous hour. I expected she'd have her tongue hanging out for the touch of a fine, upstanding organ like Iron Jack.

Instead of the old toad I saw a young army officer with a trim, athletic body – tall, unbearably handsome, languid, monocled, aristocratic. Tooley, of course. He was in full mess undress, sword and spurs all clanking, carrying the plumed tricorn of the Duke of Leeds Light Infantry on one arm. And on the other (my blood still boils to think of it) was my own sweet Kitten, laughing at his jokes snuggling against him as if beginning a fresh seduction. She was naked but for her black stockings, high-heeled boots, and a scanty black corset. But worst of all was the glow of satisfaction she wore on her skin, the shine of achievement she carried on her cheeks, and the gleam of triumph that flashed from her eyes. Not only was I forced to acknowledge that this god in uniform had spent the evening tucking his no doubt magnificent organ into my darling Kitten's tail, but also that my darling Kitten's hot little tail had fluttered in dizzy frenzy at every rapturous thrust.

And now he was doing it to me again – or doing it to Calamity, rather. Only my superb self-control prevented me from following him across the street and throwing him out – also he was older, taller, and stronger.

I went straight out to Roundhay Park to tell Kitten what was happening. However, I had cooled down by the time I got there – enough to realize that she'd know I was up to some devilment, and then it wouldn't be long before she'd worked the whole thing out. So I held my tongue and exchanged only the expected pleasantries.

I arrived just in time, in fact, for she was leaving the house as I turned in at her drive. 'Stay there,' she said as she pulled her front door to behind her. 'I'm only going next door. Come and meet them – they're awfully nice.' You'd never think we parted in a huff! I knew then that life with Tooley wasn't all singing hymns, as they say.

In that brief walk to the neighbours – a fellow called Alfred Wharton and his wife Gabriele – Kitten just had time to explain that he was a moderately successful portrait painter and that she dabbled in portrait photography. It kept the roof over their heads, she added, though the fact that they were childless must have helped too.

I said I had never heard of the man – and I had lived just

around the corner all my life until six months ago.

'That just goes to show,' she replied, giving me an odd, sideways grin.

I asked what game she was playing.

'Oh, a very old one,' she said. 'I'm quite sure you'll like it, though.'

The moment I saw Wharton I felt pretty sure he was no genius; I never met a man who tried harder to *look* like an artist. He was tall, with craggy eyebrows, and a beard that looked as if it might go off with a bang at any moment. Also he called me *mon brave*. His wife did not come out to meet us.

'And what do you do, *mon brave*?' he asked me as he led us upstairs to his studio.

'He's my macquerau,' Kitten said in the most matter-of-fact tone imaginable.

Wharton goggled at me; I looked daggers at her. She grinned and took a bundle from her handbag. 'Which reminds me,' she added, handing it to me. 'A hundred quid if you want to count it.' She kissed me warmly.

I had no choice but to play the part she had obviously assigned me in Wharton's eyes. 'Good girlie,' I said, stuffing the wad nonchalantly in my pocket.

'You unutterable swine,' Wharton said – in a surprising blend of contempt and admiration.

'I don't touch her money,' I told him, pulling out her account book, which I always carried. I showed it to her.

She whistled and grinned at Wharton. 'I'm worth nearly a thou',' she exclaimed. 'Not bad for one who was a penniless sixteen-year-old only last July, eh?' She tweaked his beard playfully as he held open the studio door for us to pass inside.

He gaped at her. 'And you earned it all by dropping your knickers?' he asked.

I tried to look as if I heard conversations like this every day.

'Most of it,' she replied, taking the book from me and consulting it again. 'Seven hundred of it. Smiler puts nine pounds out of every ten into consols and the tenth pound on the geegees. He's very good at that.'

Wharton slapped me heartily on the shoulder. 'I take it all back, *mon brave*. Capital fellow!'

I, meanwhile, was looking at his paintings. I was right in my guess – he was no artist. But he was a slick draughtsman and a competent colourist – a first-rate illustrator masquerading as a genius, in short.

'How about this?' Kitten asked gleefully.

I turned around and could hardly believe my eyes. She had slipped out of her clothes and was standing naked as Eve on the dais, which was 'dressed' to look like the corner of a luxurious bedroom. Even as I watched, she raised one leg and placed it on the bed – with the result that her gorgeous young oyster, with all its lovely folds and crevices, was on full display.

'Perfect!' Wharton seated himself where he'd get an even better view of it than me – but not, I was surprised to notice, right in front of her, where he'd get the best view of all. So I seated myself there, instead – on one of those strange stools that artists call 'donkeys' – and feasted my eyes on that fairest vision in all the world. What hours of rapture I had enjoyed, tucked up into that glorious young tail!

A moment later Wharton cleared his throat and asked me if I wouldn't mind moving farther round as I was blocking his light.

It was an absurd thing to say since his studio was illuminated by electricity from above. I'd have had to grow angel's wings to block his light. But I humoured him all the same.

'I suppose that's home from home for you?' Wharton asked lightly, nodding at Kitten's fork, which he was sketching for all he was worth.

'Ah, well . . .' I said vaguely.

'Not while Tooley's keeping me,' Kitten said heavily, and entirely for my benefit. 'That's part of the bargain.'

Wharton looked at me challengingly. 'And you take it like a lamb?' he asked. 'I was going to say 'take it lying down,' but it sounds as if that's the one thing you don't do.'

All at once I realized what he wanted of me – a subject for a drawing that would fetch ten times the price of an *empty* open quim.

Kitten put up quite a fight – all verbal, of course; but I knew she was going to yield from the beginning. She had that amused, experimental glint in her eye. In the end we reached a classic compromise. We agreed that I could slip Iron Jack inside her *but not move him once he was in!* I think she imagined he'd fall limp after a few minutes and I'd look foolish. We were both being absurd, of course. We loved each other after our faithless fashion, and yet were always trying to score petty points like that.

Anyway, Iron Jack did *not* fall slack. The moment he slipped up inside her, into that gorgeously soft, warm, lubricated cunny, he knew he was home again and he kicked, kicked, kicked for joy. I didn't need to move a muscle, so I kept to our agreement. Kitten could lubricate herself inside two seconds, whether she was roused or not; but there was no doubting her arousal now! Her vagina squeezed me and the little sticky noises made by the frilly bits of her oyster, where they clung around the base of my nightstick, echoed all round the studio. Wharton drew and drew like a demon; there was no doubting his dedication to *this* branch of art.

After several minutes of throbbing and squeezing, which brought us both close to a climax, a new idea occurred to us – so nearly simultaneously that it was hard not to believe in telepathy between us. What would it be like to make absolutely no movement at all? we wondered. What if I stopped making the Lad throb, and she stopped squeezing him? Of all the erotic variations we had ever tried (and I thought we had tried them all) that particular one had never occurred to us.

Try it, dear reader! Try it with a girl you adore – on a day when you and she are as randy as two ferrets. It is the most sublime sensation. You may think you're exploring a girl's vagina when you poke her, but you're not – not even at your slowest and most luxurious pace. What you're exploring is the sensation of poking a girl! Hold still for a moment, a long moment, and you'll begin to see what I mean. Hold still until you both come, and you'll understand entirely.

On that evening in Wharton's studio, Iron Jack seemed to fatten and grow harder with every heartbeat. Afterwards, when we held an excited recap of the event, we realized we had thrilled to precisely the *opposite* sensations. She had been aroused by the way Iron Jack *stretched* the flesh of her vagina; for me it was the resulting *constriction* of that same divine organ – hot-blooded and relentless in its stillness.

Think about it. There's no doubt that the physical activity of poking one's gristle in and out of a girl's vagina gives enormous pleasure to both parties; but it has the incidental and inevitable effect of introducing the element of time. The act of coitus becomes measurable in terms of so many hundred thrusts. Unconsciously one thinks of beginning, a middle, and an end. But when you tuck your sperm-spouter tight up into that same divine oracle and then hold absolutely still, you keep time at bay. Each moment is identical to every other. They become indistinguishable. They melt. They fuse together. You feel transported, quite literally, out of time and space – out of this world. The religious speak of paradise as an eternity of bliss. What Kitten and I experienced for the first time that evening in Wharton's studio is, I believe, the nearest a mere mortal may get to understanding what paradise must feel like.

The pose lasted half an hour. For almost all that time I was tucked tight inside her, and we both lay still as a statue. Iron Jack stayed hard as a rock, meaty and hot, stretching the almost infinitely yielding flesh of her hole to a voluptuous tension. Right at the end she made some small movement, preparing to relax, and it was enough to brim me over into the most spectacular spermspouting I had ever achieved. It just went on and on and on. The first massive spermorrhage (to coin a word for that free-flowing milt) brimmed her over, too. And the steady, throbbing fusillade kept her at fever pitch all the while it lasted. And the most curious thing of all was that – in keeping with the means by which we arrived at this stupendous orgasm – we neither of us moved a muscle, nor uttered a single cry, nor gasped, nor trembled . . . until it was over.

Kitten and I have spent our lives running from each other, deafening ourselves to that strange sexual music that plays – quite automatically – whenever we are together. But there are always those moments when we know we can never win; and that evening encounter in Wharton's studio was one of them.

'Rest,' he said at last.

I was struck by the way he glanced over his shoulder before granting us this permission – almost as if he were passing it on from some higher authority. Had it not been for that, I should never have looked to see what he had consulted in that way. Unconsciously, I suppose, I was looking for the face of a clock. I realized it would have to be a very small clock, or I should have noticed it already. And so, because my eyes were seeking something small and circular, they found it rather quickly.

But it was not a clock. It was the lens of a camera!

Wharton, having done about a dozen sketches while Kitten and I had been lost in eternity, put six of them in an envelope and gave them to Kitten. The rest he stuffed in one of those large, flat holdalls that artists use for carrying drawings, and then he left us in something of a hurry. Moments later we heard the front door slam.

I looked at the six he had given to Kitten. Two were of her torso – no head or face, just the occasional hint of a hand or foot. But the art-lover for whom they were intended would probably not even notice the missing bits for these sketches showed her thighs well parted, exposing her quim with its lips wide open, pouting for exercise. The other four were close-ups – I could even call them portraits – of her quim alone, slightly larger than life size. He could handle flesh, old Wharton, I'll give him that. Kitten being a redhead, her quim had the most wonderful aroma, vixeny and aphrodisiac. I could almost smell it off those drawings. And the gleam of the exciting wetness of her labia . . . and the dark mystery of her hot little hole, lurking coyly among the fleshy froufrou that framed it . . . I confess Iron Jack was pushing his head up under my belt, looking for freedom once again.

'May I have these?' I asked.

'Indeed, you may not!' she answered stoutly. 'Tooley would kill me. These are his.'

My ever-sharp ear detected a wistful note in these last three words; I decided to pursue the subject, but not directly. 'Where are the ones of you and me together?' I asked. 'I'm sure Wharton did several of them, too.'

'He took them away with him,' she said, thinking I hadn't noticed. 'He always does about a dozen,' she explained. 'Because he can work so fast. But Tooley thinks he only does six. Don't ever tell him there's more.'

I promised to try and remember not to. We shared so many confidences, Tooley and I!

'He sells the other six,' she went on, indifferent to my sarcasm. 'To a professor at the university. They're quite different. He always adds an imaginary partner for me on those drawings. That's why he was so pleased to have an actual model today. He gets very well paid for them, too.'

'Which he shares with you, I hope?'

From the shock in her eye I knew he hadn't passed on a penny. 'I'm happy enough,' she said. 'I get an hour's relief from the boredom, at least.'

I refused her obvious invitation to probe behind this statement; let her build up a little steam, I thought. 'And what does Tooley do with his ration of six?' I asked.

'He gloats,' she replied disgustedly. 'I often think he enjoys them more than the real thing.'

I said nothing until we were outside in the dark – my old friend. Then I murmured, 'It sounds as if life is no longer one bed of roses, Kitten.'

'Kitten!' she sneered. 'If you want the truth of it, I feel like a mangy old cat.'

'Not to me you didn't.'

She turned and flung her arms around me. 'Oh, Smiler! I was such a fool. Why did I do it? I really enjoyed the work at Lazy Daisy's – especially because I knew there'd always be *you*.'

'There still is, pet. All you need do is tell your knickers they're a yo-yo.'

She shook her head. 'Tooley would say I was betraying a trust. D'you think Madame would take me back?'

'Not from one or two rather pointed remarks she made when I saw her last.'

'You've seen her since I left?'

'Last week. I had two gorgeous young kiddies called Eleanor and Charlotte.'

She stamped her foot. 'Oh, men are so lucky!'

'No sense crying over spilt milt,' I told her.

She laughed, despite herself.

'What about a complete change of scenery?' I asked. 'How would you like to work in a high-class *maison* in Paris, for instance?'

It was as if I had put several hundred volts through her. 'Oh, Smiler! Could you arrange that for me?'

'Can we forget our childish little bet about Calamity?'

Kitten started to sneer that I was throwing in the towel, but I explained how complicated things had become. At first she would not believe that the sexual cravings of *any* girl could have brought me as low as I claimed – nor that, having got my fourth balls, I'd be at all eager to let her go. But when I'd finally convinced her – and she'd overcome her laughter – I explained that although a girl with appetites and a body like Calamity's clearly belonged in a high-class house of pleasure – especially as she had no other source of income – the girl herself was going to take some persuading of the fact.

Then I took my heart in my hands and explained further that, as a first step, I had weaned her off the idea of being faithful to me, and of seeking her pleasure only with me – by provoking Tooley into taking his revenge (as he supposed) against me.

I thought Kitten was going to fly at me and tear my eyes out. But, just as she gathered herself for the assault, she saw the funny side of life and broke down into giggles. 'So that's why you've been lurking around my gate all this past week!' she exclaimed. 'You clever stick! Because it worked like a charm, let me tell you.' But then the implications of my words began to sink in. 'So,' she said, 'you mean to tell me that at this very minute, my own dear Tooley is dipping his wick in that slut I found in your bed that . . .'

'In Calamity,' I said. 'Slut is the very last thing you'd call her now. Anyway – stick to the point! Help me prepare the girl for the life of *une grande horizontale*.'

Kitten wouldn't let me into her love nest, for fear of what might happen there, especially now that she knew Tooley would have little sexual appetite left by the time he arrived. So, for the next ten minutes we stood in her driveway and discussed our plans – or *her* plans, to give credit where it's due. Then I wrapped my arms around her and kissed her . . . and slipped a hand inside her coat and squeezed one of her splendid bubbies . . . and rubbed the importunate swelling of Iron Jack where he was throbbing to burst out of my flies and tuck himself in under that mound whose gentle protuberance was giving us both such exquisite thrills . . . until she gasped and pushed me away and rushed indoors.

I sauntered down the street until her windows passed out of sight; then, bending low, I scuttled back to Wharton's house as fast as I could. I brushed past the maid who answered the door, saying, 'It's all right – I shan't be a moment. I forgot my scarf up in the studio. I'll let myself out.' As an afterthought I added, 'Is your mistress still up there in the dark room?'

She opened and shut her mouth like a fish. Obviously people were not supposed to know about the mistress and the dark room. I smiled sympathetically and assured her I was *au fait* with all the secrets of this house.

The studio had one small light burning at the far end, but it was enough to let me negotiate my way without bumping into anything. The door to the dark room was well concealed beyond what looked like a heap of discarded paintings. I slipped behind and opened it.

But not quietly enough, for I found Gabriele Wharton staring at me with great, frightened eyes. She flinched from me as I came near her.

'I thought so,' I murmured as my eyes fell upon a washing bath full of developed prints. The water jetted in at one end and spilled out over a dam at the other, keeping the water in constant, slow circulation. The prints, of course, followed the currents, so that I was presented with an endless cataract of erotic visions – Kitten's oyster, Iron Jack, Iron Jack snuggling up into Kitten's cleft, Iron Jack stretching the frills of her labia with his oak-tree girth . . . all made lurid by the red glow of the safety lantern.

'Whoo!' I exclaimed, easing the Lad himself into a less cramped position as I turned to her again.

Whatever I was going to say I forgot it the next instant, astonished to discover that her blouse was wide open, every button undone. She clutched it feebly to her – which merely served to show up the enticing curves of her bubbies *and their swollen nipples*, which now strained against the delicate cotton of her garment. 'It gets rather hot in here,' she explained feebly.

'My hands are still cool from outdoors,' I replied, taking care not to move toward her. 'Perhaps we can be of *service* to each other?'

She took a small pace toward me. Involuntary or not, *she* moved first. Important, that.

I slipped my hand inside her blouse and felt her bubby lifting itself toward me in her eagerness; the nipple was almost as large again as her rather birdlike breast. She moved to press herself against me but I turned her gently round, facing away from me, and took both bubbies into my hands. She collapsed into my embrace and then, as if to stop herself swooning to the ground, threw her arms up around my head and pulled my lips urgently to hers.

While we kissed and kissed and kissed, exploring each other's mouths with our tongues, I raked my nails lovingly over the outer sides of her nipples, and underneath them, too, until they swelled and burned against my fingers. Gloatingly I squeezed them, pressed them, furled them – all with a tenderness that drove her to a frenzy.

She gasped. She breathed deep, and deeper-on-deep, as if she thought the atmosphere itself was about to be taken away from us. And at last, when she could bear it no more, she tore my hands from her and, turning to me, buried her face in my chest and whimpered, 'It's not fair!'

I asked her what she meant.

'Tantalizing me like that when you can't do anything

about it yourself. I saw you give your all to Miss Bossom out there.'

Since she could feel Iron Jack straining against her belly like a hickory truncheon, the words must have been insincere; yet she spoke them with every appearance of truth, and with great bitterness.

'How long have we got?' I asked.

'You mean you *can* go again?'

'If the people around me stop talking,' I complained.

She laughed and glanced at the dark room clock. 'You're a marvel! We've twenty minutes, I'd say – to be on the safe side. Better not take this off, however.'

She lifted her skirt to give me a quick flash of Old Mossyface, pale auburn, like the hair on her head. 'Don't spare me!' she gasped as she scrabbled furiously at my flies. 'Poke away! Ram hard up me, to the very hilt.'

That delicious thrill I got as the cool, slender fingertips of this randy woman closed about my tool, especially as he was all ardent and throbbing from his confinement in wool and cotton, was the first of many stupendous moments in that surprising encounter with Gabriele. The moment she yanked him entirely free she squeezed him at the base, she clasped him half-way up, she cuddled his lecherous knob and felt him kick with appreciation. Then, giving out a deep-throated gurgle of satisfaction, she leaped up six inches until her buttocks were just caught on the edge of the exposing table – and then gave a delightful new meaning to that name by scrabbling her skirts up around her waist and spreading wide her thighs. As the wondrous fragrance of her sex rose into my nostrils, the hellish red lamp showed me a quim on fire with lust – wet, fleshy, gleaming, luxurious. 'Now!' she panted.

Iron Jack practically fell into her hole, which was like nothing I had ever felt before – and I must have poked five or six dozen girls by then. The outer portion was so supple and yielding that if offered my knob no other sensation than its warmth, which was thrilling enough; the wet, tingling heat of a girl's vagina, especially to a tool that has lingered politely in the cold air awhile, is always something magical. Then, over the next inch or so, its texture changed completely, from squishy softness to a lean, firm, sinewy tube that gave way before each advance of my intruding knob only after some effort. You know when a girl takes your old man right down into her throat and then swallows good and hard? It was like that all the time I stayed up there, even when rammed to the hilt of me.

These sensations were so delightful that for several minutes I did nothing but withdraw completely from her, then poke just the tip of my knob into her infinitely soft outer vestibule, and then thrust myself with full vigour all the way in, as if trying to burst those sinewy bands that made the upper reaches of her vagina so exciting to penetrate. After a few of these pokes she caught on to the rhythm. She inhaled sharply when I withdrew, held her breath – except for little whimpering notes of pleasure – when I stirred the outer folds of softness, and then exhaled in one mighty gasp as I plunged all the way in.

After a few dozen of these ins-and-outs I tried to vary the pace, rather subtly, as I thought. But the whimpers took on a note of complaint and I soon reverted to the old rhythms; Gabriele was obviously one of those women who relish an absolutely steady poke. Some men find them boring – and so they are until you try to see it from their side.

A man's ecstasy is all focused on those few delirious inches at the tip of his knob, mostly on the underside; when the spouting sperm races through that tip, paradise explodes around it. But the corresponding pleasure in a woman can – if her lover cooperates property – consume every nerve and muscle and fibre of her being with joy. The lover who never pokes her in the same way twice, who tries to make every thrust a uniquely novel exploration of each tiny part of her vagina, denies her that supreme sort of ecstasy; for he thereby focuses *her* attention where all *his* pleasures are gathered. Only the steady, unvarying thrust, thrust, thrust of the 'boring' screw can liberate her from that concentration on her vagina and allow her joy to radiate outward through all her limbs as well.

True, the chief pleasure of the cooperative lover is in marvelling at the intensity and duration of the woman's orgasm when it finally grips her. But then comes his bonus. Few are the women who seek two such overwhelming orgasms in quick succession. (Calamity was one, but I was taking care of that.) Most of them will snuggle down quite happily to enjoy one or two, or twenty . . . or a hundred and two . . . of the more everyday kind that are sweetly confined to that tingling flesh which is now more than happy to accommodate a man and his need for change and variety.

However, on that evening with Gabriele in the dark room, there was obviously no time to reach that second stage. Manfully I pumped away at her, in-and-out, in-and-out, never varying by a hairsbreadth . . . feeling a *little* resentful, I must admit, that she wasn't more instantaneously appreciative of my consideration for her pleasure at the cost of my own – but not for long. Soon, indeed, I was lost in amazement at the sheer demonic power and violence of the orgasms that seized and shook her entire frame. She craned her neck, reaching her gaping lips to the heavens as if she'd never breathe deep enough; little collections of foam flecked the corners of her mouth. Her arms and legs closed around me like lobster claws as she launched herself off the exposing table and clung to me like a drowning woman. My fingers, suddenly tense and clawlike, bit into the soft flesh of her buttocks as I pulled her belly even tighter to me. The juice just poured out of her, bathing us both in the heady reek of debauchery . . .

And still, somehow, I plugged her in the same unvarying rhythm. And still she went on, jolting and trembling as wave after waver of thrills swept through her. At last I thought she had fainted, but it was her only way of stopping a pleasure so intense it had begun to shade over into pain – to slump upon me so heavily that she slipped off my tool and left him pressed against the outside of her sagging belly.

Once that stimulus was removed, however, she recovered rather swiftly. 'My God, Smiler – you're still stiff!'

'Can we go again?' I asked innocently.

She licked her lips, glanced nervously at the clock, and the, infinitely apologetic, said alas it was not possible.

I guessed Wharton would be a good half hour yet, but

she needed time to compose herself and deal with the prints as if she had not been interrupted.

I gave a sigh as I tucked Iron Jack away. 'Another time,' I said casually.

'Oh, please!' she exclaimed with fervour.

'Really?' I asked, as if I hadn't believed it possible.

She grew cautious. 'Not this month. Toward the end of April, perhaps – or May. We'll have lots . . .'

She didn't say *what* we'd have lots of – and I didn't ask.

I had returned to Wharton's studio angry at their duplicity, determined to claim my share of whatever money they got for the pictures of Kitten and me. In its place I had found a pleasure that money could not buy (and I had bought a great deal of that same pleasure by then, so I was well placed to judge).

There was no trace of Tooley when I arrived back at my chambers; and Calamity was nice as pie to me, pretending she was desperate for a bit of loving. Tooley must have plugged her tail well and truly, though, for I could tell that her heart wasn't in it. I told her not to be downhearted – some days were like that – no girl could be receptive to men twenty-four hours a day, seven days a week – 'Except a whore,' I added with a dismissive laugh. 'And that, thank heavens, is one thing you could never be!'

Despite all her scorn and detestation of the Noble Calling, Calamity hated being told that anything was impossible to her. 'How d'you know?' she asked coldly. 'I don't suppose you've met a whore in your life.'

'My dear girl, I was living with one until you moved in.

74

D'you remember the red-headed beauty who came here that first morning?'

Of course she didn't.

'Oh, but you must,' I exclaimed. 'She was rather uncomplimentary about you.'

It rang a vague bell with her. 'And she's a whore?' she asked.

'She was. She worked at Lazy Daisy's, which is a very high-class whore-house out in Lidgett Park. She earned about eighty pounds a week there.'

Calamity drew breath to say something but then thought better of it. I continued: 'I was her macquerau, which is a sort of special gentleman-friend. But when she found you here, she left in a huff to live with some idiot of an army officer – fellow called Tooley or something.'

Calamity was going to make a superb whore; not by the smallest flicker of an eyelid did she betray any interest in the name.

'Funnily enough,' I went on, 'I ran into her again only this afternoon. I went to see an artist friend of mine, Alfred Wharton – and there she was, having her portrait painted.' Slyly I added, 'Tooley was supposed to be there but apparently some military manoeuvres detained him.'

Again there was no response from Calamity. I even began to wonder whether he might not have given her some false name. But that wasn't his style. Besides, it would spoil his revenge.

Later, when we were in bed – and doing nothing but talk for a change – I mused aloud: 'It's a funny thing about Kitten, you know. I was her very first-ever customer at

Lazy Daisy's. We both feel very affectionate toward each other still. Yet I always knew she'd leave me one day and become Tooley's missy.'

'Dost'a hate her 'cos o' that?' she asked.

'Of course not!' I laughed at the very idea. 'No man can *own* a woman's body – especially not when she has a wonderful free spirit like Kitten's. Going to live with Tooley was *her* choice, not his. One day she'll up and leave him, too. Free as a bird – that's Kitten! Yet – as I said – I knew, almost from that very first day at Lazy Daisy's, I knew she'd go and stop with Tooley sometime.'

After a lengthy pause Calamity asked, 'How?' She hated my talking about Kitten in these flattering terms but curiosity got the better of her.

'Tooley was the girl-taster for the Young Turks. He picked her to go and pleasure them on only her second day. They gave her the most wonderful time, too. Just imagine – a dozen randy Young Turks and a beautiful fresh girl who's just awakening to the pleasures that lie in ambush between her thighs! D'you know who the Young Turks are, by the way?'

She shook her head. 'And what's a girl-taster when it's at home?'

'I'll come to that. The Young Turks is a club of all the junior army officers in the Leeds garrison – about a hundred and fifty of them. Life in an officers' mess is arranged for the convenience of the older members, which makes it very dull – stuffy and formal. So they've got this clubhouse out in Headingley where they have six pretty waiter-girls – who divide their time between serving at table and being served (in the stud-farm sense) in bed.'

Calamity's thighs clenched involuntarily together and the pupils of her eyes went large and dark. I decided to pile it on.

'Being military types, of course,' I said, 'it's all highly organized. There are always one or two girls entertaining the cardinal. So there's only four or five available for service. They start work at two in the afternoon, when the club opens its doors. The rule is that there can only be one girl being rogered upstairs at any given moment. The others must be downstairs, serving drinks and snacks and things – because it is, after all, a club as well as an officers' knocking shop. So the officers take the girls upstairs strictly on a rota. If young Dawkins is panting to sink between the thighs of Lily and she's only just come down from a brisk canter on the back stretch with Willoughby-Smythe, poor Dawkins has to wait while Vane-Trumpington takes Dora upstairs for a joyful thrash, and then Cholmondeley-Smithers takes Millie up to her room for a spread of hot gentleman's relish, and then Farquharson-Brown takes little dark-eyed Joan up for a quick dip in paradise – and only *then* can Dawkins take Lily up to her bedroom and put four quarters on the spit.'

By now Calamity's fingers were busy at her fork; she tried to hide it from me but her breathing alone was enough to give her away. 'Go on,' she urged. 'Tell me some more.'

'There's not much more to tell,' I replied. 'Between ten and midnight the rules change. If there are four officers with their tongues hanging out and four pretty waiter-girls available, they can all vanish upstairs at the same time. So for the first ten hours of their day, each girl knows fairly accurately when some randy young fellow is going to take her upstairs to her bedroom and give her the ancient cure for melancholy. But for the last two hours of her day it's a free for all. She might be taken upstairs only once – or she might lie on her back the entire time and help as many as half a dozen lusty young lads improve their shooting.'

Calamity let out a huge sigh, but all she said was, 'I think it's disgusting.'

'Not the sort of life *you'd* like to lead, eh?'

'What were that girl-taster-thing you said?'

'Oh yes! On Wednesdays and Sundays two of the pretty waiter-girls get the day off. Their place is taken by two pretty young whores from Lazy Daisy's – who don't do any waiting, of course. Being thorough professionals, they're on their backs all ten hours, from two till midnight, taking all comers in their stride.'

Calamity closed her eyes and shivered. 'Eay! It's hard to imagine.'

'Aye,' I agreed, 'it takes a special kind of lass, does that. Anyway, the officer who selects the two young whores from Lazy Daisy's is called the girl-taster – and that's what this Tooley fellow does at the moment. *He's* the one who decides which girls get to spread their legs for the young officers and which girls don't.'

'It's definitely on for tonight,' Kitten told me when we met at Leeds Central that Saturday morning. About ten days had passed since our extraordinary session in Wharton's studio. I had called on Wharton himself a couple of times, hoping to find Gabriele alone and available once more – but no such luck. The second time he grew suspicious and I was forced to commission a painting of me and Kitten *in flagrante* – if he could remember it well enough, I said, for I was sure Kitten would not agree to repeat the pose. He assured me, without a trace of a smile, that he had an absolutely *photographic* memory for that sort of thing. And so there it was – to deflect his suspicions I was compelled to buy a painting I could never hang.

I also had another strange encounter with Miss Campbell – again on our stairway; again, too, she was ahead of me though this time we were both going down. We had now progressed from grave bowing to spoken greetings, smiles, and smalltalk. She was chatting away about the joy of early Communion or something and had just reached the bottom step when she stumbled. She would have fallen completely if she had not clutched at the newel-post. She gave a little cry and said, 'Oh, my ankle!'

I stood anxiously nearby and gave her elbow a reassuring squeeze, at which she shot me a look of enormous gratitude, saying, 'I do hope it's not broken.'

'What may I do?' I asked. 'Shall I run and fetch a glass of water?'

Shyly she protruded her booted foot from under her long skirts. 'Does it look alright?' she asked. 'I know you won't take advantage of this awkward situation.'

I stooped and gingerly took her boot in my hands. The moment I touched her she gave that same cry she had given when I carried her satchel. And again she stared at me in wonder as she snatched her foot back into respectable cover and said, 'The pain is quite gone! Ye *are* a healer. I thought as much when ye cured my hand. Dinnae ye ken ye're a healer?'

I shook my head.

'Well, ye are,' she replied – and sailed out of the front door with the most fetching smile.

Again, I dismissed the incident almost at once. I had other problems on my mind without responding to Miss Campbell's rather blatant come-all-yous – chiefly how to keep Kitten on my side and organize Calamity's seduction by exploiting her, Calamity's, boundless gift for deceit.

My conversation with Kitten during that period was reduced to two brief exchanges in her driveway – that is, *I* was in her driveway, *she* was leaning out of a window; however, we managed to convey the essentials. She told me that Tooley was going to complete his revenge by smuggling Calamity into the Young Turks one night – not the whole night, just the two 'free-for-all' hours between ten and midnight. All I needed to do then was to let Calamity know I'd be away one night and her unique combination of treachery and sexual desire would do the rest. I told her I'd be away until about two in the morning on the following Saturday. 'I hope to make a killing at Sedgefield races,' I explained.

She, being careful rather than suspicious, wondered why I'd be away so long.

'If I win, there'll be quite a celebration.'

'And if you don't?'

'Then I shall have to drown my sorrows.'

She gazed at me with all the scorn of the reformed

drunkard for the occasional binger; but my story was accepted.

In fact, Kitten was to accompany me to the races (since revenge is a two-edged sword), and we would be back in Leeds by eight that evening.

So when Kitten said, as she joined me on the train, that it was definitely on, she was merely providing the final confirmation. 'Really,' I told her, 'my doubts were dispelled last night when Calamity rifled my pockets and found this.' I held up my railway ticket.

'What a very careful girl she's turned out to be,' Kitten said coldly.

I agreed. 'She's the very soul of deception and trickery. The smile on her face was something to behold – the smile of a girl who knows she's going to enjoy some fairly heavy rogering.'

Kitten's lips curled in a sneer. 'She sounds an out-and-out little whore!'

'Oh God, Kitten!' I reached across and squeezed her arm affectionately. 'I just hope you're right. She talks as if whoring were the foulest, most disgusting thing she ever heard of, but the *idea* of it obsesses her.'

'A bit like your friend Rachel,' Kitten pointed out.

I shook my head. 'Rachel doesn't think it's disgusting.'

'No, but she is obsessed by it. She'd love to spend a single night as a *fille de joie* at Lazy Daisy's. Or taking on a dozen Young Turks. But she'd never turn professional.' She grinned maliciously. 'Maybe your precious Calamity's the same.'

'Don't talk like that,' I grumbled. 'You're supposed to

be on my side. The great thing about Calamity is that she gets addicted to things. It was alcohol that time you met her. . .'

'Oh is *that* what it was?' she asked heavily.

I ignored the sarcasm. 'Then it was Iron Jack and lots of sticky.' I sighed. 'We shall just have to make sure this high-class *maison* in Paris offers her plenty of scope for an addiction of *some* kind.'

We had a splendid day at the races and I did, indeed, make a killing of about five hundred pounds – and I won a further five pounds on the train back south, playing poker with three Roman Catholic clergymen. I took Kitten straight home from the station. The cab journey to Roundhay Park was about twenty-five minutes and I'm sure she expected me to try to seduce her on the way. She would have repulsed me, of course; bourgeois ideas about loyalty reign in places that would shock most bourgeois citizens to hear about. I had quite a battle over it with Iron Jack, who – with his mind on that dear, soft, warm, wet little hole of hers, not twenty-four inches away – was engaged in his usual muscular struggle with fly-buttons and worsted. The Worsted War, I called it – or the Serge Struggle, depending on what I was wearing at the time. But this time I won it. Kitten was not going to have the pleasure of hearing me beg while she proved her moral superiority by saying no.

For my noble self-restraint I was granted the extraordinary privilege of washing and changing in her bathroom. Her maid was Tooley's spy and had hopes of getting Kitten dismissed and then taking her place between the sheets, so Kitten must have known that word of my invasion would get directly back to him; in her own way she was telling me she was getting ready to move on.

'Thank you for a wonderful day,' she said conventionally enough as we parted, and then she added, 'It was the first really *free* day I've had since you left me.'

Since *I* left *her* – note!

By the time I reached Headingley I was assailed by two great hungers, both of them below the belt. A quick snack at a fish-and-chip shop took care of one of them. The other, I told myself, would have to wait for another day; tonight was strictly for voyeuring. (Which, as you will see, only shows the futility of planning ahead in affairs erotic.)

It was nine o'clock and fully dark by the time I crept into the grounds of the Young Turks clubhouse. Knowing Calamity's impatient nature I felt sure she'd have nagged and nagged until Tooley agreed to let her start at half past nine instead of ten, so I had, at best, a mere half an hour to determine the lie of the land.

I had only clapped eyes on the house once before – and then only from the road. The view from the back was quite a surprise – and filled me with some dismay. The ground floor was ablaze with light; I could hear laughter, banjo music, a piano, and the click of billiard balls. The floor above it, however – where I expected the pretty waiter-girls to do their solo entertaining – was in complete darkness; yet I distinctly remembered that Kitten had described some rather sumptuous bedrooms on that level. By contrast, several of the windows along the top floor – presumably where the pretty waiter-girls slept – were bathed in a soft, seductive light. The inescapable conclusion was that they not only slept in those rooms but performed the horizontal part of their duties there, too. It was a daunting climb, with nothing but drainpipes and ivy to help me.

Looking back on it now, I cannot understand why I was surprised at this arrangement. It is so obvious when you think of it. Those upper-class officers grew up in large houses bustling with young female domestics, all of whom slept in the attics. Their adolescent fantasies (and occasional adventures, too) must have involved ten thousand ascents to those garrets of slumbering temptation. The Young Turks clubhouse was where their dreams came true, night after night. Of *course* they took their pretty waiter-girls up to their proper bedrooms in the attics! (But the high-class *fille de joie* from Lazy Daisy's was another kettle of fish, for she was part of a different fantasy; her proper milieu was the sumptuous boudoir up on the first floor.)

Scouting round the side of the house I found a ladder leaning against the wall of the stables. With its help I soon reached a balcony outside one of the darkened boudoirs. From there I was able to use some heavily cut recesses between ashlar stones, piled in a column – together with handholds of ivy and, near the top, a diagonal run of cast-iron drainpipe to reach the parapet that ran all along the garden side of the house. It formed the outer wall for a generous lead-lined gutter, about eighteen inches wide, beyond which the roof rose steeply to an apex of pierced ridge tiles. The windows of the garret rooms projected outward from this roof, finishing at a vertical level with the inner edge of the gutter. I was thus able to walk the full length of the house, needing to duck only as I passed each window.

There were seven in all, four lighted, three dark. As it happened, they were in perfect alternation – lighted, dark, lighted, dark . . . It seemed obvious to me that the lighted rooms were the ones in use. A gentleman may be obliged to poke his wife in the dark, but when he's poking for pleasure, he wants to enjoy it with all his senses alert. I remained cautious, however; many a plan has come unstuck on assumptions that seemed obvious at the time. So I scurried along the gutter (the right place for a voyeur, I thought) and began my observations at the far left of the house. Fortunately the night was overcast and there was no moon to give me away at the darkened windows.

Confirmation came at the very first peep. A young redheaded waiter-girl, rather tall, was standing fully dressed in maid's uniform, which in those days was down-to-the-ground black with a white pinafore. She was leaning against the wall beyond her mean little fireplace, where a generous fire was blazing. Her expression was blank as she watched a young officer undressing himself. He was standing beside the bed, a highly ornamental affair of cast-iron and brass, wide enough for two. They could only just have come into the room, for he was barely halfway down the twenty-odd buttons that fastened it. After he had fiddled with about eight of them, she came forward and helped with the rest. He had no shirt underneath, just a long-sleeved woollen vest. She started on his flies but he shooed her away – in a friendly fashion – and waited for her to resume her position against the wall. Now she leaned down and hitched up her skirts at the front, showing a large expanse of frilly white petticoat and her black-stockinged calves.

Only then did he start undoing his flies. His tool, when he fished it out, was stiff as a ramrod and pointed straight up at the ceiling without support. The knob was bright scarlet; I could almost feel the heat off it from where I stood. He gave it a few loving strokes with his fingertips as he advanced toward her, grinning lecherously. When he reached her he fell to his knees and, hooking his thumbs under the hem of her petticoats, lifted them to expose her knees – which he kissed with all the fervour of a lovesick swain.

Slowly, inexorably, his lips rose up her stockinged thighs. Her garters were high, only inches from her quim, and I saw flashes of bright red beaver among the frills of her underwear as his excited hands fumbled with the material. When his lips reached that brief expanse of naked thigh, his tongue came out to join the exploration. I could almost smell the heady reek of her sex from out there in the cold; Lord knows what havoc it was playing with his senses, only inches away.

At that moment she took the hem from him and spread the garment wide so that it fell down over him, confining him inside the tent of her petticoat. From the movement of his head and the way her body dipped as she spread her thighs for him I could only imagine what a feast he was making of her oyster. And what a dilemma for me – desperate to discover whether Calamity had already arrived, and equally desperate to see what this couple would do next!

The girl's behaviour intrigued me most of all. For a brief while she stood there, staring impassively at nothing in particular; but when she first parted her thighs to let him get his tongue right into her fig, she bit her lip and clenched her fists, as if willing herself *not* to be roused by him. She stood a moment thus, opening and closing her hands and then, finally, clasped his head to her through the petticoat and surrendered to the pleasure. She closed her eyes and raised her head toward the ceiling. He simply continued feasting at her fork, his head darting this way and that in little movements that reminded me of a grazing rabbit.

Next she unbuttoned her blouse and took out her bubbies. They were small but nicely rounded and with large, swollen nipples, which gleamed like pinkish mother-of-pearl. She caressed them with her fingertips, scratched them lazily with the edges of her nails, and cupped them in her hands stroking them with a slow, sensual, upward movement. When a girl is flying high on that level of pleasure it's hard to tell when she rises to a full orgasm. I think this particular filly had several before her lover's mighty tool decided it could stay out of her no longer. Then, with a lithe, animal movement, he ducked out from under her petticoat and, catching its hem on the fiery tip of his ramrod, lifted it with him and he rose. His whole face gleamed with his slaver and her juices, which he wiped off into the sleeve of his vest.

She, waking up with a jolt to what was now coming her way, grabbed the petticoat from him and tucked it deeply into her open blouse. She held her bubbies up to him while at the same time she clenched the tops of her thighs tightly around his gristle; they, too, were soaked in her juices. He still had his trousers on but she slipped his braces off his shoulders so that they fell to his knees at least, where they crumpled, concertina-fashion, upon the tops of his cavalry boots. It was going to be a genuine, military-style knee-trembler, all right – the sort of encounter you see in the shadows round any barracks gate, five minutes before curfew.

He rooted his weapon around in the soft stickiness between her thighs for a while, getting it well and truly lubricated. The moment he was ready she knew it and, hugging his neck for support, threw one leg up around his waist. Happily, it was her near leg from my point of view so I was able to see her labia smiling for him; they were engorged with blood both by her present letch and by the heavy traffic they endured each night. His tool made several stabs at her cunny but, being so well lubricated by now, missed and slid up between the cheeks of her bumhole instead. She laughed and, relaxing her raised leg a bit, got him well and truly bunged up her on his next frantic thrust.

She gave out a strangled cry of joy and redoubled the strength of the leg that encircled him; her heel was digging into his waist on the opposite side, so that even if he had wanted to withdraw he could not have done so. But withdrawal was now the last thing on his mind. He plugged away at her like a well-oiled steam engine, withdrawing only half his piston each time and then plunging it back up her cunny as if his pressure vessel was about to burst. Her labia were so swollen with her pleasure that they furled and unfurled with each reciprocating movement of that mighty rod. The firelight flickered lasciviously on her wet thighs and the flesh of her quim.

There was no doubting when he reached *his* orgasm. She felt its onset and timed her movements perfectly, lifting her other leg around him and ramming her vagina down tight on his spermspouter at the very moment it lived up to its name. That she didn't break his spine was a marvel. His pelvis writhed and twitched in that unstoppable spasm, packing his gristle yet tighter into that gluttonous space – so much so that the milt of his ecstasy and the juices of her bliss were forced out of that frenzied confinement in wave after wave, soaking his balls and underwear.

At last he collapsed against the wall – or against *her* against the wall – and her thighs released their grip and slid to the ground. She fished a large, man's handkerchief out of her pinny pocket and, folding it into a pad, plugged it to her quim just as his organ shrivelled and fell limply out of her.

He kissed her gently on the lips, then on each of her nipples, before he reached for his braces and pulled them up over his shoulders again. His knob was still quite swollen and red but the column of his tool was no bigger than his finger. It was shrivelled, too, like skin that has soaked a long time in water. He stared down at it and uttered a sad, mock-sigh. She stooped and gave it an affectionate kiss before she tucked it away for him. As she straightened up she lifted his wrist and consulted his watch. It was twenty past nine. She uttered a sigh that was far from mock. In forty minutes' time she'd be up here with some other young man, doing it – or something very like it – all over again.

My fairy godmother was smiling upon me that night. I traversed the full length of the gutter without being discovered. Indeed, discovery would have been a miracle, for all the rooms – darkened or seductively lit – were empty, which, with the one-girl-on-her-back-at-a-time rule, was only to be expected. However, I arrived at the last lighted window, at the farther end from the little drama I had just witnessed, at the very moment that Tooley ushered Calamity into that room.

The little deceiver was barely across the threshold when she raised her arms above and behind her head, putting them around his and pulling his lips down to hers. His hands closed around her bubbies, and her chest began at once to heave with passion. I feared I was about to witness Tooley exercising some sort of *droit de seigneur*, but a moment later she giggled and fended him off. She wagged a finger and said something to him; he pulled a contrite face and started to point out certain features of the room – the cupboard with fresh sheets, the wash basin, the long mirror, extra cushions and pillows ... and so on. He stoked up the fire before he left. At the door he wagged a finger back at her and uttered some jocular warning; she laughed and blew him a kiss.

The moment she was alone she raced out of her clothes and, delving in a bag that Tooley had dropped just inside the doorway, produced several items of provocative underwear which *I* had bought her! Pale-blue silk stockings that hugged her thighs like true skin. They were held up by a narrow suspender belt of the identical hue; it had a lacy top, and tassels of slightly darker blue all round the lower edge; the way her curvaceous moons and fine-haired beaver shimmered through it made me sweat already. Next came a brief chemise of fine gauze – 'woven air,' the salesman had called it – so brief that it ended in a fringe exactly on the line of her nipples, which now and then poked saucily through the strands. Then a pair of ermine slippers – and that was it! She was 'sweet, clean, and ready for service,' as the mesdames always say.

She began to pace up and down. She jiggled with excitement to make the fringe tickle her nipples, which swelled to bursting with her elation. Now and then her finger strayed into the dimple that split her Venus mound but, as if that pleasure were too acute, she snatched it away again every time.

In fact she had not long to wait. She had just started the fourth up-and-down when there was a knock at the door. She ran to the bed, stood near its foot, and quavered, 'Come in!'

I almost fell off my perch when the door burst open and I saw what stood there. He was a short, hairy Scotsman who looked as if he could toss the caber clear across Loch Lomond. He was wearing the kilt (of course) and the black Montrose jacket with the lace ruff and lace dripping out of the sleeves. He already had his sporran off and in his hand – no doubt because on the way up it had chafed the huge bulge that already swelled the pleats of his kilt, making him look eight-months gone. He had a wild red beard – and an even wilder red gleam in his eye as he advanced toward Calamity. He hung his sporran and that dagger thing they tuck into their socks on the bedpost as he passed. And she just stood there, her fringe and tassels trembling with the mighty beat of her heart. The way the bed was angled, they were three-quarters-on to me so I could see them both in near-profile, with more of his back and more of her delightful front.

The diamond-shaped silver buttons were decorative. The hook-and-eye fastenings came undone with just four deft tweaks and the Montrose fell off him, taking the lacy bits with it. He stood before her, a hairy oak-tree of a man, naked but for his kilt. Calamity sat down heavily on the bed and prepared to discover the *second* great secret of life – what a Scotsman wears under the kilt. She lifted the hem and discovered that *this* Scottie had nothing there but an impressively knobbly caber, eight inches long and thick enough to need both her hands to get round it; the one-eyed knob on the end of it would have made a good job of packing the powder into a short howitzer.

Gently he took her head in between his hands and coaxed it down toward that object of awe. Fortunately Calamity had generous lips and a wide mouth. Moments later he jerked in a spasm of delight and threw his head right back, giving out a roar of joy. Instinct alone guided his fingers to the buckles of the strange two-ended belt that holds a kilt up. The moment it fell from him, Calamity's hands began an excited exploration of his body. That and her skill with her tongue made him suddenly fear for a premature conclusion so he jerked his organ out of her mouth and bore gently down on her shoulders, pushing her backward.

In a trice she was flat on her back with her arms and legs waving in the air. With her pale flesh and her blue underwear her movements were so enticing I thought of some beautiful undersea creature of the coral reef, waving its parts to lure an unsuspecting minnow to its doom. The folds of her quim, so well known and so dear to me, looked especially oyster-like and enticing.

His rammer was certainly no minnow, though. It was now so stiff that he had to arch his back and press it down to the point of pain to get it into her cleft. There, although it was still dripping from her saliva, he ran it up and down, up and down, several times, to pick up that extra-fine lubrication that only a young girl's quim exudes. She rested her heels on his shoulders and left the moment of penetration to him.

To my almost certain knowledge his tool would be only the third such organ in her life to slip up inside her – and it was by far the fattest and chunkiest. Tooley's might be as long (from what Kitten had told me) and the knob on Iron Jack might be as swollen, but this was two-hands'-girth of solid gristle all the way. I wondered how she'd be able to take it all in.

At last he braced his legs apart and arched his back still further and I knew that the moment had come. Calamity's hands went down to her bottom, her fingers crawled across her buttocks and pressed into her crevice, one from each side. Then they drew her labia apart – wide as could be – so that the dark flesh of her vagina gleamed in unaccustomed exposure. A second later it was masked by that importunate red knob of his as he slipped the first inch into its natural home.

He grinned steadily down at her, she grinned steadily up at him, as, bit by bit, with dozens of tiny thrusts and withdrawals, he worked the whole of his stupendous weapon into her. When he got it all the way in, she threw back her head until she was staring upside down at the wall behind her and let out one great gurgle of joy. Then, as if he were still not deep enough into her, he leaned forward, bending her double, so that her knees touched her shoulders, and started piledriving his great belly-ruffian in and out of her.

'And what the hell are you doing out there?'

The voice – female – came from behind me. I spun around and found myself face to face with an angry young Juno who was leaning out of the window of the darkened room next door. Except that it was no longer darkened, for she held a candle in her hands, shielding her own eyes from it but blinding mine.

'Ssh!' I responded and ran to her with a finger to my lips.

'Peeping Tom!' she said, half-way between whisper and speech.

'No!' I assured her. 'Just looking after my property. That's one of my girls in there.'

There was a long pause before she said, in a tone of quiet intrigue, 'One of your girls?' She rested the candle on the sill and now I could see her face, which was round, strong, and pleasant – though not at all pretty. A country wench, built for stamina. ''Oy!' Her eyes lit up. 'Are you that . . .' She clicked her fingers in momentary frustration. 'Smiler!'

'How d'you know my name?'

'Yon girl's tooken my place tonight. I should be lifting that Scottie's kilt next door.'

'That's not an answer to my question.'

'Are you the famous Smiler, then?'

'Yes, but how d'you know?'

She sighed. 'It'd take too long to explain, love. Happen I'll tell thee someday. I'll tell thee this now, though – I've known about thee since last year, when that Kitten girl first come here. So maybe that'll let thee guess the rest.'

While she spoke she kept looking toward the window of the room next door – and suddenly I realized what had brought her there. 'D'you want to watch?' I asked. 'Want to join me?'

She bit her lip and looked uncertainly at me. 'I've done it that often,' she said, 'but I've never seen it done. Can tha credit that?'

'Come and see, then.' I reached with my arms to help her climb out of the window. She giggled as she half-fell into my embrace. There was lots of flesh on her bones but it was firm and strong, not fat. She half-crouched to absorb her jump and then pressed tight against me as she stood up. Her thighs were stout and lusty and her bubbies large and firm; she had not bathed that evening and a delightful milky sort of odour rose out of her bodice and bathed my face. Iron Jack began the fourth Worsted War of the evening but I put all such thoughts resolutely from me.

'I'm Dido, by the way,' she said.

When we returned to Calamity's window I got the shock of my life. Only a few minutes had passed since I had left my vantage but already the Scottie had gone. Now she was standing on the floor, legs apart, leaning forward over a huge pile of cushions on the bed while a thin officer plugged away at her from behind. He appeared to be fully dressed – though obviously his flies, at least, must be undone.

'What happened to the Scotch fellow?' I asked, peering this way and that to see if he and this new fellow were taking it by turns.

'Didn't tha know?' Did asked. 'Yon Tooley asked her how many she wanted to take on toneet – and she said she's take on t'whole lot, if they'd a mind.'

My stomach fell. 'And how many is "the whole lot," Dido?' I asked.

'There's only twenty-five in toneet,' she replied. 'Saturday's compulsory dining-in for a lot on 'em. 'Ere, is it true what they say about thee, Smiler?'

'She couldn't take on all twenty-five in two hours,' I exclaimed.

'Two and a half,' she corrected me. 'She could if they only had six minutes each – ten to an hour. Is it true, then?'

'Six minutes!' I echoed incredulously.

'That's about as long as most on 'em can make it last, anyroad,' she sneered. 'They just chuck a girl on her back and toss theirsels off into her belly. Is it true about thee – that tha can make it last two hours?'

The prospect of watching Calamity being plugged

through two-dozen-odd quickies for the next couple of hours or so had no appeal whatever.

But Dido had.

'Easy,' I assured her – thinking that two hours would hardly take me to midnight and I'd still have another two hours to fill before I could return to my chambers.

'I don't believe it,' she scoffed – though we both knew what she was really saying.

'Three hours – if you wish,' I said.

She swallowed heavily.

'*Do* you wish?' I asked. And then, 'Will that bedroom I found you in remain undisturbed if we use it?'

Dido was *big* in every way – big of heart, big in appetite, big in warmth, big in her demands. She was a country wench, only nineteen, but straight off the farm and built to go any distance on the flat. There was not an ounce of flab about her; a gentle pinch would raise less skin on her than it would on many a more angular filly. Big, firm, warm, and glowing – that was Dido. She was not, as I said, especially pretty, but she had the most beautiful hair, long and glossy and blue-black, like a raven's breast. Since I was to make good my boast that I could go three hours with her, I was in no hurry to press on with the first act. I presumed it would suit her, too, to hasten slowly, since her complaint was all at the hustle the Young Turks made of the business. So, while three more of them whanged their meat into the boastful Calamity next door, Dido and I did no more than kiss as chastely as any two lovers on a park bench of a Sunday afternoon.

It's an odd thing to confess now but I had never before
in my life spent twenty whole minutes doing nothing but
kiss a girl on her mouth. At the end of that time Dido's lips
seemed to undergo a strange transformation. Not that they
became some kind of crude substitute for those other lips,
endlessly smiling their hidden smile down there between
her magnificent thighs, but they came to symbolize her
sexuality itself – not, I repeat, her sex, but her entire
sexuality . . . that exciting brew of warmth and passion, of
desire and fulfilment, of all the physical and all the
spiritual sensations that cluster around the act of sexual
love. Dido became – or, rather, stood for – all the willing
females in the world . . . and yet while I held her in my arms
she was the only woman I could possibly desire. Yes! The
mere act of kissing her filled me with such loving tenderness that I would have lain with her a month and done
nothing but pleasure her big, gorgeous body – if she had
but asked it. Perhaps it was as well for both of us that she
already considered three hours an eternity!

We were lying on the bed, both fully dressed except for
our shoes and my jacket, and every inch of me was on fire
for the touch of her. I loosened one button of her blouse and
slipped a tentative finger inside. I was miles away from her
nipple – barely into the softness where her bubby began –
and yet it seemed the most impudent intrusion! When she
responded by loosening one of my shirt buttons, I felt I
must be the most privileged man on earth that night. Until
then I would never have believed that, simply by removing
the mechanical assumption between us (that I would
inevitably roger her and she would inevitably open her legs

and let me in), we could endow these simple actions with such powerful erotic force. It was every bit as exciting to me to loosen the second button of her blouse as it had previously been to slip Iron Jack into any of the dozens of fillies I had rogered before that night. Between us Dido and I had restored the primal magic to the sexual act.

And so it went, with one magical moment following another – the first touch of her nipple, which was distended and perspiring with her craving by then; her discovery that my nipples were as sensitive as any woman's and enjoyed the same sort of play; the moment when my finger slid down into the glossy black forest over her Venus mound . . . on into the hot, wet crevice beneath, there to find her *coquille* swollen to the size of a big, juicy escargot – and so exquisitely tender that the merest touch was enough to send that old, mad electricity coursing through her limbs. And the moment when I buried my face in that fragrant fork, astonished at the firm pink bananas of her outer labia and the contrast they made with the delicate folds and frills of the inner ones. And the melting clench of her tight little vagina as my tongue went questing in. Perhaps three or four cocks had already preceded me there that day but to me that was meaningless. I was the first who ever brought her to that peak of lechery; she was then the only girl on earth for me.

We explored and toyed with and pleasured each other for the best part of an hour before Iron Jack finally got his way and tucked himself tightly up into her tail. It reminded me at once of something I had completely forgotten. When I was about fourteen my Uncle Tommy and I (he being sixteen and a kind of god to me) used to go out and tickle cocks on the golf course. One day I went out to meet him there but he was being punished and could not join me. So I gouged a hole in the soft peat beneath the gorse bushes, pushed a handkerchief into it, and poked my immature but oh-so-randy little cock into the recess. The sun had baked that spot all afternoon so the earth was as hot as a real live woman; the sensation was so delicious that I started coming at once. Usually Uncle Tommy and I went on until we'd had half a dozen orgasms each (or had given each other blood-blisters from the friction); but this was so stupendous that I didn't need to go again. I just lay out flat on my huge Mother Earth and filled her with my empty spending – for I had no wet spunk at that age.

And that is what I remembered the moment Iron Jack slipped up inside the big, warm, all-female body of Dido that night; and a moment later I was filling her with enough wet spunk to float a cruiser.

And a moment after *that* she was beating at my shoulders with her mighty fists, crying fit to drown herself, and calling me every name she could think of – telling me I was no better than the rest and I hadn't even gone one hour, let alone three.

However, the moment I jiggled inside her a little and she felt Iron Jack still hard as hickory, her arms went about me and her legs flew up around my waist and she gave my shoulders a hundred little love-bites and she gurgled in her pleasure. 'When tha said tha can make it last three hours,' she murmured, 'tha meant . . . *it!*' And she squeezed the walls of her vagina tight against *it*.

'Of course,' I replied. 'What did you think I meant?'

'I thought tha meant *it*. Tha knows! *It*.'

'Actually, I meant both,' I said – and we passed the next two hours in most joyful proof of *it*.

When I explained to Dido why Calamity was there that night, and my hopes of getting her settled in a high-class house of pleasure in Paris, she begged me to take her, too. I saw at once that she was the missing element in my strategy. The idea of taking just two girls – Kitten and Calamity – to France had always filled me with unease. I contemplated it only because the alternative – to take Calamity alone – was quite unthinkable. But Calamity, Kitten, *and* Dido was a different matter altogether. I saw at once how I could manage the whole thing then, and agreed without more ado.

The fact that, at a single stroke, I would be depriving Tooley of his mistress, his clandestine bit of fluff, *and* one of his pretty waiter-girls played almost no part in my decision. I am not a vengeful man and I bore him no malice. Still, I did enjoy the occasional quiet laugh when I thought of it.

It seemed best to write to Madam ffrench, founder and proprietress of the world-famous *Maison ffrench*, a magnificent palace of pleasure in the southern suburbs of Paris*. It was easy enough to tell her about Kitten and

*I have already edited and published Charlotte ffrench's two-volume memoirs under the titles *ffrench Pleasures* and *The ffrench House*, uniform with this present volume. – FR

Dido – all she needed to know was a brief description of their physical beauties, their social graces, their background, education, aspirations, and dedication to the Noble Profession. But what to tell her about Calamity?

I decided to write as if I were not actually offering her for a horizontal position at the *Maison ffrench* – merely that she was a complete enigma to me and that I would welcome her opinion and advice as a woman who must by now know every variety and condition of female on this planet.

Madam ffrench wrote back by return of post, a brief but charming letter saying that, while she could not guarantee a regular place for any of my girls she was always looking for extra ones in springtime, when the demand for willing girls increased to dizzying heights. If my descriptions of them proved trustworthy, she would offer Kitten and Dido ten weeks' work with the prospect of a more regular place thereafter. And she could hardly wait to meet Calamity, who sounded *most* intriguing.

So all that remained was the matter of buying our train tickets and arranging our clandestine flight – though, unlike the Mozart opera, this was to be a flight *into* the seraglio! And, oh yes, there was also the matter of persuading Calamity to come at all!

Of her night at the Young Turks, where she successfully accommodated twenty-five lovers in the space of a hundred and fifty minutes, she breathed not a word. When I returned home at three that night – allegedly from the Sedgefield races – she even tried to seduce me, and complained when I said I was too tired (the first time I had ever said such a dreadful thing to a woman in my life!). So, if she was going to remain stubbornly insistent that I was the only man who ever had or ever would take horizontal refreshment with her, I had no choice but to play along.

'You'd be bored to death,' I told her. 'You know how you loathe whores and anything to do with prostitution. It would be absolute misery to you to be cooped up with two such girls and to hear them boasting day and night of how they're going to work in the most luxurious House in Europe . . . and the fortunes they're going to make . . . and the grand, important men they're going to pleasure . . . emperors, kings, presidents, not to mention the young aristocrats and army officers . . . you'd *hate* it, Calamity!'

'I needn't listen,' she snapped. 'And I should like to see Paris.'

'I'll take you another time.'

And so the battle raged for days, with me refusing to contemplate it and her giving me all the high-sounding reasons for changing my mind. At last she produced the *coup-de-grâce*: If I went to Paris without her, and took those immoral girls to that house of iniquity, I'd be tempted by the whores of Babylon who lived there – so she'd swallow all her misgivings and accompany me to keep me pure. I made her promise she'd be nice as pie to the two Unfortunates, Kitten and Dido, and, with the greatest (show of) reluctance, I capitulated at last.

The night before our departure I had yet another odd encounter with Miss Campbell next door. This time it was nothing to do with healing – at least, not the healing of her person. Her bathroom geyser had given up the ghost.

Could I possibly come and look at it as she was afraid it might explode? She had conveyed this request to Calamity while I was out. Naturally I went round at once; there had been a spate of exploding geysers in Leeds recently so it was no far-fetched nightmare.

I was more than a little surprised to find her wearing a dressing gown, a creation of pure, virgin-white towelling; however, it covered everything between her neck and her ankles, so she no doubt felt she was decent. But she had tied it so tightly about her slender waist that it was clear she had nothing on underneath.

'Ye're all a-tremble,' she murmured in her husky Highland voice as I removed the draught shield from the geyser.

'The pilot light's gone out,' I said. However, there was no sniff of gas.

The meter showed she had a good shilling's-worth left, and there was a strong supply to the cooker; so the problem was confined to the geyser. Turning on the pilot-light valve made no difference – there was still no flame.

'And you say it just went out half-way through filling your bath?' I asked.

'Aye.' She stooped over and felt the temperature of the water.

My eyes nearly popped out of my head for the cleavage of her dressing gown fell open and a pair of the most beauteous bubbies I ever saw hung like ripe fruit for all the world to see. The display continued for almost half a minute while she stirred and stirred, apparently lost in some reverie. I just stood there transfixed while Iron Jack

fought yet another valiant skirmish in the old Serge
Struggle.

At long last she appeared to notice what had happened
and straightened herself up with a jolt, blushing furiously.
'Och, what must ye think of me!' she moaned. That sweet
Highland quaver always sounds slightly ironic. 'I hope ye
don't think badly?'

I assured her I did not.

She calmed down at once and told me I was being very
sensible. After all, weren't our bodies given to us by the
Almighty? It was only Satan, putting mucky thoughts into
our heads, who made them sinful. Good Christians should
reclaim the beauty of our bodies for the side of righteousness
– and would I be interested in joining the Kirkstall Naturist
Club, of which she had lately become a member?

At last I twigged what Miss Campbell was all about. I
could just see her driving the men to distraction behind
those tall, tight-clipped hedges of yew at Kirkstall. I closed
my eyes to her charms and stopped my ears to her winsome
prattle. The gas tap in the pipe that fed the geyser had, as
I immediately suspected, been turned off – something that
could not possibly happen by accident. I turned it on again,
smiled at her, relit the pilot light (with the very last match
in the box), waited for it to heat the safety bimetal, and
turned the geyser back on. Of course, it burst merrily into
life. '*Voilà*!' I said, leaving it running so as to fill her bath.

'Would ye like tae become a member?' she repeated.

I challenged her, then. 'Very well. If you're so convinced
the naked body is pure and innocent, show me yours!'

And by thunder she did!

I've been to nude-bathing clubs; I know how girls behave when they're genuinely unselfconscious of their charms. I've also been in the boudoirs of some of the finest courtesans in the world; I've seen how girls behave when they know their own bodies down to the last corpuscle, and the power they have to command men's eyes. But I have never known one with Miss Campbell's ability to combine the air of the innocent with the skill of the courtesan. She had the sort of body that men would gamble whole empires to possess. I surveyed her without a word until I'd got over my heart attack, my sense of disembowelment, and my shivering fits – which was long enough for me to realize I was looking at a body without a single blemish. There was not a line I'd alter, nor colour I'd change, nor form I'd remould. She was perfection.

In a humbled, awestruck voice I said, 'It is the most beautiful body I have ever seen, Miss Campbell. And what about that adorable smile *between* your legs?' I was pleased at how steady my voice sounded. 'Will you show me that, too?'

She sighed and shook her head, as sensible women do when faced with incorrigibly naughty boys. 'I'm sure ye think ye're no end of a wag, Mister S.,' she said.

'Ah, perhaps the Almighty *didn't* make that bit, eh?'

'He did, of course,' she replied icily. 'But He hid it a-purpose, as ye ken fine well.'

'He didn't hide the male equivalent though.'

'Naturally. Women are made sweet and pure unless man defiles them. Ye may be sure an undefiled woman's thoughts never stray in that direction. But men are impure in their very nature. So isn't it the mark of a loving Creator that He put men's inflammatory parts oot there in the full light o' day, where we puir females can see them – and be well and truly warned when their thoughts stray toward lascivious deeds!'

She knew precisely how infuriated I was by her specious arguments; she knew I was longing to turn on my heel and go storming off, flinging an oath over my shoulder; but, although she no longer held her dressing gown wide open, she left it with the belt dangling loose, granting me the most stimulating glimpses of her ravishing young body – and so she knew I had no choice but to stay and take it.

'We must talk about this when I return,' I told her. 'I am quite sure you are wrong.'

'Return?' she asked, alarmed at the implication that I was going away.

'I'm off to Paris tomorrow.'

'Paris,' she echoed suspiciously.

I grinned. 'I'll leave a set of keys to my chambers in your letterbox downstairs. Then, if you hear anything suspicious, or simply run out of matches again,' – I shook the empty box – 'you can pop in without difficulty.'

She thanked me with slightly ill grace, annoyed that I had somehow recovered the initiative, and tied her dressing-gown girdle tightly around her waist. Now that I knew what perfection lay just beneath it, however, those towelling curves were still enough to bring me out in a sweat. 'By the way,' I said as I retreated, 'if you see a young man – two years older than me – around the place, don't be alarmed.

He's my Uncle Tommy. I've told him he can use my chambers while I'm gone.'

By 1898, the year of which I write, most express trains had through corridors; but there were still some first-class carriages that had full-width compartments of the old pattern; they were usually coupled in near the front of the train. I booked one such compartment for our journey to London, which departed just before half-past two (allowing for a nice long luncheon) and arrived at St Pancras at six-fifteen (in good time for dinner); for fillies with weak bladders there was just one stop at Leicester.

I must confess I felt proud of my three young beauties as we strolled down the platform to our compartment. Two of them might have had accents as common as dirt but they held themselves like queens and sailed along like three stately galleons. I was the focus of many an envious look from male fellow-passengers and many a quizzical sidelong glance from the females travelling with them. And I? Well, I strode like an Oriental pasha out with his hareem. What a fool I was!

And how unfathomable are the ways of women! Consider:

Kitten was a whore. Dido was a whore. And Calamity, who was something of a gourmand for high-cockalorum herself, knew they were whores. Kitten had enjoyed many a melting moment with me. Dido was desperate to work her hairy oracle on me again. And Calamity still liked me to measure her insides half a dozen times a day. Each of these facts was known not only to me but to each of them.

We *all* knew precisely what our situation was. We all knew why I had reserved a compartment in which, once the train started, we should be as isolated as if we were at the North Pole. And what was the result?

Nothing!

I might have been a nancy boy and they three nuns for all the advantage we took of our situation. Kitten and Dido did not even talk about Paris and the *Maison ffrench* and the way it might change their lives. I blame all three girls, of course, but mainly Calamity. When females get together they seem to organize among themselves – quite automatically – a competition to conform to some common ideal; they want to draw together, to agree, to be more like their unconscious model of femininity, whether pure or foul. Sometimes that model can be deliberately foul. I have heard whores competing among themselves to reveal their most disgusting experience . . . the vilest cock they ever sucked . . . the biggest shit they ever shat on a man's face . . . and things unprintably worse. But those poor girls were an embattled group, surrounded by disapproval and needing to prove their toughness.

My little 'pasha's hareem' was quite the opposite. Two of them knew they were guaranteed a certain amount of well-paid work, and I had guaranteed them their fare back if it proved uncongenial; they had no immediate worries and nothing to prove. The three of us were consumed by one overriding purpose – to get Calamity safely to Paris and hope for a miracle once she was there and saw which side her bread was buttered on. Meanwhile, she was the queen of the castle. If she saw her rôle as protecting me from wicked girls like Kitten and Dido, what could we do but nod and applaud? And prove how *un*wicked we really were!

In a nutshell, she ruined our whole journey from Leeds to Paris, which could have been one long orgy, with brief pauses for sleep and food. Calamity turned it into a celibates' gala, so I shall say no more about it.

At our first sight of the *Maison ffrench* a kind of reverential hush fell over us. It was a glorious spring day and we were in an open carriage, winding its way up a half-mile drive to the grand portico. In the eighteenth-century it had been the Château Bougival, though it was more of a palace than a château. It bordered on the grounds of the palace at Malmaison, where Josephine lived apart from Napoleon, about five miles out of Paris in the south-western suburbs; in those days it was open country and villages all around.

We were greeted on our arrival by a flunkey in a silk tunic, knee breeches, and a powdered wig; the girls felt like princesses already. And there was no going in by the tradesmen's entrance, either; the fillies here were the cream of the cream; they ranked equal with the gentlemen who came to enjoy their favours. Our royal treatment continued indoors, too. We were ushered through the magnificent portals and barely had time to catch our breaths at the sumptuous interior, which seemed to be all palm trees and white marble with gilded inlays, when another flunkey said that Madame ffrench would see us at once.

We had all expected a much older woman but Charlotte

ffrench was not yet forty, very handsome and vivacious. Her House, as we already knew, had then been in business for about fifteen years – and prodigious business it was, too, for she was already worth milliards in whatever currency you cared to name. The sparkle in her eyes when they lighted on Kitten and Dido told me they were already over the first hurdle; my descriptions of them had been reliable.

After a brief conversational opening she took the two girls into her boudoir and interviewed them closely for about twenty minutes, leaving Calamity and me to enjoy some Russian tea and bonbons while we leafed through a generous assortment of newspapers and magazines. I apologized several times to Calamity for subjecting her to this ordeal and promised her we'd soon be gone; she made some very peevish replies.

At length the two girls rejoined us in a state of high excitement. Madame ffrench had shown them two sumptuous boudoirs upstairs and there were several gentlemen who had heard rumours of two new girls starting that afternoon – eager to try them out. Madame proposed they should have two lovers each, who (and which) would occupy them for two to three hours; then they were to return to Paris for one more night at our hôtel. She would give them copies of her book, *A Young Girl's Guide to the Maison ffrench*, which they could read tonight and tomorrow morning and – if they still desired it – begin full-time work tomorrow afternoon.

'These gentlemen will pay *twenty pounds* for the privilege of being our first lovers!' Kitten said breathlessly.

'And we can keep half!' Dido added. 'Ten quid!'

[*The reader may smile patronizingly at their enthusiasm, but the pound sterling of 1898 was worth about £50 in our devalued modern currency. In other words, the two girls were going to return to Paris that evening with something like £1000 each in modern terms! – FR*]

'Tut, tut, and tush!' I sighed as they skipped away for the first of these costly assignations.

Calamity, for once, made no reply.

'Who said the wages of sin is death?' I asked.

Still she said nothing.

I turned round only to discover that she had swooned right away. I bent to try and revive her but she was out to the world.

'I feared something like this might happen,' said a woman's voice behind me.

I looked up and there was Madame ffrench. 'Have her carried into my room,' she told two of the flunkeys.

One of them immediately opened some panelling and produced a stretcher, which I later learned is an essential item in any house of pleasure – many a gentleman who dies with 'a certain smile' on his face has had his obituary tidied up, thanks to a handy stretcher. As they carried the unconscious Calamity into the inner sanctum, Madame gave me a delighted wink.

She repeated the gesture ten minutes later when she returned and told me: 'She's sleeping now. It's probably something she ate. We'll let her sleep it off, eh?'

I responded to this with a somewhat skeptical frown.

She laughed. 'That's what I promised her I'd tell you. And now I'll tell you the truth. She asked if she might be given a trial here, too, and I have agreed.'

'You actually *want* to take her on?' I asked in amazement.

'I know what you mean, Smiler – may I call you that? All three of your girls did, and they speak of you with *such* affection.'

'It's mutual,' I assured her. 'Please do.'

'As to your Calamity . . . I honestly don't know. Some instinct tells me she'll be one of our very top girls in next to no time. But I've been wrong before and will be again, no doubt. And that same instinct also tells me that to be wrong about Calamity is to be *disastrously* wrong. Isn't that so?'

'Calamitously wrong,' I said.

She took my arm. 'I can't wait for my friends to report. I must go and watch this girl for myself. Would you like to join me?'

I was already half a pace ahead of her.

We went through her inner sanctum, which – like Madame's at Lazy Daisy's – was lined with ledgers. She was very proud of it. 'Every girl, every lover, every little preference, every soul!' she said, waiving a hand vaguely over those crowded shelves.

'How many séances does that add up to?' I asked.

She held my arm as if to steady me, not her. 'About forty thousand a year for the last fifteen years. D'you enjoy mathematics, Smiler?' She opened some panelling and pushed me ahead of her up a narrow staircase; the House was full of secret ways.

'I live by it,' I replied. 'I'm a gambler by profession – and professional gamblers are either cheats or they are mathematicians.'

'Ah – you very delicately answer the one question I have been wanting to ask you.'

'Just as I, Madame, have been racking my brains for some way of assuring you I would not dream of asking a sou for bringing you these girls.'

'How about a quid, instead?' she asked teasingly as we arrived in a narrow, ill-lighted corridor on the floor above. Then she added, 'A quid pro quo?'

'A séance with one of your girls?' I asked. 'A *quim* pro quo, don't you mean?'

She hugged me delightedly. 'Oh, Smiler, you are everything your girls say you are. We talked mostly about you, you know. They think the world of you.'

She opened a door, peeped inside, and said, 'Oh, stupid! It's at the far end, of course. Actually' – she crooked a finger – 'come and have a look at this girl. She has a most interesting method.'

The door led into what I can only call a viewing gallery – something like a box at the opera but with two narrow viewing windows, about one foot wide and four feet high. They appeared to have some film of dust upon them, which I tried to wipe off – until Madame explained that there were three panes of glass between me and what I was trying to wipe off (which was why we didn't need to whisper) and that if I was in the room I would swear I was looking at panels of dark, slightly streaky marble.

But my eyes were already rivetted on the girl and her

lover (all patrons were called lovers at the *Maison ffrench*). She was in her early twenties, slender, olive-skinned, a Creole of some kind. She lay on a sumptuous gilded bed with acres of pink silk sheets, not quite face-down – in fact, with her face toward us, eyes closed, and a most seraphic smile on her lips. Her lover, a man in his fifties to judge by the little we could see of him, lay behind her with one hand caressing her bubbies, the other toying with her Venus mound and beaver, and his short, chunky cock slipping in and out of her vagina in a slow, lascivious motion. She had one leg up and resting on his to make his penetration easier.

'The laziest girl in the House!' Madame said crossly. 'And the men adore her. The minute she lies down with a lover she stretches out in that sumptuous fashion, gives a sigh as if she's already starting to come with joyful anticipation, closes her eyes, fixes that simpering smile on her lips – and then does nothing but sigh and moan with pleasure. And some men can't get enough of her. Come on! It makes me sick to watch!'

She led me out and into the next viewing gallery along the passage. There we saw Kitten sucking valiantly on an outsize tool held proudly for her – like a lance – by a young cavalry officer who was still only half undressed. He was lazily fondling her bubbies and, from the expression on his face, there was no doubting the commendation he would give when he reported back.

'She's a real find, Smiler,' Madame said. 'I'm surprised you can part with her.'

'I doubt I'll ever part with Kitten, Madame,' I replied. 'Nor she with me. We cannot live together for long, and nor can we part. We shall alternate between those two impossibilities all our lives, I feel.'

Dido was next. Her lover was a wiry little fellow in his sixties with a bristly moustache and a weaselly face. Had we arrived in the viewing gallery a second or two later, I would have had no idea as to his appearance, other than that he was on the small side. He was lying on his back on a bearskin rug in the area of floor immediately in front of our see-through panels; if the glass had not been there, I could have reached through and tweaked his toes. He had a long, rather gnarled old tool which, viewed from beneath, anyway, curved to his left before becoming straighter at the top – a veteran vagina visitor, no doubt, bowed with use and years of pleasure. And his pleasure that afternoon was to be half-suffocated under Dido's big, warm body.

Only moments after we arrived, as I said, she rolled herself on top of him and wriggled her mighty frame so that every big, firm curve of her did something to delight him. From where we sat we were looking almost straight up between her parted thighs, which remained parted only long enough to make sure his gnarled old cracksman was within a tantalizing inch or two of her crack. Then they clenched around it in a mighty squeeze. Only the fiery purple helmet remained visible, looking like the head of a drowning man between great, rolling billows of white swell. I could imagine the old boy's head at the other end, too, fighting for breath while her two big, soft bubbies threatened to suffocate him.

Then Dido began a series of remarkable gyrations of her hips and thighs – parting, closing, pumping up and down

— during which the plethoric knob was less and less visible.
The likeness to a drowning man in a turbulent ocean grew
ever stronger. The hole at the heart of that feverish wet
crevice in which the column of his tool was now engulfed
was like a whirlpool, sucking him in. At last it succeeded
and we, the voyeurs, could tell the precise moment when
he drowned in joy, right up inside her belly, for they both
jerked in a spasm of uncontrollable pleasure — not the high
peak of an orgasm but one of its major foothills,
nonetheless.

Madame ffrench nudged me. 'See those pink blotches
on her back?' she asked. 'That girl's genuinely enjoying
this.'

'Is that bad?' I asked, for her tone was quite neutral.

She shrugged. 'I've heard every opinion possible on
that particular question. It's the one subject on which we'll
never agree. Some girls never come; some come almost
every time; but neither sort, in my experience, is particularly
happy about it. About themselves I mean. Most of us are
in-betweenish. If it happens, *c'est la vie*! It adds a little
spice.' She chuckled. 'I come every time, of course — but
then I only go with the ones I like in the first place.'

I goggled. 'You mean . . . you still . . .?'

She gave a gamine little grin in which I saw the girl she
must have been at twenty. 'Not too often,' she said. 'Once
a day, perhaps — if that.' She rose. 'We'd better go and look
at your Calamity. She must be about ready by now.'

'If not half-way through,' I commented as we returned
to the passageway.

But Madame shook her head. 'She would have required

117

Faye Rossignol

all this time at least to prepare. Or be prepared, rather.'

When we entered the gallery to Calamity's boudoir I saw what she meant, for I hardly recognized the girl on the other side. Her long hair was piled up in an elaborate coiffure, her face had been made up to give it an almost Oriental cast, her fingernails and toenails had been painted deep scarlet . . .

'It took six *manicuristes* to achieve that,' Madame told me.

Most extraordinary of all were the clothes she had been given. A flimsy peignoir of peach-coloured satin circled her neck and shoulders but so brief that it only just covered down to her nipples, which peeped brazenly out among tassels of gold; beneath them her bubbies hung unadorned. Indeed, from there she was naked right down to her Venus mound – except, I saw, for a fine gold-filigree chain about her slender waist. This made the swelling of her hips and the luscious contours of her derrière especially alluring. Around her hips – so low that wisps of her beaver poked out over the top of it – was a broad band of some kind of elasticated and brightly embroidered silk, again with an Oriental quality. This band was, in fact, the belt of an unusual pair of trousers – hareem trousers, as they are called. The word *pair* has always seemed an odd one for a single garment; but it was perfectly apt on this occasion, for the two legs were, indeed, quite separate. They overlapped for about two inches at the front, where a few tassels provided a sort of teasing concealment of her bush and cleft, and they met side-by-side at the back; but they were perfectly open – delightfully open – right through her

118

fork. They were made of the finest bolting silk; a girl could wear three or four layers of it and still feel naked as a babe. The single layer of these trousers did nothing but envelope Calamity's long, slender thighs and legs in a kind of silvery aura.

And there she stood, all alone, gazing at herself in the tall, free-standing mirror beside the opulent bed, running her hands lightly over the material, and up and down over her naked body, as if she (like me) could hardly believe what a transformation there had been.

'Why did you take so much trouble to change her but not the other two?' I asked.

'Because,' she replied slowly, 'I think *your* Calamity could never bring herself to do what that transformed creature in there is going to be asked to do over the next two or three hours.' There was a powerful tension in her voice. 'I only hope I've guessed correctly,' she added.

Poor Calamity was on the very edge of her nerves. In between staring at herself in the mirror she paced up and down, wiggling her toes between the golden thongs of the flimsy sandals on her feet. She took a chamber pot out of the cabinet, right beside our viewing panel, and tried to use it, but nothing came. However the parting of her thighs, so close to us, revealed a further detail of her dress – namely that the borders of the opening through her fork were all embroidered with lacelike patterns of flowers and butterflies, and, as a centrepiece, one on each side, flew a dainty little hummingbird with its cruelly curved beak darting upward as if it, too, were eager to sip at her honeypot. I could see her breasts and the tassels of her peignoir shivering with her racing heart.

She returned the empty chamberpot to its cabinet and went to sit on the bed. There she spread her thighs again and rubbed her finger gently up and down her furrow. She took it out and sniffed it, pulling a face. She opened a small pot of lotion, standing on the cabinet, and swiped a fingerful. Then she lay back on the bed and, spreading her thighs as wide as they'd go, started to rub it into her quim with a slow, sensual motion.

Beside me Madame gave out a sigh, though whether of sympathy or annoyance I could not tell. A moment later she nudged me again and this time nodded away to our left. I tore my gaze from the little solo drama on the bed and saw that the door was open. Calamity, with her eyes closed and that faraway expression on her face, was not aware of it, but the doorway framed an army officer in full rig – cape, kepi, baton, and all; but the most astonishing thing to me (as it no doubt would be to Calamity when she woke up to it) was that he was as black as the Niger night.

I looked with amazement at Madame ffrench, who nodded gravely and repeated her earlier remark: 'I only hope I've guessed correctly!'

'Who is he?'

'A very old friend. Major Obispo of the French General Staff. He's from Sénégal.'

I licked my lips nervously. 'Aren't they said to have very large . . .'

She smiled grimly. 'You'll see!'

Obispo took in the scene at once. He doffed his hat, like a man who had recognized something to revere, and watched Calamity briefly – an affectionately lecherous smile playing on his lips. Then he stealthily closed the door behind him, took off his cape, his tunic, and his shirt – all without alerting the girl on the bed. *How typical!* I thought angrily. *Only Calamity could vanish into some private erotic world of her own at a moment like this!*

'Did you ever see a more magnificent body?' Madame asked, leaning forward, eyes a-glow.

I had to allow I hadn't. We could see only his torso, of course, for he still wore his trousers and shoes. He was lithe as a panther and hairless as a carving in ebony. His muscles rippled at the slightest movement – as now, when he eased off his shoes without unlacing them and started to loosen his belt and flies. All his movements were completed with such panache – and with such quiet drama – that I already suspected he knew Madame would be watching; the tantalizing way he was doing everything possible to loosen his trousers without once displaying his tackle would seem to confirm it. He had delicate, prehensile toes that removed his socks in one scoop.

At last he was ready – barefoot, belt dangling like a treesnake, flybuttons like seven dead eyes, buttonholes gaping like old whores' quims. Quiet as a shadow, clutching his trousers loosely to his belly, he moved to the bedside, until he was standing level with her head. He was to her left, which was the far side from where Madame and I were watching, spellbound and hardly daring to breathe. He bent low over her – to kiss her, I thought, and awaken her like Sleeping Beauty. Perhaps he did, but his main purpose was to slip out of his trousers and spring upright again and stand before her in all his sudden glory.

I cannot say I have *never* seen a more magnificent tool than Obispo's, but I have certainly never seen one so awesome on a man of such average height and build. To envy the circus giant who can lift two dozen men is absurd; but to envy the fellow of modest build who can nonetheless tear phone-books in two is eminently reasonable. I think the envy I now felt for Obispo's champion was of this second type. I won't go on and on about it; I'll just say that if a hundred men all sat down and wrote to Father Christmas, telling him what sort of organ they'd like, he'd probably say to each and every man, 'Oh, you obviously mean one like Obispo's!'

It was the first thing Calamity saw when, awakened either by his kiss or by the palpable heat that great, randy tool must have been pouring down on her, she opened her eyes and stared up. To her it must have seemed he came there by magic.

And magical, too, was the way they now seemed to work together. She gave him a ravishing smile and reached up her dainty fingers to touch his wand with a kind of reverential awe. He knelt on the bed, wriggling his ankles until his trousers fell completely off. She lifted her head, reaching her lips eagerly to kiss the thing her hands could hardly hold. He stuffed two pillows under her neck and pressed down on his tool, using it like a truncheon, like a giant horse-bit between her teeth, to press her head down; then he relaxed the pressure while she ran her lips and teeth and tongue the full length of its tender underside, from the base right up to its swollen helmet, which glowed like a hot coal.

His left hand began a gentle, fingertip caress of her belly and the bottom of her ribs. With a swift, urgent movement of her hand she plucked up her satin peignoir, laying bare her breasts. His spidery black fingers stretched wide so that his thumb and little finger touched both her swollen nipples at once, where they began a maddeningly gentle fondling. It proved too gentle for Calamity, who arched her back and, holding his baton by its two ends pressed it down into the softness of her bubbies and squirmed violently, exciting her nipples with its fiery hardness. The sight of that superb black rod half-buried in the milky softness of her delectable bubbies almost had me coming in my trousers there and then.

He let her have her way awhile and then, crouching over her on all fours like some predator over its kill, whispered something in her ear.

Calamity grinned wickedly.

'Oh, no!' Madame exclaimed in disappointment. 'I hope I'm wrong.'

Calamity turned to lie face-down on the bed, wriggling her lovely round bottom excitedly and plucking the hems of her hareem pants as clear of her fork as they'd go.

'I'm not wrong,' Madame said glumly. 'Dear Obispo has decided she's *in*. He knows I'm here, watching everything, so he's cutting out all the hors d'oeuvres and going straight for the main course. He'll enjoy the rest another time, when I'm too busy to watch.' She sighed, but it was a sigh of resignation.

Obispo took an inordinate time to ensure that his 'main

course' had a perfect *présentation*, as waiters call it. First he knelt between her lightly parted thighs and ran the tip of his tool up and down her crevice, picking up a lavish head of her juices. Then, without pause, he slipped it right up into her, lying down at full stretch upon her at the same moment. He gave her a few experimental pokes and decided it wasn't quite right.

Out he came again, his huge ebony rod now shining with her sap, and tucked another pillow under her belly, lifting her *derrière* still further into his groin when, once again, he mounted her and stretched fully out.

And again it was not quite right. More pillows. Tuck in tight, one more time. Thrust, thrust, thrust . . . Better, but still not quite . . .

Seven times he went through that rigmarole. I could not imagine what difference he felt between one trial position and the next, but at last, when her whole body was buoyed up on pillows and cushions, he found the perfect fit. Then, sinking gratefully down upon her once again, with his tool almost falling into a vagina that must now be as wet and steamy as never before, he stretched himself luxuriously upon her, obviously relishing every little curve and flutter of her lithe young body, and lay still a long, satisfied moment.

His face was half-turned from us but Madame said, 'He's telling her that he's sorry but this séance is now about to become very boring for her. He's saying: "I'm going to roger you in this one position, without pause, for the next twenty minutes or more. I want you to lie absolutely still. You are not to move in any way, except as

I may direct. You are not to wiggle, or tremble, or sigh, or laugh, or gasp – or do anything to respond to what I'm doing to you. I ask you, mam'selle – do you understand?" That's what he's whispering in her ear.'

. The timing was perfect for Calamity nodded solemnly just as Madame asked the question. I wondered whether she knew these things because that was what Obispo always asked a girl to do, or whether it was merely part of a new-girl test they had devised between them. I hoped it was the former; I did not relish the thought of my Calamity giving her all to a man who could test her as coldly as that.

And for the next twenty-*five* minutes that is all that happened. Calamity lay completely relaxed on her tummy, her generous and curvaceous *derrière* thrust up by silken cushions, while Obispo stretched himself full length upon her and pumped his pride and joy to its hilt in her infinitely receptive vagina. Boring it may have been – in the dirty-joke sense – but tedious, no! I never realized there were so many ways of going in and out of a woman, just in that one position. Sometimes his firm, male buttocks fluttered like a butterfly in a web; sometimes they rammed so furiously I expected to see the tip of his tool come out through her mouth; or they pumped so deliberately slow they hardly seemed to move at all, literally like the minute-hand of a clock; or they swooped with a side-to-side swing, right to left . . . left to right . . . on alternate thrusts. Knowing how Calamity loved to feel a hard cock nuzzling against the wide walls of her vagina, I could only imagine what *that* did for her self-control.

I don't suppose Sénégalese muscles are any more

powerful than English or French ones, but the *impression* of power they radiated as they rippled beneath that gleaming, ebony skin of his was fearsome. And when, at the end of a thrust, he would tuck his tail in tight between the soft, quivering moons of her bottom and the muscles of his buttocks would writhe and knot with his lust to pack yet more of himself up into her, the sheer physical pressure inside her vagina must have been prodigious.

At other times he lay rigid and used the balls of his feet to push himself back and forth, letting the elasticity of her buttocks act as a sort of roller-pivot. Or, still keeping his whole body rigid, he raised himself up and down with his hands spreadeagled beside her flattened bubbies.

'Red patches on *her* back, too!' Madame commented with a kind of grim satisfaction.

I was too fascinated watching his dark, glistening pego moving back and forth, almost vertically. It was like those long, cylindrical weights that hammer building piles – just at that moment when the pile has vanished into the ground and you see the piledriver going in and out – or in-and-not-quite-out – of the hole.

These variations were not as random as my listing of them makes it seem. They were, indeed, part of a superbly choreographed buttock-dance, which ran the gamut through jig, gavotte, waltz, polka, sarabande . . . and every rhythm imaginable. It had a shape, too: a measured beginning, a joyous middle, and a wild, wanton end. There was no doubting the moment when he began to rise toward his climax; it was one long crescendo of increasingly urgent thrusts at an increasingly frantic pace. At last his gleaming, sweating body performed a most astonishing manoeuvre. He clenched his buttocks so tight, and bent the small of his back forward in such a curve, that he suddenly looked more wasp than human – the way a wasp will curl its tail right under itself to push out its sting. I could just imagine that promethean ebony sting of his, tucked deep in her belly, squirting its liquid fire into the very core of her.

How she was able to accommodate it, I could not imagine. But I saw, to my utter amazement, that, right at the end, she disobeyed the orders she had followed so magnificently until now and arched her back still further, making her cunny gape even wider, and thrusting the tube of her vagina down upon his rod to the ultimate-ultimate limit.

And even through the thickness of three panes of plate glass, I could plainly hear her triumphant cry of ecstasy.

Of course Calamity tried to make him stay and roger her again – and no doubt, if he had, it would have been again *and* again. She tried every trick she knew. No doting mother about to be parted from her baby ever caressed and kissed it as she caressed and kissed Obsipo's ebony wand – and its tumid condition left no doubt but that he ardently wished to yield. It was the only time he glanced our way, giving a kind of hopeless shrug, while she fondled and kissed the bright red knob of his fast-reviving tool.

All Madame did was laugh, and Obispo eventually left. His final act was to push her back on the bed and very deliberately place a number of gold coins between her belly button and her Venus mount – twenty in all. She protested at the touch of the first few and then lay there, mesmerized. Madame watched intently.

'English sovereigns!' I murmured.

'You've got good eyesight,' she remarked.

'I have where gold is concerned. Why does a French officer pay in English coins?'

'I thought it would have more meaning for her.'

I felt rather foolish then.

A maid came in, a stout, elderly dame who helped Calamity tidy up and then changed the sheets. Calamity put on another, identical, pair of hareem pants and changed her peignoir for something a few inches longer, just about covering her bubbies.

'You wouldn't believe our laundry bills,' Madame murmured.

'Who's next?' I asked.

'A Russian artist called Malakoff. There he is now.'

You couldn't imagine a greater contrast. Malakoff was a stocky, well-built fellow of slightly less than average height. He was swarthy, hairy as a bear, with a Prince-of-Wales moustache and goatee beard. He wore a gold-rimmed monocle and flashed two all-gold teeth – his left eye-tooth and the one behind it. His fingers were festooned with rings, all sporting uncut gems in the Russian manner.

Following that, I feel I ought to go on and say he looked the complete Russian, with astrakhan-fur hat and collar, grey silk spats, silver-tipped ebony cane in one hand and a massive cigar in the other. Actually, all he wore was a silk dressing gown, dark maroon in colour, and dark red carpet slippers. He carried his clothes over his arm and arranged them with care over the back of a chair before he did anything else.

Calamity was still running a brush through her hair. He waved a hand at her and obviously told her not to stop. Meanwhile, he ran his eyes over the room, taking in every detail.

'Clever,' I said.

'Mmm?' Madame pretended not to understand.

'Two gentlemen, both so far outside the experience of a provincial English girl as to be potentially quite frightening to her – yet each highly interesting in his own way. You not only want to make her jump, you want to see in which direction too!'

'And how would you manage it?' she asked, thinking my tone a little patronizing.

I grinned and reassured her. 'Like all acts of genius, Madame, it is so simple and obvious once the genius herself has done it!'

She linked her arm in mine and leaned her head on my shoulder – remaining thus rather longer than a gesture of such minor reconciliation required, I thought. And even when she raised her head again, she left her arm loosely linked in mine. For the first time I began to think of her as a woman – I mean as a possible partner in bed – but of course I put the thought from me at once.

Malakoff's eyes took in the rugs, the cushions, the provocatively curved little bellystool, and he gave an approving nod. Then he glanced over toward our right and I saw a silk-upholstered daybed I had not noticed earlier. He came over and drew it nearer, so that the foot of it almost touched our viewing panel. Then he placed two of the long mirrors near it and moved the third to stand beside the bed.

'Good man!' Madame said quietly, and I realized he had placed them to increase *our* viewpoints, not his.

Calamity had stopped her brushing by now and simply sat there, watching him in amazement. He paid her no attention whatever, even though he passed within inches of her on his way to the sofa. From it he took two cushions, brought them back toward us, and dropped them side by side at our feet – or, rather, at the foot of the daybed. He contemplated the arrangement critically and then, going once again to the sofa, returned with two more, which he placed on top of the first pair.

At last he turned to her and bowed, obviously introducing himself. She rose and did a little curtsey. He crossed the room, took her by the hand, and led her to the daybed. He gave her a gentle push, causing her to sit. He clasped her shoulders and pushed until she was leaning against the sloping backrest. He knelt and lifted her legs until she was seated completely on the daybed. He behaved precisely as if she were an artist's model whom he was placing in a particular pose.

Then he sat beside her and ran his fingers gently over her naked ribs. He moulded his hands around her waist and nodded gravely in appreciation. In the same unhurried manner he took the hem of her peignoir and lifted it right up, laying it to rest across the tops of her bubbies; Calamity raised her arms and interwove her fingers behind her head. His fingers were meanwhile on her nipples fondling them tenderly, running his thumbs up the soft undersides –

smiling to see them harden and swell.

By now his tool was lifting his dressing gown like an army tent. She pretended to notice it for the first time and her eyes went wide with the pleasure of the discovery. One hand crept down and her fingers stole in among the folds of his dressing gown ... those sly little fingers teasing that most exquisitely tender gristle. I knew precisely how she was running the knuckle of her middle finger up and down the spermspouting tube on its underside and back and forth along the groove between knob and column. His jaw slackened as if he were breathing heavily. I wished it were possible for us to hear as well as see.

Then he leaned slowly forward and licked and suckled her nipples. She slipped her other hand behind his head and ran her fingers dreamily through his hair. And in that way they continued quite some time. He suckled her breasts and she fondled his tool, as if it was all they ever wanted to do.

'She is superb!' Madame breathed. 'She doesn't put a foot wrong. She knows exactly what each man wants of her and she adapts herself completely to provide it.' She turned and stared at me, almost anxiously. 'How much of it is cool calculation and how much is sheer instinct, Smiler?'

I shrugged hopelessly. 'I haven't the first idea – and nor, I think, has she.'

Madame nodded glumly. 'I'm sure you're right.'

Malakoff now made Calamity take up a new position, with her legs parted astride the bed and her feet on the floor. He did likewise, straddling the bed and facing her. He edged forward, slipping his thighs under hers and continuing

131

to approach her until their wide-splayed forks were almost touching. Then he tweaked the cord of his gown and let it fall away; though his back was to us, blotting out all direct view of the action, we were able to follow it in one of the mirrors. His tool was about the size of a banana and almost as strongly curved; if he could have pissed at that moment, he'd have soused his navel. She had her fingers round it now, squeezing and caressing it with long, loving strokes.

He returned to his worship of her bubbies, gently licking her right nipple while fondling the other in his right hand. His left hand stole down into the opening of her pants, where he let the backs of his fingers graze in her bush and stray in small caressing movements over her mound. She closed her eyes in pleasure and curled her back, pouting her sex toward him. Her fine labia, usually so milky pale, were inflamed red from the hammering Obispo gave her. Malakoff picked up some of her moisture on his knuckle and started a delicate massage of the labia around her *coquille*.

It was not that no one had ever done those things to her before. I of all people knew that! But no one had ever done them with such languorous finesse, with the suggestion that time had ceased to exist, and haste was a word with no meaning. For twenty minutes he did nothing but tease her little rosebud; he no longer suckled her nipples but sat upright, caressing them both between the outstretched fingers of his other hand, staring at her upturned face, enjoying her obvious pleasure.

At last she was so carried away she forgot to cuddle his tool; he leaned forward and poked it where his fingers

132

were, by her clitoris, and gave a sharp prod. She came to with a start and gave him a naughty smile. He leaned forward and kissed her tenderly on her mouth. She responded with love bites on his lips and cheeks. They continued kissing hungrily for some minutes.

When they stopped he gripped her round the hips and eased her along the bed into a more horizontal position, until her shoulderblades were at the base of the backrest and only her head tilted up. He eased up her *derrière* and pushed two of the cushions under her. He spread her thighs as wide as they'd go and pulled the material of her trousers away from her quim all round. Her gaping oyster was carmine red, partly, as I said, from Obispo's pounding, but mostly because it was now well and truly engorged with her own excited blood. I never saw her rosebud so swollen – like the prickle of a newborn baby boy. He placed the third cushion as a rest for his chin and, kneeling on the fourth, went down to feast on that pungent, meaty spread. After a good long gobble he slipped his arms beneath her thighs and reached up for her bubbies, which he tormented once again with his expert fondling.

The position must have been tiring though he bore it as well as a man half his age. But at last he fell away and lay gasping on the bearskin rug immediately in front of us. Calamity did not give him a moment's rest but fell upon him, snuggling herself down on her belly between his thighs, thrusting them roughly apart. And at once she started persecuting his staff of life with her lips and teeth and tongue. He never knew what might be coming next – a dainty little bite, a rapid series of small sucks, a long stupefying lick, spilling her hot breath all around the swollen knob of him . . . Or would she suddenly engulf it – ram her mouth all around it, swirling her tongue up and down, side to side? Sometimes when she did that she'd pause suddenly, open her lips, still with most of him inside her mouth, and breathe in sharply, stunning it with the sudden shock of the cold, wet air all around it. Then she'd dowse it quickly once again in the fever of her hot little mouth.

Fire, ice, fire, ice . . . she drove him mad, to the verge of orgasm. And then suddenly she'd go all calm. For a moment he'd think nothing was happening and then he'd get that sweetest sensation of all as he realized she was slowly swallowing him. She could make it last ten minutes, spitting him out . . . starting again. But at last she got him deep in her throat and started swallowing hard . . .

He jerked himself sharply out of her, sitting up, pulling his tool out of her reach, blowing fiercely on it, fanning it with his hand . . . just managing to stop himself spending.

'That's one thing she'll have to learn,' I commented.

Madame, who was still holding my arm, gave a little squeeze and said, 'Now I wonder who taught her to suppose that a man can come, and come, and come again?'

I just grinned modestly.

'Smiler,' she said, 'you get more interesting by the hour.'

Malakoff had by now brought Calamity back to the daybed – in fact, beyond the head of it from our vantage point. There he placed her with her feet apart until her fork rested against the top of the backrest. He bent her forward, over the backrest, away from him and toward us.

'Damn!' I said. 'He's jogged the mirror. We shan't see a thing.'

Without a word Madame rose and drew aside some curtains, revealing that this viewing gallery had more windows than I thought. There was another pair so perfectly placed that if I cared to kneel down, my nose would be within twelve inches of the invitingly open cleft of Calamity's bottom.

'No chairs in here, I'm afraid,' Madame said. 'But we can stand, eh? I see part of you is already doing so, in fact. And quite a *large* part it is too!'

'*À vot' service, Madame,*' I told her, but she merely smiled. Well, it had been worth a try.

Malakoff stretched the opening in her hareem pants as wide as it would go. I could see wisps of pale beaver, glistening wet, curving out between the sinuous folds and rilles of her labia, which were soaked by now in the secretions of her excitement. But he was still not satisfied with her position and pressed down heavily in the small of her back, making her quim gape wider still. Then at last, with enormous deliberation – like a sculptor about to place his chisel for the first whack at a virgin marble – he offered his tool up to the trench between her vertical smile. With equal deliberation he ran it up and down, soaking it lovingly in her saft.

Then, entirely without preparation or warning of any kind – just when it reached the declivity of her vagina – he rammed it home, right to the hilt, deep into her belly. He did not withdraw, either. In fact, he grasped her hips and pulled her tight against him, keeping his gristle as far inside her as it would go.

Madame ffrench put a finger to her lips, warning me to hush, and then, grasping a lever in the wall, turned it through an arc. At once we could hear the sounds from the room next door – Malakoff gasping at the thrill of being deep inside her at last and Calamity making encouraging moans and purrs of satisfaction. Air wafted through from the boudoir, too, bringing with it the reek of debauchery – perfume, sweat, the ancient spendings of men and girls, and those exciting odours that are special to a woman's sex.

For a while Malakoff simply stood there, half-in, half-out, luxuriating in the warmth of a vagina whose sweetness I knew only too well. Then he tightened his buttocks and rammed himself to the limit again.

'May I inquire if I cause you severity, please, mam'selle?' he asked.

'Eay!' Calamity cried. 'Thou may do *that* till the middle o' next week, sir!'

'Be certain you speak honesty,' he warned. 'I now desire I give you thirty-forty... 'ow you say?' He withdrew until only the tip of his plaything rested in the outer vestibule of her vagina and then rammed it back in again as hard and as far as he could. 'Punch?' he tried. 'I give you many punches, please? But not if I cause you severity. Yes?'

'Oh yes, yes!' Calamity cried in high excitement.

'You like?' He seemed surprised.

'I like! I love! Punch away m'sieu – bang, bump,

smash, wallop, and whack! I adore! Only please begin
. . . *please*!'

He pulled back out of her very slowly and then . . .
wham! What a piledriver! The whole daybed jerked
forward with the violence of his thrust and Calamity gave
out a cry of astonished delight. Again he withdrew in little
twitches and jerks, swaying from side to side, feeling his
way along every millimetre of her darling hole. And *wham*
again!

This time he gripped her firmly by her hips to stop her
ricocheting away him at the lustiness of his thrust, which
struck another cry of joy from Calamity; you'd imagine
she'd never had a bit of hard inside her filet mignon before.

When Malakoff said 'thirty-forty' he meant sixty! His
eyes went all glassy and his face hung slack in an erotic
stupor – a man after my own heart; I learned so much from
watching him – mainly that orgasm is *nothing* but the path
to its achievement is *all*.

After an eternity he took his hands from her hips and
caressed them all the way up her pink-blotched spine to her
shoulders, grasping her tenderly there and pulling her
upright again. The hands went on down to her bubbies and
fondled them. She was gasping still from the exertion of
just standing there, legs spread, *concon* gaping, taking
each one of his 'thrusts of severity.' Little beads of sweat
rimmed her upper lip and brow. She lightly scratched the
backs of his hands to make him fondle her nipples more
forcefully.

Madame closed the lever and turned to me with an
expression of wonder. 'She is an absolute natural,' she

said. 'One could teach her nothing.'

'Except French.'

She waved my objection aside. 'Three months for that! But I don't think you understand what I mean, *cher* Smiler. The way a girl offers her body to a lover is the very essence of our trade. It must be done with *feeling*. It can be bad feeling – scorn, disgust, tears even. It's all equal. There are men who seek out each of these. Such girls find a market. Unfortunately, girls are taught to hide their feelings. They come to me, seeking work here, and they think it's enough to be pretty, to have beautiful bosoms and a supple young *vagin* and to open it without fuss and let a man do what he likes best down there. So I tell them to *feel!* Give feeling too! It needn't be real but it must be there. And they can't do it. Girls who can lie in their teeth – who can tell an ugly friend she looks beautiful and charming – turn into the worst actresses in the world! They think feeling is all in the face. But you watch my little Calamity here, with Malakoff's hands on her bosoms, and her hands on his. She says *yes!* with her hands. She says *more!* with her hands. With her whole body she speaks. She responds to his every move. She *knows* how he feels. This is so-so-so rare in a girl – to know intimately just how a man feels through every little moment of a séance. Who taught her, Smiler? You? Tell me all – I wish to know all about her.'

Malakoff had one hand down in Calamity's crevice now, stroking her labia tenderly each side of her rosebud. He was still poking her from behind. The tops of her thighs were pressed against the daybed backrest and she was leaning slightly backward, into him. His thrusts were erratic now, some fast, some tantalizingly slow, some barely going an inch into her vagina, some delving all the way. Each one was a surprise and Calamity's body duly responded, with the subtlest little movements, which I would probably not have noticed if Madame ffrench had not pointed them out.

And while we watched I told her what little I knew of Calamity's history and her time with me. It was rather disjointed, I'm afraid, because I could not tear my eyes away from the drama that was unfolding in the boudoir next door.

Malakoff grasped her hips again and exerted the faintest turning force upon them. She twigged at once and, still keeping his pego lodged firmly inside her, wriggled her bottom on the backrest and raised the thigh nearest him, holding it aloft under her arm, like a can-can dancer. He bent his back forward and clenched his buttocks hard, getting right in under her and tucking himself firmly up into her tail. He threw back his head and gave out a roar of satisfaction that we heard even through the closed louvres.

Neither could hold the position for long and soon she kicked her leg right up toward the ceiling and brought it down on the side of his body nearest us – so that she had, in effect, turned round to face him, and all without losing his happy home inside her!

She was on tiptoe, her buttocks high on the backrest, her body leaning sharply back so that their heads were about two feet apart, grinning at each other in shared triumph. His hands went at once to her bubbies while she, dropping

139

her head and smiling up at him like a naughty little girl, slowly let her derrière slide down over the backrest. Since he was already well and truly tucked into her, this slide had the effect of stretching the soft flesh of her oyster, pulling it forward and upward, and rubbing her rosebud against the fuzz of his bush.

They kissed affectionately. The peignoir fell down over her bubbies and he fondled her nipples through it; she did the same to him, through the silk of his gown. She raised the leg near us and clamped it round him. I bent down, peeping under her raised thigh to watch his ramrod go in and out of her. It was drooling with her juices now, causing her labia to cling to it. At each thrust, those complex folds of skin around her hole vanished with his tool into that delicious dark; and with each withdrawal they stretched and stuck to it as if they would caress him to the last.

Soon she raised both her legs and hugged him between them. Suddenly his powerful, spadelike hands slipped under her derrière and held her motionless. Bearing all her weight he waddled, with her *still* impaled on his lance of love – head back, laughing – to the other end of the daybed.

When Madame ffrench and I returned to our original seats we found Malakoff siting on two of the cushions at the very end of the bed with Calamity, unplugged from him at last, standing with her back to him – that is, with the backs of her knees just brushing his kneecaps. His hands were fondling her hips while he gently eased down the embroidered belt of her hareem pants – she responding to every touch with dainty, sensuous gyrations of her hips.

At last the belt fell free, catching round her knees. She

bent double, keeping her legs straight and her knees together, to step out of the garment altogether. Fine strands of hair and delicate folds of glistening-wet labia peeped coyly out between the firm clench of her moons. He leaned forward and kissed them reverently, rubbing them with his nose and tongue, growing more excited and pushing his tongue into her while she remained doubled up. Then on up her cleft to her bumhole. Licking her cleft vigorously. Licking her bum. Scrabbling with frantic hands over the beautiful globes of her backside. Pulling them apart . . . licking, licking, licking.

When that little storm passed he sat upright again and grasped her hips in a most businesslike way, like a gunner sighting a cannon. His own cannon was raised like a howitzer, throbbing with anticipation and aimed directly at her crack, which was now all lathered by his drool. With infinite slowness he drew her back toward him, massaging her hips all the way, revelling in the perfect curves of her girlish and now delightfully naked *derrière*, and the provocative ways she could move it.

Naturally she could not move nearer him without parting her legs each side of his. She understood exactly what tantalizing glimpses of her oyster this offered him; by kneeling down and using one of those strategically placed mirrors I could see it for myself. The frills of her most tender flesh hung in that widening hairy gap like dolls-house laundry on a miniature line. The excitement it gave him, only inches away, must have been intense.

The nearer her dumb glutton drew to his excited tool, the wider she had to part her thighs, for she now had to spread her feet each side of the daybed, too. And naturally, the wider she parted her thighs the lower her fork sank toward him – so that by the time she was all the way there, the engorged helmet of his tool was separated by barely an inch from her holey of holeys.

He tightened his grip on her naked hips; she resisted. He pulled harder. In response she began a slow gyration that held him spellbound. At first it was an almost perfect circle but bit by bit she diminished the side-to-side element and began to emphasize the forth-and-back motion – the pelvic thrusts. Now her entire vertical smile was brushing his knob with its gentle moisture; and she did it with such skilful and lascivious slowness that he must have felt every nook and cranny, every fold and wrinkle between her *coquille* and her bumhole.

And then she sat down on him – *wham!* – a delightful revenge for that earlier surprise of his. It was like a cymbal crash in music, marking an abrupt change from *lente* to *poco vivace*. And if any girl ever knew how to *poco vivace*, it was Calamity! She wriggled and squirmed with her lithe young *derrière* like a dancing dervish – until he clamped her tight against him and forced her to be still, fearing, no doubt, a premature conclusion; though how anyone could call it premature after almost an hour of playtime I don't know!

The crisis over, he slipped her peignoir off her shoulders so that, apart from her gold sandals and the filigree chain round her waist, she was now entirely naked. He ran delighted hands all over her body, scratching her back, fondling her arms, caressing her breasts, tickling her nipples – all the while easing her round through a quarter-circle, until she was sideways on to him – facing us. She began squirming and wriggling again, much more slowly now, while he continued to stroke her all over – her thighs, belly, arms, neck, bubbies . . .

She was waiting for that moment when his fingers would stray down over her thigh and hook her under the knee. When it came, she pushed him back on the bed and swung her leg over his torso, so that now she was straddling him – and the daybed, too – with her thighs as wide as they'd go. She slipped the dressing gown off him and caressed his body the way he had stroked hers. He reached up his hands, fingers spread, and held her bubbies in a gentle, rhythmic squeeze.

After a while she gripped him by the elbows and leaned backward. He took the same grip upon her and let her falling weight raise him, until they were both at forty-five degrees to the bed. Now she straightened her legs, too, so that she clasped his hips between her outstretched thighs. Then she leaned back all the way, coming to rest with her head hanging back between his knees. He goggled in delight at what a Chinese brothel keeper once described to me as 'Number-one pretty-sight in Universe' – a pair of slender thighs parted to reveal a young girl's juicy quim, also parted to exhibit its form in every wanton detail – especially that bone-hard inch or so of your own joystick which is not, at that moment, luxuriating in the hot, amorous squeeze of her vagina.

Calamity did nothing to distract him during this long moment of euphoric contemplation. He ended it by giving her gold chain a little tweak. She raised herself slowly and then stood up. The room was warm but his tool was steaming with their mutual heat. Grinning, she reached down and gave it an answering tweak. He sat up at once and took her hand. She turned her back to him and led him across the room, wriggling her *derrière* provocatively at each step; she was making for the bellystool, on the floor between the daybed and the bed proper (if anything in the *Maison ffrench* could be called *proper*!).

'She must be telepathic,' Madame murmured, watching her avidly. 'Has she ever used a belly stool before?'

'I'm sure she's never seen one in her life,' I replied. 'I certainly haven't. I've been trying to work out how one uses it ever since I saw it an hour ago. And now I have, I may add, I can't wait to try one out!'

Calamity must have been doing the same, for she showed no hesitation when they reached it. She glanced at him, raising her eyebrows and smiling that naughty smile again. He nodded eagerly and held his breath as he watched her lie down and arrange herself over the low hump of the stool. The twin globes of her bottom looked so appealing that I was hard put not to break through the glass and possess her myself. She took as much care to arrange her bottom for a man's pleasure as Obispo had taken earlier. And Malakoff just stood there, gazing down, and waggling his stiff cock in excited anticipation.

At last he knelt down, straddled her, and then threw himself flat, covering her completely, slipping into her perfectly aligned tail without a moment's pause. After only a few gentle pokes in this position Calamity rose to an obvious orgasm. Madame ffrench opened another set of louvres – apparently there was one for each viewing window – and we heard her choking and gasping between whimpers of 'Oh! . . . oooo-ooh! . . . no-no-no-ooo . . . oh God, oh God, don't stop!'

He kept her on that plateau of ecstasy until she stopped moaning at him not to stop. Then he lifted her up in his powerful arms and carried her over to the bed, where he laid her gently down across the mattress, with her fork at the edge and her feet on the floor. He knelt between her thighs a while, pushing them wide apart and feasting once more at her open fig. Then he rose to a kneeling position and got himself lodged inside her again. She came back to life at once, wriggling with excitement, throwing her legs wide, grabbing at his every thrust with her quim. We heard his grunts of pleasure, her sighs, and lots of little sticky noises as his piledriver frothed up her juices.

Then, with the smallest break in his rhythm, he withdrew entirely, slipped her over, and rammed himself home again. I realized with amazement that he was going for his climax now – rodding away with great vigour. Somehow I had expected him to try every position known to Adam, Eve, and the Serpent.

Madame ffrench realized it, too. She closed the louvres and leaned forward, watching avidly to see what Calamity would do.

And Calamity, to my surprise, did nothing. That is, she held her body as rigid as a piece of furniture and let him thrust away with ever-increasing eagerness and force.

I cast an anxious glance at Madame, thinking that this,

of all times, was not the moment for a girl to turn herself into a passive horse; but Madame's mouth was an open smile and her eyes sparkled with appreciation.

Malakoff came at last – with a cry to raise the roof and a series of muscular spasms as if ten thousand volts had seized him; and still Calamity did nothing but keep her body *there*, infinitely available for his pleasure.

Madame ffrench exhaled in one long sigh of admiration. 'Smiler,' she said, 'that is the hardest thing to teach any girl in this trade – to be as passive as possible when her lover has his *grand plaisir*.'

'D'you say so?' I responded with surprise. 'I would have thought Malakoff would grumble heartily.'

'Malakoff won't even know she did it. If we were to ask him later how Calamity behaved while he was filling her, he'd swear she went wild with a passion of her own. And I'll wager she's done the same with you – without your ever noticing it! Either that or she discovered it for herself during that night with your Young Turks.'

I tried to remember my moments of ecstasy with Calamity – and realized that Madame ffrench could very well be right. 'Talking of which,' I said to change the subject, 'have you ever known a girl take on so many lovers in such a short time? Twenty-five in a hundred and fifty minutes? Only *six* minutes each!'

'Dear Smiler!' She laughed and brushed my cheek. 'Once upon a time in my life – when I set myself the task of learning every aspect of this business – I worked for a season in a house in Hamburg where I and six other girls regularly *did* a hundred men and more. Each! And

146

day after day! Six minutes would have been a long time there.'

It seemed an impossibility – until I thought about it from a sailor's point of view . . . coming ashore with one thing in mind after six months on the briny. 'It must have cost very little,' I remarked.

'Cheap and cheerful!' She grinned at me. I found it impossible to imagine this elegant and rather beautiful woman in a place like that.

I continued: 'But then I suppose that, after months without a woman, those sailors would have been very disappointed to pay for the usual half-hour and shoot their load within three minutes.'

'Ah me!' she sighed. 'The difference between men and women! You understand the reason at once. I worked there for six weeks before I realized why the sailors all came to us first. A new ship would tie up and there'd be fifty of them standing in line down the stairs. Sometime I did the same matelot three times on his first day ashore.'

'After six weeks!' I mused. 'That would have been after doing . . . four thousand seven hundred men. And only *then* you twigged?'

'Oh!' She came back at me with good-natured belligerence. 'You're a genius at mathematics, too!'

'No,' I confessed, 'I'm not in the genius class – not like Calamity. She'll do any sum you want, just like *that*!' I snapped my fingers.

A broad grin spread over Madame ffrench's face. 'The perfect answer!' she exclaimed. 'Calamity will never admit to you that she's going to work here as a *fille de joie*.

Not after all she's said on the subject. All while we've been sitting here, I've been racking my brains, trying to think of a way round it. And now you've found it. She'll tell you she's coming back here to work as a book-keeper. And you'll believe her – yes?'

I glanced over Madame's shoulder and murmured, 'After *this* I'll believe anything!'

Malakoff had let his tool soak for a few minutes and was now rogering away again. Calamity was flat on her back in the middle of the bed and he was on top of her, poking away as if they'd spent the past hour just dreaming about it. As Madame ffrench turned round to see, Calamity raised her legs high in the air, one each side of him, kicking exuberantly before she clamped them round him like a wrestling champ.

'Ah, good,' was all Madame said.

This was straightforward, joyous copulation now – hedonistic, cares-to-the-winds fornication, with lots of thrashing around, rolling over, hasty changes of position . . . heavy breathing . . . red faces, laughs, cries of joy and encouragement: 'Yes, oh yes! Now! More! Aa-aah!' Sometimes it was her pale, girlish bottom lunging away, mooning the air; sometimes it was his hairy, masculine buttocks, piling every inch of his ramrod into her belly. Then they were both on their backs, gazing ecstatically at the bed canopy, her on top of him, and his hands straying all over her perspiration-soaked body, tormenting her nipples, teasing her *coquille*, making her come at will. And finally they were back where this second séance started: Calamity on her back, with Malakoff face-down on top, plugging away like a maniac. Only this time he had his thighs outside her, clamping them tight together in a cavalryman's grip.

He was lifting his bum high in the air before each thrust. Surely, I thought, his tool was not as long as all that? He must have been pulling right out of her each time. But by then her juices must have been whipped to such a creamy lather he could hardly miss.

And at last he jabbed her one mighty jab and stayed plugged, tightening his buttocks and tucking in so hard you'd think he was trying to vanish up there. And once again she lay quite passive, smiling seraphically at the ceiling, letting him take all the joy he could possibly want of her.

Ten minutes later, before he went along to the bathrooms, he took a large leather purse from under his pile of clothes and counted out thirty sovereigns onto the sheet at her side. When he had gone she picked them up slowly, one by one, and, when both hands were full, showered them down upon her bubbies, her belly, and into her groin.

I knew beyond doubt I was witnessing the birth of her second lifelong addiction.

It was a splendid feeling to assist my three freshly bathed young beauties to climb back into our carriage outside the *Maison ffrench*. They looked so bright and pretty – and so respectable, too – now they were dressed again in their new finery, the very latest in Paris creations. And what admiring looks they received from a newly arriving party of young swells, who gazed at me in envy as I took my place among them and drove off! To be honest, I even envied myself. Calamity was at my side, with Kitten and Dido facing me. My mind was full of thoughts of their dear young *concons*, no doubt still all a-tingle from the two solid hours of all-too-solid adoration they had just received.

What a powerful and mysterious organ it is, a girl's vagina! We think of it as soft and tender, warm and wet and infinitely receptive. And so it is. And we think of our own ramrods as hard and brutal, thrusting and conquering. And so they are – until they meet their match in the mighty, invincible vagina! She can take on dozens of him and quell them all – *ten* dozen, if what Madame ffrench had just told me was true. Ten dozen a day! And she left them all powerless and flaccid, beating a retreat to gather strength for yet another engagement, yet another defeat.

No wonder that throughout history we men have sought to keep the possessors of these all-conquering organs in subjection!

'Penny for your thoughts,' Kitten said.

I replied, 'I was just thinking what a lovely world this is. And I wouldn't change a thing!'

I listened to their excited prattle all the way back to the Bristol – our hôtel in the Place Vendôme. Kitten and Dido were so full of pride at what they had done – and were going to do – that I thought Calamity must surely capitulate and confess that she, too, was now among the very cream of Parisian courtesans. But she held her peace and smiled serenely while the other two gushed on in the manner of whores the world over – not about how young and handsome and well-endowed their lovers had been but about how *important* they were, how many lives they could shatter at a single pen-stroke, and, of course, how generous and grateful these lords of the earth had been to them for granting the Ultimate Favour. And they showed the money they had been allowed to keep – twenty pounds! – and counted and recounted it as if they feared they'd soon wake from this gorgeous dream.

'And you?' I asked Calamity when the other two had exhausted their boasting. 'Are you feeling better now, my dear?'

'Aye, ta,' she replied weakly.

'Why? What happened?' Kitten asked.

'Yes, what did *tha* do while us was havin' us fun?' Dido chimed in.

'I painted me fingernails,' Calamity replied, smoothly drawing off her gloves. 'Look! And me toenails, too – I'll show you them when us get back t'Bristol.'

'We shall have our nails painted every day from now on,' Kitten said.

'We're to spend all tomorrow with the barber and nail polisher,' Dido added.

'*Friseur* and *manicuriste*,' Kitten corrected her. 'D'you know, Smiler, the girls at the *Maison ffrench* are only allowed to go with *four* lovers a day? It's six at the moment because its springtime. But normally it's only four. Four! I can't believe it. We often did twelve at Lazy Daisy's – and that's reckoned to be the highest-class house of pleasure in the North. Mind you – the things you have to do to pleasure a gentleman here . . . you wouldn't believe! I'm tired enough after only two. I should think four would be quite exhausting, don't you, Dido?'

'And what did *tha* do, Smiler?' Calamity interrupted. 'Tha'rt asking us all t'questions. Did tha just sit and twiddle thy thumbs, or what?'

Kitten laughed. 'I'll bet it was 'or what'! I can't see our randy young Smiler visiting the finest bordello in Europe and just twiddling his thumbs!'

'You are cruel and heartless females,' I protested. 'If you think I could go off and enjoy myself while two of you were undergoing the most important test in your lives and the third was lying in a faint in some darkened sickroom – for all I knew, I mean, I didn't know you were painting your nails somewhere. Anyway, it was out of the question for me to enjoy myself – and I'll give lusty proof of it tonight to any girl who disbelieves me still.'

'Ooh!' Kitten guffawed and stared at me with dancing eyes. '*I* disbelieve you! Don't you, Dido? Of course you do!' She linked arms with her. 'We'll accept all the proof you can give us tonight – and still demand more!' She looked defiantly at Calamity – for they still did not know what she had really done that afternoon, and nor was I going to tell them, either.

'What's it to me?' was all Calamity would say.

'However,' I cut in. 'I didn't exactly twiddle my thumbs, either. If you must know, I enjoyed a long and fascinating conversation with Madame ffrench.'

'*She'd* like to take you up to one of her boudoirs,' Kitten said.

I laughed at the very idea but both Kitten and Dido swore it was so. 'Ye could see it in her eyes,' Dido assured me, adding, 'One of the girls said she's t'richest woman in Europe – or the richest what never got her money by inheritance.'

Kitten said, 'She told me that we could expect to stay in the Noblest Profession – that's what she calls it – to stay in it ten years. She says there's a whole ring of high-class houses where they move the girls around, to make a change, you know. About every eight to ten months, or a year, depending on how restless the girl is. She told me I could expect to work in Paris, Rome, Milan, Vienna, Berlin, Constantinople, Saint Petersburg . . . cities like that. She said it's hard work – twenty-three days on, five days off, right round the year, no holidays . . . how many days a year is that?'

'Two hundred and ninety-nine,' Calamity said at once. 'Three hundred in leap year.'

The other two just stared at her.

'Did she talk to thee about it, and all?' Dido asked.

'Nay, 'course not,' Calamity replied scornfully. 'But twenty-three twenty-eighths of three-sixty-five is two-ninety-nine. Any fool can tell thee that.'

'As you have just proved,' Kitten said icily. 'Anyway, she said we can earn ten pounds a day in those houses. Eight after all deductions. What's eight times two-ninety-nine?'

'Two thousand four hundred, all but eight pounds,' Calamity said. 'And that's for only fifteen hundred fooks!'

'Is that right?' Kitten ignored her deliberate crudity and questioned me.

'If Calamity says so, it's so,' I assured her.

153

Calamity went on: 'In ten years at that rate tha could put by t'best part o' twenty-four thousand pounds. Invested monthly at four percent, it'd rise to twenty-nine thousand, four hundred and fifty. And all ye need do for it is fook fifteen thousand men!'

They stared at her, jaws gaping; she had found the one topic that could reduce them to silence. [*In modern currency they were talking about something close to a million and a half pounds. – FR*]

'How do you know all that?' Kitten asked; there was no longer any scorn in her tone.

I turned to Calamity and said, 'You might as well tell them now, love. They'll know tomorrow, anyway.'

She stared sidelong up at me with huge, frightened eyes and I saw she feared I had been told everything and was about to blurt it out. To spare her misery I said, 'Calamity is to be the new assistant to the treasurer at the *Maison ffrench* – there now!'

She was so flushed with relief she raised her fist and punched me hard on the thigh. 'How dids'ta know that?' she asked. 'Who told thee?'

'Madame ffrench. She said you had the best head for figures she'd ever come across. She asked me if I'd agree to let you go. I said no at first. She had to fight very hard to make me relent, I can tell you. So now! If you've been screwing up your courage to break the news to me gently, you needn't bother.'

Tears sprouted in her eyes – but it was her own fault for insisting on living in such a tangle of lies.

'And if you wish to thank me,' I added, 'you can join

these two *filles de joie* in my bedroom tonight and say a proper farewell.'

The three girls shared a room at the Bristol; for propriety's sake I had a single room next to it – but, this being Paris, there was a well-oiled connecting door. On our return that evening they went into their room to change for dinner while I continued up the corridor. I had barely reached my own door before I heard shrieks of girlish laughter and I reached my room only to find Kitten standing in the connecting doorway, a wicked smile on her lips as she beckoned me to see what prompted all their amusement.

The moment I saw it I burst into hearty guffaws, too – for there, side by side in the middle of the rich turkey carpet, nestled three little bellystools with gilded legs and red-velvet upholstery. Pinned to each was a note, crested with the device of the *Maison ffrench*. Each note bore but a single word. Taken together they read: *Enjoy! Enjoy! Enjoy!*

Madame ffrench must have remembered my remark about how eager I was to use a bellystool now I'd worked out its function. And she must have dispatched them while the girls were bathing, half an hour before we left the *Maison ffrench*.

'But how did she know!' Kitten asked.

'What are they?' Calamity had the presence of mind to inquire.

Dido unpinned the note on one and gave a fully-clothed but graphic demonstration. Calamity turned to me, her eyes all dark and liquid, and said, 'Oooh, Smiler – just *think!*'

There was more in the way of erotic accoutrements from the *Maison ffrench* but they didn't find the parcel until I'd returned to my own room; and they didn't tell me of it until . . . well, I'll come to that.

We sat long over the most aphrodisiac of dinners – out-of-season asparagus, *filet de boef en croûte* with oysters, green figs from North Africa, black coffee and turkish delight; and for wine we had those two most reliable leg-openers of all: Imperial Tokay and Pink Champagne. To linger over such a repast with three young girls at their most desirable age, all peaches and cream in their low-cut evening gowns, and each filled with excitement at the life of luxurious and well-rewarded venery that now beckoned her, was an unforgettable experience. The monstrous reservoir of letch that had built up in my loins all that afternoon was swollen to bursting as we took the new electrical lift up to our floor, and had it not been for a respectable German couple hobbling along the corridor, I should have gone straight into the girls' room with them.

As it was I raced through my room to the connecting door – only to find it bolted from the other side. As I rattled the handle I saw a note being pushed under the door. 'Wait!' it read in Calamity's firm but untutored hand. Below it Kitten had added a more soothing: 'and you won't be disappointed!'

I raced out of my clothes. I shaved again. I gave myself a quick all-over flannel-wash. I soaped Iron Jack in every wrinkle and got him cleaner than a surgeon's hand; never had he blushed more fiery red nor stood to attention with such pride. I applied a little judicious powder here and there. I slipped into my blue silk dressing gown and, with my great bowsprit cleaving the air before me and threatening to unbalance my walk, returned to the door, where I gave a hesitant knock. 'Is it all right now?' I asked.

'No!' came three high-pitched shrieks.

I returned to my dressing table and took a small dab of petroleum jelly, which I rubbed into Iron Jack's swollen head – not that he would need it among the juices that were, I doubted not, even then flowing freely next door, but it made him look so splendidly hot and urgent. Then in the corner of my eye I saw a second note being slipped on top of the first. 'Count slowly to twenty,' Kitten wrote, 'and enter.' Beneath it was Dido: 'And enter!' And beneath that, Calamity: 'And enter!!!'

In ten seconds I counted twenty millennia. Then I pushed the door slowly open, hardly daring to imagine what lascivious sight might greet my eyes. I had guessed, of course, that it would have something to do with those bellystools; but never in a lifetime would I have divined the rest. And *divine* is the *mot juste*.

It seemed that Madame ffrench had also sent three sets of those hareem costumes I had seen Calamity wearing with Obispo and Malakoff. And my three lovelies had powdered and perfumed their bodies and put them on, and now they lay side by side, face down, each on her own bellystool, and each perfectly aligned on me as I stood transfixed in the connecting doorway.

I sweat and the pen flutters in my hand as I recall it even

now. Three curvaceous *derrières*, each beautifully pneumatic in its own darling way, uplifted and split for my delight. And tucked into those splits, bearing the *Maison ffrench* crest, three notes saying : *Enjoy! Enjoy! Enjoy!* And beneath each note, gloriously exhibited in the wide open fork of three hareem pants made of woven air – three sinuous vertical smiles, glistening wet with an excitement to match my own. And lurking in the depths of those smiles – three lush vaginas on the eve of setting out to conquer the world, each tingling in eager anticipation of the hot gristle that would soon set them all a-fire and wreak havoc with their senses . . . I fell upon them, and oh, what a Fall was there, my cuntrymen!

No man should die before he has taken simultaneous pleasure of three young *filles de joie* who know what they're doing. To pass from vagina to vagina to vagina – one muscular and lean, one soft and yielding, one full of voluptuous textures, and all hot and juicy and cooperative! To explore them lovingly, luxuriously, with fingers, nose . . . and sinuous tongue, and rampant tool! To have two girls suckle your nipples while a third does her best to swallow your Nimrod, your Mighty Hunter – and to have them take turns at being that energetic third! To take the measure of all three at once with finger, tongue, and cockalorum high! To lie at peace between one séance and the next, with one girl forked over your left leg, one over your right leg, and one over your middle leg, with warm bubbies pressed across you from elbow to elbow! To drown under six ripe young bubbies! To riot on ocean billows of girlflesh, not knowing which orifice you have entered, nor caring, either, for all are hot, hot, hot and welcoming! To swoon in joy, drowning under girlish curves and swellings and bumps and softnesses, lithe, wriggling, quivering with limitless passion! To feel one eager filly rise to her orgasm and set the others off – and then yourself, too – so that you deafen one another with cries of ecstasy, moans of pleasure so exquisite it borders on pain . . . gasps of astonishment that this can go on and on and on . . .!

Try it!

It is not to be wondered that our mood was rather somnolent the following morning – not to say downright sombre. The girls had a thoughtful, rather faraway look in their eyes as we set off after luncheon to return to the *Maison ffrench*. In their case, of course, it was for good. (And in mine, for *something* good, I hoped.) I guessed that Calamity's taunt about the number of men they would have to *fook*, to use her crudity, was beginning to sink in. Fifteen thousand *fooks* is a daunting figure to contemplate all at once, especially when you are only a seventeen-year-old girl – and will still only be twenty-seven by the time you've notched up that tally. 'Four gentleman-lovers a day,' sounded like a summer breeze in comparison.

Some such thought must have been on Dido's mind when she piped up with: 'Why is it six lovers a day in springtime, I wonder?'

'To cope with the demand,' I said.

'Aye, but *why*? Why does the demand go up in spring?'

'Do *you* feel even randier in spring, Smiler?' Kitten

asked me. 'I wouldn't have thought it possible. Explain it to us.'

I stared at her in amazement. 'But Kitten – you already know! You can't have forgotten, surely?'

'What?' She stared at me blankly.

'You remember at the back-end of last year, when Rachel wrote down her charming phantasy about having to pleasure all the seamen in a ship? You wrote down a phantasy, too.'

It rang a distant bell with her. 'Something about having my photograph taken?'

'That was the first bit, but then you wrote about quim-power – don't you remember?'

She shook her head and I could see she had genuinely forgotten.

'What did she say?' the other two clamoured to know.

'Well, you may have forgotten,' I said, 'but I've thought about it a lot since then, because I agreed with every word you said. I'd express it slightly differently, though. I think – you know all these wireless telegraphy experiments they're doing, where people send out electrical messages across enormous distances without wires? Well I think living flesh can do the same.'

'They call it telepathy,' Calamity said solemnly. 'I read a bit in *Modern Woman* about that.'

'Yes, but telepathy's a message from mind to mind. What I'm talking about is from body to body – and particularly from girls' bodies to those of men. I think all the female quims in the world are sending out little messages all the time – saying, 'I'm here! Desire me!' But

because it's body-to-body, we're not aware of it. I mean we
don't actually hear the words. Our minds don't have the
special receiving apparatus that's needed – the aerial, as
the wireless people call it. But our bodies do! Or men's
bodies, anyway. Did you know that most men, all round the
world, wake up with a stiff pego?'

They shook their heads and listened with rapt attention.

'We call it *piss-proud*, because we think it's to do with
bursting for a piss. But that's not the reason at all. We wake
up with stiff cocks because *that's* our aerial! All night long
it's been receiving those messages your shy little *concons*
have been sending out – "I'm here! Desire me!" And our
piss-proud aerials are telling us to wake up and *do*
something about it! But what *can* they do, most of them?
With wives who say twice a month is more than enough,
and friends' wives they'd be mad to touch, and sisters or
daughters they daren't touch at all . . . what are they to *do*?'

Kitten and Dido grinned happily at each other and said,
'Us!'

'Yes, you,' Calamity agreed.

'*Your* quims send out the strongest marching orders of
all,' I pointed out. 'Especially in springtime, when the
atmospheric conditions are just about perfect and even the
ones with rusty old aerials can hear you loud and clear.
D'you realize – there are men just waking up in America
now – piss-proud like the rest of mankind? And the
thought that flits through their minds as they rise and shave
is, *Must go to Yurrup, soon. To Paris. Must try the girls
at that Charlotte ffrench's sporting house*. And men in
India, too – saving penny by penny in the hope they'll one

day be able to afford you. And in Australia, South America
. . . all over the globe. Just think of that every time a
gentleman says, "May I take you upstairs, *ma petite*?" – as
if *he* had the slightest choice in the matter! *He* is not
choosing *you* at all. Days, weeks, *months* ago your
invincible *concons* sent out the marching orders that
brought him there. In one hour you will leave him limp and
exhausted. It will take him days to work up the strength to
try again – days during which you will defeat a dozen more
proud pricks. And all of them summoned by the secret
powers that radiate night and day from your vaginas!
Remember that and be proud! Yours is the power that rules
the world. Most *filles de joie* suppose that their greatest
piece of play-acting is the orgasm they duplicate on cue
with each lover. But they are wrong. Your greatest pretense
will be to allow your lovers to think they came to the
Maison ffrench of their own free will – and that they freely
chose you! Small wonder that in return for preserving that
grand delusion they will make you rich beyond your
wildest dreams!'

Perhaps it was mind-over-matter or perhaps it was that
time of the month anyway, but Calamity started entertaining
the Cardinal during that morning's drive out to the *Maison
ffrench* – so she was put to doing some calculations for
Madame ffrench and was spared having to reveal her new
profession to me during the five days I spent there.

For bringing me three such splendid English roses
Madame ffrench said I might have three séances with three
girls of my choice. Of course, I had used up the offer by

mid-afternoon on the following day, and went on to enjoy the others – one in the afternoon and one each evening – at my own expense. It is all a bit of a whirl in my mind now . . . well, it was then, too, to be honest – I was absolutely intoxicated with the exotic females who brought to that house the sexy traditions of every continent.

I remember a naked Indochinese girl who rubbed an oil with a powerfully aphrodisiac perfume all over me and then lay on top of me and squirmed and wriggled her body all over mine – and had an orgasm while doing so, though she did her best to conceal it, and then produced an insincere imitation later, when I rogered her in the more traditional fashion.

And there were twin Indian maidens who worked only as a pair. Dear little monkeys they were with velvety hair on their lips but no hairs at all around their quims. They bit me all over – hundreds of little love bites that left my skin tingling and sensitive as never before. Even their vaginas were identical, which was a bizarre sensation.

I remember an American girl with long fair hair and sumptuous bubbies who rode me like a wild mustang, and made me feel like one, too. And a plump little Turkish nymph, shy as a gazelle and ticklish, too. And a fiery beauty from Mexico who had the finest skin I ever saw – and flashing eyes and a dazzling smile and a body that was full of passion. And a tall, statuesque blackamoor girl from Morocco, who managed to keep me going for almost two hours while she took her pleasure of me in a wild, hedonistic way.

And, naturally, I had Farah, that 'lazy' girl Madame

ffrench had pointed out to me on our way to watch Calamity with Obispo and Malakoff. Farah was amazing and I could understand why men flocked to her, though she did so little work for her money. I think she realized quite early on in her career that she looked like the sort of girl who was born to say no – the keep-off-the-grass girls, who have got humankind's sexual marching orders all wrong. I don't mean that she was sour or prickly – quite the reverse. She was exceptionally pretty, delicate as porcelain, neat in every feature and movement – the sort of girl one meets, sadly, all too often in daily life. Invest five minutes of elementary seduction on them and you know beyond doubt that they are *never* going to open their thighs for you. With Farah you got that same conviction after a mere five seconds. What on earth was she doing as a *fille de joie*? you wondered. Curiosity alone induced you to choose her and take her upstairs.

The moment you were out of the salon, however, she would look all around – as if she didn't want any of the other girls to see this bit – and then flash you a dazzling smile, giving you the impression you had just turned her day from hell into heaven. And she'd hum a happy little tune as you went upstairs and keep on smiling to herself until, unclothed at last, she'd spill her nakedness over the silken sheets and offer you the Ultimate Favour as if she'd kept it all these years just for you. And from the moment you started kissing her, caressing her, fingering her, she kept up a steady outpouring of murmurs, sighs, little gasps of amazement – suggesting that you alone, out of all the men she had known, had somehow found the knack of breaking through her reserve and hitting the button of her pleasure. And when it came to rogering her . . . well! I never knew a girl with a greater repertoire of shivers of ecstasy, moans of ecstasy, gurgles of ecstasy, yelps, whimpers, gasps, and sobs of ecstasy than Farah. She seemed to experience one long, delicious orgasm from the moment you touched her. So you left her company thinking not only that you had had the immense privilege of seducing a natural keep-off-the-grass girl, but also that you must be one of the finest lovers in the world to give her such monumental satisfaction.

I know damn well she was actually half-asleep during most of my time with her; but it made no difference; one doesn't think less of a great actor's Romeo because one knows he's not really in love with Juliet. If I had lived in Paris, I would naturally have been a frequent visitor at the *Maison ffrench* and Farah — one of that fair city's outstanding actresses – would have been high among my frequent choices.

If I seem a little brief in describing my séances with the high-class courtesans of the *Maison ffrench*, it is because one encounter overshadowed them all. On my final day in Paris, Madame ffrench herself took me by the hand and led me up to her finest boudoir, where we enjoyed a séance the gods themselves must have envied. She was twice my age, and though I now look upon women of forty as mere chickens, 'just beginning to get interesting,' they then seemed as old as my grandmother to me. Also, I could not help reflecting that she was a veteran of close on forty thousand *fooks*, to borrow Calamity's blunt phrase, so there was nothing I could do to surprise or amaze her; if it was anatomically possible, she had done it before. It was the first time in my life that I had gone into a bedroom with a female, knowing I was going to poke her, but with an Iron Jack who would have been more aptly named Macaroni Marmaduke.

But there is something bewitching about a vagina that has welcomed forty thousand comers before yours; they are surrounded by an aura of stiff prick. Approach within six feet of them and . . . *boi-oi-oing!* Up he comes like magic – Captain Standish at your service ma'am!

And there is something enthralling, too, about a woman who has been the focus of so much intense pleasure over so many years – ecstasy has made her its natural home. Thrills hide within her, waiting to ambush the next intruder, as if they had nowhere else to go. And she has adapted her favours to so many that your particular desires are second nature to her, just as if you had been her sole husband all those years. When, years later, I took my first drive behind the wheel of a Rolls-Royce, I thought at once of my single séance with Charlotte ffrench. It was the same when I first set eyes on the Bay of Naples at sunset. That hour between the thighs of one of the world's greatest courtesans was one of the great moments of my life – the standard by which all other peaks were measured.

And, strangely enough, because that séance with Madame ffrench was so utterly perfect, it had the effect of turning me against lesser *filles de joie* for a long, long time – several weeks, in fact. I returned to my chambers in Leeds some hundreds of pounds poorer than when I left – not that I begrudged a penny of it, and not that I was approaching destitution, either. Indeed, I still had quite a few thousands put by. But I had no reliable means of refilling my coffers, being badly out of touch with recent racing form; and so I spent my first two days sitting up in bed, immersed in *The Pink 'Un* and other bibles of the turf.

Toward the end of the second day I developed the uncanny feeling I was being watched – and in particular from the direction of Miss Campbell's apartment, for my bedroom shared a party wall with her chambers. I had knocked at her door several times – to get my keys back – but, receiving no reply, had assumed she was away. All that evening the sensation, or perhaps delusion, grew stronger. At last it was powerful enough to make me carry out an inch-by-inch survey of the panelling on my side of the wall. There were several hair-cracks in the ancient oak but a peeping Tom, or Tomasina, would have needed to put her eye directly to such a crack – which was out of the question in this case, for, not only was there the equivalent panelling on her side, there was also half a ton of sound-damping oyster shells (how appropriate!) sandwiched in between.

I did not discover it until I put out the light that night – which I did rather abruptly. For a moment I saw what looked like a glowworm, half-way up the panelling and directly opposite my bed. Yorkshire glowworms being slightly less common than hens' teeth, I sprang up and leaped across to the point in question – and was just in time to see a knot being pushed back into the hole in the panelling. In an instant all was clear. The minx next door had taken advantage of my absence to remove a section of panelling on her side (boxing it off, no doubt, to prevent an avalanche of crushed oyster shells) and had turned one of the knots into a stopper for an eyehole. It was well chosen, too, for it lay deep in the shadow of a heavily framed oleochrome of *The Rokesby Venus* by Velasquez – a much more likely focus for my eyes than a bit of ancient fumed oak.

I waited awhile and then gently pushed the knot out, back toward her room. I heard it fall inside the boxed-off section but all I could see was a faint light at the top, shading off into pitch blackness at the bottom; it took a little time to work out that I was looking at the back of a framed picture, leaning slightly forward. And that, for the moment, was that.

When I awoke the following morning I was, of course, piss-proud. I was just about to throw off the bedclothes when I remembered the spyhole opposite my bed. A surreptitious glance revealed that the knot was absent from its hole – but that might merely mean she had not yet discovered it had 'fallen out.' On the chance, however, that she was spying on me, I simply eased the covers to the foot of the bed and lay on my back, stabbing the air with Iron Jack, who was by this time so stiff he was almost ready to snap right off.

And for the next five minutes or so I gave her (if she *was* watching, that is) a living tutorial on the male priap – all his tender places and all the delicious things she could do to make him sing the oldest, most gladsome song on earth.

It concluded with a sudden, heavy thump next door, followed by a high-pitched shriek – which I would probably have heard even if she had not removed a section of the oyster-shell filling in the oak sandwich that divided us. My first instinct was to rush to the spyhole and see what was happening, but an imp of cunning whispered to me that if she had merely toppled a chair to the ground and faked her cry of pain, I would give away my knowledge of the spyhole at once. So, studiously ignoring it, I hastened into my dressing gown and slippers and ran down the passage to her apartment door.

There was no answer to my knock so I tried the door and found it unlocked. I opened it and called out her name. The only answer was a low groan from somewhere up the internal corridor. 'Miss Campbell?' I cried again as I advanced cautiously into her territory.

There was a more lively moan from her bedroom. 'Are you all right?' I asked. 'I heard a crash.'

'I twisted my ankle and fell. I think I passed out.'

'Where's Miss Monteith?'

'She's away today, I'm afraid. My ankle's destroyed.'

When I entered her bedroom the first thing I saw was a large, framed text saying *Thou, Oh God, Seest All*, hanging slightly awry over the place where the spyhole would be. Miss Campbell, still in her nightdress, was lying in a heap near the foot of her bed and a low stool was lying on its side near by. 'I was trying to straighten the text,' she explained in a weak voice.

'It certainly needs some straightening,' I said.

From the outset, of course, I had suspected that Miss

Campbell was resuming her prick-teasing ways now that she had a prick to tease once more. And the moment I discovered there was no swelling in her supposedly 'destroyed' ankle, nor even any particular warmth, Iron Jack started putting naughty thoughts into my mind. For instance, he whispered, what if *he* took over the task of caressing her ankle? He painted a picture of his hot, crimson head snaking up the division between her ankles, her calves, her knees, her slender, shapely thighs . . .

'I'm gey sorry tae bother ye, Mister S.,' she said winsomely, 'but could ye bear me tae ma bed?'

The moment I lifted her up she put her arms around my neck and laid her head close to mine. The darling, girly smell off her body almost gave me an orgasm on the spot. And she knew the effect she was having on me, too, because I could not lift her beyond the reach of Iron Jack, who kept prodding her bum within inches of where any sensible beard-slitter would want to be – and she kept squirming her *derrière* to feel him do it again.

The moment I laid her on the bed she murmured seductively, 'Ye *do* have the healing touch, ye know. I never felt it stronger.'

'How nice,' I answered, reaching for her covers.

But she put up a hand to stop me; her girl's fingers on my wrist. Girls' fingers are *so* erotic. We all know where they've been – small wonder the female tribe is so particular about wearing gloves in public! And thank heavens they are, or we'd all be driven mad. 'I'd consider it a grand favour tae me, Mister S., if ye'd heal my ankle entirely afore ye gae.'

While I obliged she lay on her back, legs loosely parted, closed her eyes, and sighed like a girl enjoying those *petits tressaillements* that signal the start of her long and enviable journey into ecstasy. 'Och, ye have such wonderful hands,' she murmured. 'I think I struck my knee in the fall, too. Could ye . . . aye! Och, aye, ye have it there!'

By now Iron Jack was telling me not to be such a bloody fool – lift her nightie and get stuck in. The woman was begging for it. And if not, she was certainly asking for it! But I was *au fait* to Miss Campbell by now and I knew 'gey well' that one overt move to seduce her and the doors would slam in my face. It was far more amusing – in rather grim sense – to see how far she'd go if I continued to hold back at each new provocation.

And provocation it was. If I had not already seen her divine form in all its delightful nakedness, I would have been left in no doubt as to its glories by the way her nightdress now clung to her – I could even see how her lovely, soft bubbies shivered like jellies to the beat of her pulse, which was spirited and fast.

'My, but ye've taken away every twinge, Mister S. – if you aren't a living marvel!' She rolled away from me, onto her side, and, taking my hand in hers, transferred it to her hip. 'Just a wee touch there, if ye'd be so kind. I feel a twinge there, too.'

With her other hand she must have secretly gathered her nightdress more tightly to her for suddenly every curve and bend of her figure was visible, as if the material had stuck to her skin. And so, with a heroic display of self-control, I caressed her hip until she realized I wasn't going to try any funny stuff. Iron Jack, disgusted at me, fell limp between my thighs and refused to rise again even when Miss Campbell 'accidentally' turned onto her back, causing my fingers to try their healing magic on a well-known 'wound' in the medial pelvic line (to keep it medical) – a wound that has been there since the days of Adam and Eve and which all the loving attention in the universe has never yet healed.

After one or two strokes (or perhaps more) during which I pretended to be so preoccupied that I did not notice the change, I said 'Oh!' rather calmly, and rose to take my leave. Miss Campbell did nothing to stop me.

When I regained my own bedroom, however, I noticed that the knothole was coloured pink – the very tone of her wallpaper. It could only mean that the framed text had been removed and that her head was not in the way. Gingerly I approached it and darted my head past the spyhole, pausing barely half a second to see what was going on in there. And what I saw in that brief flash of vision, brought my eye back at once and kept it glued there for the next . . . I know not how long. Time was suspended.

Miss Campbell was lying as I left her – on her back, clad only in her nightdress. She was running the tips of her fingernails gently and lasciviously up and down her body, from her knees to her nipples. When she fondled the insides of her thighs, she forced them lightly apart, teasing herself because the tightness of the material prevented her fingers from delving deeper. Then to her Venus mound, where the little fingers played in the opening of her labia while her other fingers and thumb drummed pit-a-pat on the mound itself. Then to her flat little belly, where her nails stroked up and down, up and down, while she clamped her knees tight together and wriggled her hips by clenching tight the muscles of her *derrière*. And finally up to her bubbies, where she tantalized herself to the edge of madness by caressing them round and round and up and down in toward the middle, like the spokes of a wheel, and out again without ever touching her nipples. By the time she finished they were so swollen they looked quite painful, even through the thin material of her nightie.

At last, when she could bear it no longer, she slipped her buttons undone and laid those two creamy dairies bare. She pinched her nipples firmly in her hands and tweaked and furled them until I could hear her gasps of pleasure even through the stout oak of the panelling. And then she did one or two of the buttons up and started all over again.

I then became aware of a draught coming through the spyhole and reluctantly went to find a piece of glass to place over it otherwise I knew I should pay for my brief spell of voyeuristic heaven with an eyepatch and days of hellish pain. I found one beneath my shaving mug, cleaned it up, and returned to my vigil. By now Miss Campbell had lifted up her nightie and was lying with her legs half-parted, fingering her crevice with long, lingering strokes of all ten fingers and thumbs. No wonder she had removed the text from the wall, for even I, with only a tiny knothole to aid me, could 'see all' without the slightest effort!

She had one of the most perfect quims I had seen during the nine months or so since my quim-spotting days had begun. The outer labia were blubbery and supple, dark with excited blood and generously forested with her fine, blonde hair. The inner pair were silvery pink in colour, finely drawn and silky smooth; at their bottom end they curled round like the lower lip of a suckling baby – and where the mother's nipple would have been there lurked the dark hint of her vagina.

So near – and yet so far! I seethed with anger that she should flaunt these precious possessions at me and yet deny me the smallest share in them – I, who was willing to share *my* corresponding possessions without stint.

Wider and wider went her thighs and more and more excited was the play of her fingers, until at last her limbs stretched in a single line and she resembled a dear little frog, lying on its back. Now her quim was wide open, the inner labia parted and the astonished O of her vagina pointing at me like the barrel of a gun. I was so afflicted with tunnel vision that I only vaguely noticed her hands scrabbling under the pillow; when they returned into my field of view they were holding something long, pale, and cylindrical, with a barely-sugar twist – which it took me some time to recognize as a candle. It was as well I needed no stool to stand on, or I should surely have tumbled off it then.

For a while she ran it up and down between her labia, the way she had tormented them earlier with her fingers; and then, when the whole of her fork was gleaming with excited juices, she started inserting it in the gaping nook of her vagina. What followed was one long, excited tutorial in how she would like to be poked, *if* she ever let me in. She wanted to begin with dozens of short stabs, penetrating her holey of holeys no more than an inch but entering from every angle, so that all four sides of her vagina were equally stimulated. Then she'd like me to plunge deep inside her, all at once. I was amazed to see the entire candle, which must have been seven or eight inches long, vanish up there. Then she clamped her thighs tight and rolled over on her side, drawing up her knees so that her bum was now facing me and I was looking at her labia, squeezed between the backs of her thighs.

Somehow she expelled the candle without the aid of her hands; when two inches of it were back in the light of day her hand slipped down into her fork and started diddling it quickly in and out of her – then slowly – then changing the angle again. Almost the entire skin of her back turned bright pink as she flushed repeatedly with her pleasure. And finally her hand vanished, only to reappear at once over her hip as she rolled still further, ending up on all fours, with her bum in the air and her labia squeezed into the grand old vertical smile. Her free hand plucked the candle from her and stabbed it back again – but this time in her bumhole. Two or three long, lecherous pokes were enough to brim her over into one of the most stupendous orgasms I ever saw in a woman. She practically had a fit before my eyes.

And when it was over, and her scattered wits were restored to her once again, she rolled on her back and smiled me a sweetly wanton smile that said, 'Enjoy it, Mister S., because that's the nearest you'll ever get!'

My anger rose to new heights when, later that day, my

Uncle Tommy came round to thank me for the use of my set while I was away. He told me of the fillies he had brought there and I told him of my Parisian successes; and the superlatives were just beginning to fail us when he suddenly said, in a rather offhand manner, 'Who is this Miss Campbell who lives next door, by the by?'

'She lives next door,' I replied, pokerfaced.

'Ah,' he said, equally solemnly, 'that explains it, of course. I suppose you know everything about her?'

I considered the matter carefully. 'No,' I admitted at last. 'There's one thing I don't know.'

'And that is . . .?'

'Does she or doesn't she?'

'Ah!' he said heavily.

'Did you have any, er, *connection* with her while I was gone?'

He shook his head ruefully. 'And it wasn't for want of trying, I can tell you. The day she fell and twisted her ankle – and got me to massage it better for her – did you know I have healing hands, by the way?'

'I suspected it the moment you mentioned her ankle. You thought you were *in* that day, eh? And what about when the geyser conked out? And she was only wearing a white flannel dressing gown? You still can't understand where it all went wrong, I'll bet!'

He stared at me in amazement. 'Did she tell you all this, Smiler?'

I shook my head. 'She *did* it to me, too. She's still at it. Every day there's a new hint of seduction in the air – she's the original prick-teaser, the prick-teaser of all time. But

I no longer respond. Now it's driving *her* mad. God knows how it's going to end.'

'Someone should give her a good hiding,' he said.

'Or a good rogering!'

Our eyes met, daring each other to turn the joke into a strategy and the strategy into a plan.

'She did the same to poor Reggie Morgan when he joined me for supper one evening.' Tommy cleared his throat rather shamefacedly and added, 'She somehow induced the pair of us to join the Kirkstall Naturist Fellowship. It was the most embarrassing evening of our lives, I may tell you.'

'I can imagine!'

'Oh no you can't! She has a figure like ...' He searched in vain for a simile to express it. 'Gad! Just like the Rokesby Venus there. Enough to desanctify half the saints in the calendar, anyway. She walks into the room and twenty men have to sit down and read magazines suddenly. And she bloody well knows what she's doing! Somebody *ought* to give her a good rogering!'

On that point, at least, we were agreed.

Our chance came a few nights later and it was, of course, provided by Miss Campbell herself. She waylaid Tommy one evening as he left my chambers and inquired sweetly after Reggie. 'We've not seen much of ye at Kirkstall lately,' she simpered, adding, 'Not that we see much of ye when ye *are* there, either!'

After more badinage she ended by inviting the three of us to join her and Miss Monteith for dinner the following evening. We accepted, of course, but when we arrived she told us that poor Miss Monteith had sent a telegram to say she was detained at Scotch Corner; we were not shown the telegram, however. It occurred to me that, though I had occasionally seen Miss Monteith, from a distance, I had never seen the two of them together. She had her room, her clothes, her knick-knacks were about the place – and I had often sorted out letters for her from the pile in the hall, including one from the income-tax office. But even so . . .

All went well until we sat to the table and Miss Campbell lighted two candles. 'I always think they're so romantic, don't ye all?' she asked, glancing at the three of us with a flirtatious sparkle in her eyes. 'Compared to the deadening brilliance of oil lamps or the incandescent gas.'

But I was staring in horror at the candles she had just lighted. They were . . . well, you must already have guessed; pale, about eight inches long, twisted like barley-sugar sticks, and curiously smoothed over, as if they had been stored in a hot cupboard. And in case I still entertained the slightest doubts, the aroma that assailed our nostrils a few moments later dispelled them utterly. It was the fine, fishy odour of all the most desirable quims you ever kissed, licked, tasted, plumbed, and enjoyed.

And it was driving us *mad*!

How we endured it throughout the meal I do not know, for it grew stronger and stronger with each passing minute – the stink of most glorious debauchery. Miss Campbell had ordered in the meal from an excellent restaurant just round the corner in Headrow; the waiter who brought it sniffed the air and gave us the strangest glances, which grew increasingly wild as he returned with each new course.

Miss Campbell wore the most modest dress imaginable; it buttoned right up to her neck and reached all the way down to her wrists – and, of course, completely concealed her feet. But when you have a figure like hers, in a dress that looked as if she had been sewn into it that evening, *modesty* becomes a most relative term indeed. And she lost no chance to flaunt her modestly covered charms before our goggling eyes – nor to tease us with elegiac descriptions of the joys of naturism and the Great Cleansing that comes when we accept nudity for the purity and liberation it brings. She predicted a new revolution for mankind – a Nude Rising that would sweep the globe and usher in the new Twentieth Century, which would turn all our stuffy old outmoded Victorian values on their head . . . and so forth.

It was over the sorbet that my Uncle Tommy finally exploded. He wiped his lips, threw down the napkin, refused the coffee, refused a turkish delight, and, rising to his feet, said with quiet deliberation, 'Miss Campbell – you have no need to wait until the new century to see this great Nude Rising, for I can show it to you now!'

And without further ado he ripped open his flies and . . . 'there it was!' as the chorus girl said after Act One – an ugly-looking gap-stopper, gnarled in service, and red with lust. It was nude beyond a doubt – and it was most certainly rising!

'*Mister* D.!' Miss Campbell's face was livid with fury.

'I beg ye will remember where ye are!'

'I know very well where I am,' Tommy said, grasping his truncheon and waggling it at her like a policeman. 'I am at the table of the finest prick-teaser the world has ever known. But tonight the pricks are tired of being teased. Tonight the pricks come into their own – or, rather, they'll come into *your* own! Am I right, lads? They'll come and they'll come and they'll come!'

Reggie and I, having already surreptitiously eased our flies, stood in unison and let our two belly-ruffians bay the moon alongside Tommy's.

Miss Campbell stared from one to the other with her wide-open eyes – eyes that filled with terror even as we watched. Poor girl! She had only ever practised her wiles on gentlemen – who had all, until now, obeyed that steadfast code which protects young ladies even from their own folly – in fact, *especially* from their own folly. Until that evening, I swear a young lady – a *true* young lady – could, through some unimaginable chain of circumstances, have been forced to sleep naked in a four-foot bed with any one of us, and her honour would have been as safe with us as if she passed the night with her own sister.

But tonight Miss Campbell was to discover she had traded on that stern code once too often; it had broken down at last and the three gentlemen who had sat down to her table now rose from it, a company of wolves, with hot lechery in their veins and hot spermspouters in their hands, determined to take in reality what she had offered in cruel jest.

'No!' she gasped, shivering with fear, staring from face

to face, seeking one sign of pity but finding none. 'Oh please, no!'

'To the bedroom,' Tommy said.

I moved round one side of the table, Reggie took the other, Tommy ducked underneath. Miss Campbell, hobbled by that tighter-than-tight dress, made a pathetic attempt to trip and skip away. 'I'll scream,' she warned, but she did not carry out the threat. She fell when she reached the door and sprawled headlong down the corridor. (Only later did it dawn on me – when I was reliving that extraordinary incident in my mind – that she sprawled in the direction of her bedroom. I suppose a charitable person might say that a girl's bedroom symbolizes privacy and security to her; but even in her panic Miss Campbell must have known that safety lay entirely outside her chambers on that night.)

Reggie and I pinned her by the wrists while Tommy caught her round the ankles; together we lifted her, struggling like a wildcat, and carried her unceremoniously down to her bedroom – where Tommy locked the door and pocketed the key. He began undressing as he crossed the room to the bed, where we had unceremoniously dumped Miss Campbell. Taking our cue from him we were all stripped down to the buff in no time, while she just lay there, staring in horror at our brawny young bodies and the three rampant piledrivers that were about to take an hour or two's revenge of her for all those days and weeks of torment.

'I appeal to you as gentlemen . . .' she began.

'Wrong!' Tommy interrupted. 'You *taunted* us as gentlemen. You appeal to us as men. You appeal to us very much, too. Now! You can either have that dress ruined by letting us tear it off you – or you can undo it like a good little girl and we'll . . .'

'Never!' She flared up. 'You will never be able to say that I lifted a finger to help you.' She struggled to rise, though no one was holding her down.

However, that gave us the idea and, a moment later, all three of us were holding her down – me pinning her right wrist, Tommy her left, and Reggie holding her feet. Tommy and I required only one hand each for that particular job, so our two free hands made short work of her buttons.

It came as little surprise to any of us to discover that she was completely naked underneath the dress, but it was something no amount of bluster on her part could explain away – and, to give her credit, she did not try. Her next move, however, almost brought our revenge to a sudden and premature halt. She ceased her struggles and went completely slack. 'Very well,' she said as we slipped the dress off her shoulders and started to draw it free of her arms, 'I shall neither assist you nor oppose you. I shall lie here as lifeless as a side of meat in a shambles and you may do your worst. If you are the gentlemen I know you to be, you will very soon feel ashamed of yourselves – and you will be begging my forgiveness before you leave. And I, as a good Christian, will naturally give it you.'

We eyed each other uncertainly as shreds of the gentlemen we had been not an hour earlier began to reassert their influence. But Tommy, catching sight of her splendid bubbies as he pulled one arm free of its sleeve, recovered his spirit and said, 'And then we'd know no peace until we took the emigrant boat! Oh no, Miss Campbell, you don't trick us so easily!'

I had her other sleeve free by then and Reggie drew the dress neatly down over her feet. For one stupefied moment we stared at her naked body, thinking we have never seen anything so seductive and stimulating in our lives.

'Very well, then.' She sighed as she let her thighs fall slackly apart. 'Do what ye think ye must – and just see if it brings ye any pleasure!'

To Tommy's surprise she grasped his rampant tool and jerked it, not at all painfully, in the direction of her crutch. She closed her eyes and an expression of seraphic calm filled her face. He climbed onto the bed and was just levering her thighs wider with his knees when I dashed to my clothes and returned with three lambs' bungs in my hand.

She opened one eye – then both. 'What are those?'

'We're here to teach you a lesson,' I told her. 'Not to give you a baby.'

'Teach her a lesson?' Tommy asked scornfully. The inflamed animal in him was angry at this restriction, though the last remnant of the gentleman saw the sense (not to say self-interest) of my action. 'We're not here to teach her a lesson, man. We're here to fuck her tail off!' He had the bung on by now and was thrusting her thighs apart with his knees once more. 'We're going to split your cunt in two, little prick-teaser!' He lowered himself upon her and lifted his buttocks for the first great thrust. 'We're going to pile meat inside you until steam comes out of your ears!'

Wham!

Down went his arse and a couple of pounds of solid gristle went piling into her belly, bidding fair to carry out all his threats.

He lifted his head and stared into her eyes. She gazed past him at the ceiling. Her face betrayed no expression whatever. He moved his head to intercept her line of sight. Her eyes did not refocus.

'Oh, you're having the time of your life, aren't you!' he sneered. 'You think you can beat us this way!' He kissed her forcefully but she simply permitted it.

It would be wrong to say she was like a block of wood, for there was no resistance or stiffness about her at all. (There was a stiffness *in* her, of course – but it was all Tommy's!) She was more like a limp rag doll. What is more, I could see she was clearly going to win. Something drastic had to be done.

Casting my eyes about I noticed a hook and pulley in the ceiling, right over the bed; probably there had been an elaborate oil lamp there when these apartments had known better days. Leaving Tommy to fight his losing battle I raced to the kitchen and returned with a length of washing line, which, after several attempts, I managed to get through the pulley. Miss Campbell tried to snatch it out again but I held it beyond her reach until I had formed a noose from one of its ends. I passed it at once to Reggie.

'Turn her across the bed,' I told Tommy, 'with her crack at the edge of the mattress, and let Reggie slip the noose over her ankles.'

She struggled then, all right, but it was useless. As soon as the noose drew tight I hoisted away, pulling hard until her bum was almost off the mattress. She gritted her teeth in pain but refused to cry out. I slackened off again and told the others to put a towel round her ankles, inside the noose; I had only wanted her to feel what it would be like without such padding. She did not struggle the second time.

That was the point about Miss Campbell – she'd accept whatever you did; and if you took the trouble first to show her something worse, she'd accept it without resistance. 'Now you two take turns to fuck her,' I said. It is not a word I enjoy using but I had noticed the effect it had on Miss Campbell, whose pupils went wide and dark at the very mention of it. 'Really ram your meat into her, turn and turn about. Give her no rest. Show her no mercy.'

'And you?' Tommy asked.

'I'll take my revenge up this end,' I said, moving along the other side of the bed toward her head.

I knelt down and put my lips to her ear. As I started to whisper I reached my hands across her supine body to caress her bubbies, which I did exactly as she had demonstrated when I watched her through the spyhole. 'Miss Campbell,' I whispered, 'you have the most fuckable body of any young woman I've ever known. Every bit of you is fuckable. Your cunt is fuckable. Your mouth is fuckable. Your hands are fuckable. Your armpits are fuckable. Your bubbies are fuckable. And if you're wondering, Miss Campbell, how these parts of you can possibly be fucked, we are going to show you before we kiss you good night. And don't think I've forgotten Miss Brown – your gorgeously fuckable bumhole! We're saving that till last. I just thought you might like to know.'

By now she was in the grip of the most colossal orgasms, wave after wave of them. I could hear it in her breathing. I could feel it in her heartbeat. Yet not by one flicker of an eyelid nor one tiny tremor of her lips did she reveal it to the others.

'I shan't give you away,' I whispered. 'But I also think you are one of the most magnificent girls I have ever had the privilege of knowing.'

That almost finished her.

Tommy and Reggie poked her twice each, using just about all the orifices and bodily parts I had listed for her delight, except her bum. She made no outward response at all, which drove them to new frenzies of poking and pumping. They kept suggesting I should join in, but I told them I was keeping something special for the end – which produced the first and only sign of alarm in her.

'You may break and defile my body,' she said, 'but my spirit is beyond your reach for ever!' She had been freed of her ropes for some time but had given no struggle.

Tommy guffawed. 'Talking of 'something special for the end,' we haven't pumped beef in her arsehole yet.'

'No!' she begged, struggling for the first time to escape – but succeeding only in flipping herself over onto her belly and wriggling her *derrière* into a convenient position for him. 'Anything but that, please!' She looked over her shoulder at him, which had the effect of stretching her lips into what looked almost like a welcoming grin.

He tore off his lamb's bung and – his tool being well lubricated in his own milt – thrust it into her with an exciting squelch. She farted round his pego, which annoyed him into poking her savagely and without stopping, until he came.

Then Reggie leaped upon her and did it all over again.

And at last it was my turn.

'Now we'll see what this something special is,' Tommy said scornfully. 'And I'll tell you this, Young'un – it had better be good!'

'Oh, it's good, all right,' I assured him. 'What d'you think is the best answer to a prick-teaser?'

'We've just given it to her,' he replied.

'Have you?' I said. 'I doubt it. What happens when the irresistible force meets the immovable object – by which I mean what happens when the irresistible prick-teaser meets the immovable *cunt*-teaser? Well, little Miss Campbell here is about to find out.

I flipped her over on her back and parted her thighs wide, meeting no resistance from her. 'Now you two fellows take a nipple each and suckle it as lasciviously and gently as you know how,' I said as I dived into her muff and started to dine out on her fabulous young fig.

All the erotic skills of my whole body I now concentrated in those muscular zones around the tip of my tongue. She hadn't a chance as I furled it and twisted it and made it writhe like an eel among those most wanton inches of her sex. There came a point where she flung aside all her previous reserve and began to moan and gasp – the very picture of a woman rising to the pinnacle of a mighty orgasm.

Judging my moment perfectly, I lifted my head just in time to deny her that final release and said, 'Good! That's enough for tonight, then. If she wants more, she knows where it's kept – and she only has to ask.'

Miss Campbell let out a great cry of rage and frustration. I bent over and kissed her warmly on the cheek. 'You only have to ask,' I repeated.

By heavens but they're made of stern stuff, those Scots lassies! Three days she held out, when I had been convinced she'd cave in after one. And what precipitated it was something quite incidental – a parcel that arrived for me on the second morning after our three-man tutorial in her bedroom. It was an embroidery sampler that had been worked on by several of the girls at Lazy Daisy's – Miriam (my first-ever partner), Sarah, Yvette, Virginie, Kiddy, Gazelle, Tendresse . . . and others. Each had signed her name beneath the appealing message, pinned to the cloth: *We miss you dearly, Smiler – come and enjoy the real thing!* This was a reference to the embroidery, which showed my name, Smiler, with the i modified to suggest . . . well, judge for yourself from my drawing of it below:

(The girls did needlework every afternoon between two and six, when a casual visitor would have been forgiven for supposing he had strayed into a respectable ladies' finishing school rather than a high-class brothel! The clients during those four hours were mostly bishops, judges, clergymen, senior officers, and professors – all of whom were surrounded by respectable young females they dared not seduce and so they needed an effective substitute.)

As soon as I saw this 'text' I realized what a splendid counterpart it made to the one hanging on Miss Campbell's wall; so I had it framed, moved the *Rokesby Venus* to another wall, and hung the text up in its place – naturally ensuring that it covered the spyhole this time.

And that was all it took!

Miss Campbell, denied the chance to spy on me and watch my resolve slowly crumbling away, suffered that fate herself. The following morning I was awakened by an aroma of fish and warm girlflesh. I opened my eyes blearily and found that my field of view was entirely filled by a pale, well-forested Venus mound, pressed hard against the edge of my mattress, only inches away.

I reached my lips across those inches and gave her a passionate kiss there, letting my tongue slide out and start to ramble in her bush. Oh, the taste of it! But she pulled away, spun herself round, and bent over, away from me, pushing her pneumatic but firm young buttocks tight against the mattress where her thighs had just been. It was not, however, her buttocks that rivetted my attention so much as the sinuous lips of her vertical smile – meaty, rich, and inviting . . .

I flung an arm around her midriff and stabbed at her furrow with my tongue. What a breakfast! Ambrosia and nectar all in one. Heaven is fish-flavoured, let me assure you of that! I had in mind a long, lascivious feast at that divine chink of hers; but she had a different idea – as always. However, I did not complain, for her idea was to push back with her bum, rolling my head until she was sitting fully on my face. Simultaneously she twisted herself round toward the head of my bed, with her thighs gripping tight against my ears, and her heels under my shoulders. While I drowned in juicy quim I reached my hands up and found her bubbies – their nipples already swollen to the size of egg-cups and begging for my caresses. When they received them, she gave out one long sigh of contentment and leaned back, back, back . . . until her elbows were beside my hips and Iron Jack was thrumming the air beside her head.

But not for long! She turned her face sideways – and gave a new meaning to the name of 'mouth organ,' playing him exactly as a performer plays that instrument, but getting notes of ecstasy out of him higher and more shrill than anything the concert version ever gave.

For the next two hours we stayed between the sheets (thank heavens I had risen and pissed my bladder void an hour before her arrival!) and we exhausted the entire geometry of copulation – and all without a word spoken. Once or twice early on, when my mouth was not filled with quim or clitoris or nipple or her lips and tongue, I drew breath to speak – only to have them stopped again with quim or clitoris or . . . one of the rest. After a while I saw her point. The silence between us opened up every other channel of communication quite splendidly. Touch assumed an importance it had never held for me before; our bodies responded to minute variations of touch that would otherwise have passed unnoticed. And odour, too; the fragrance of her armpits, her hair, her sweet breath, her fork – these were obvious enough. But then there was the small of her back, her wrists, the soft backs of her knees . . . every part of her had a spice all its own. This strange, silent lassie was leading me into wonderlands whose existence I had never even suspected.

After two hours I was desperate to come inside her and I scrabbled in my bedside cabinet to find a lamb's bung. But she would have none of it. She snatched it from me and popped it in her mouth, leaping across me at the same time and engulfing my spermspouter in her smooth, slim vagina. Three wriggles of her *derrière* and it was too late. To me, with my eyes closed and my body racked by spasms of an ecstasy that bordered on agony, it seemed as if I were lifting her, like those pingpong balls on fairground waterspouts, on a great fountain of semen.

Almost immediately we curled up in each other's arms and fell into a profound slumber, which lasted about half an hour. We rose, washed, and took breakfast – all without speaking, which now seemed the most natural thing on earth between us. Then, some further ablutions out of the way, we returned to my bed and there she lay on her belly and made it fairly plain she desired me to roger her in the bumhole – which I did, using all the movements I had observed Obispo making when he poked Calamity at the *Maison ffrench*. She loved it especially when I lay out at full stretch upon her, with the knuckles of my toes pressing hard against the soles of her feet, and the rest of my body

191

struggling to touch as much of hers as possible, and then just let my bottom rise and fall, rise and fall, in a slow, steady, relaxed sort of rhythm, clenching my buttocks hard when I was deepest into her, to give each poke that extra little tingle for her.

After another brief sleep we rose for a luncheon of sandwiches, which I fetched from a nearby teashop while she brewed a reviving cup of coffee. Again we ate in that strangely relaxed silence and returned to bed for more nookie. This time she lay on her back and opened up to me while I repeated all those earlier movements – except that now we were face to face and could kiss as well, and, of course, Iron Jack was in his proper element, which is the hot juice of an excited young girl's vagina. And when I say *excited*, I discovered a new standard for the word as she writhed and gasped with pleasure beneath me for the next hour or so.

We slept long and deep after that and did not awaken until it was time for dinner. I took her out to the Café du Nord, which had the finest cuisine in the North and, more important, boasted the most sumptuous *chambres privées*. I took one, not for the usual reason but because I thought we could eat there without breaking that most relaxing silence we had enjoyed all day. But (have I said it before?) Miss Campbell had other ideas.

'Now let me explain, Smiler, pet,' she said as soon as we were alone.

'I don't feel there is anything you need explain to me, dear Miss Campbell,' I began. But her raised finger halted me.

'Not aboot the past – that may come later, perhaps. But aboot the future, d'ye see.'

'Ah . . .' I fingered my collar nervously.

She let me flounder awhile and then laughed. 'Relax, mon! It does'nae involve ye at all. The truth is, I'm to be wed next week, and so I'm leaving Leeds for ever tomorrow afternoon . . .'

It took quite a while to get the full story out of her but the gist of it was that she was betrothed to an insufferably dull prig of a Scottish minister who, she felt sure, would put on gloves and a blindfold whenever he was required to perform his matrimonial duties – which would probably be about three or four times a year – like collecting a rent.

I asked her why she did not call it off, in that case.

She told me that, not being a woman, I could hardly understand her point of view, but there were many advantages to this marriage for her.

And there we left it – except that on returning home to my chambers she added, as if our conversation had flowed without a break. 'Also, if ever I feel like *shrieking* with boredom, I can just fish out the happy memory that a man once told me he was going to fuck my tail off . . . and split my cunt in two . . . and pump meat inside me until steam came out of my ears. And another young man whispered to me that I had the most fuckable body of any young woman he'd ever known. Every bit of me is fuckable, he said. My cunt is fuckable. My mouth is fuckable. My hands . . .'

'Yes, yes!' I laughed.

'And most wonderful of all, Smiler, pet – he later fucked me right roond the clock tae prove it!'

193

And so I did!

She left Leeds the following afternoon, as she had promised, and I thought that was the last I should ever see or hear of her. But three weeks later a large piece of wedding cake arrived for me in the post. On eating it I discovered a small tube of paper in my mouth. I unfurled it to read, in Miss Campbell's prissy little hand: *Oh, Smiler, it's bliss – he fucks my tail off every night till the steam comes out of my ears!*

I had helped Miss Campbell to pack on the morning of her departure. She took everything, including the framed text, which, I now learned, had been a birthday present for her intended. She was very worried about the yawning depression in our party wall, which, together with the removable knot, would reveal her dirty-minded antics to Miss Monteith. I merely grinned, for I fully expected Miss Monteith to be exploded, like Algernon Moncrieff's 'Bunbury' in *The Importance of Being Earnest*. However, to humour Miss C. I promised to make good the damage – and I kept that promise in a most ingenious way, I think.

I bought a mirror that was silvered but not red-leaded on the back – which made it a see-through mirror. On it I painted a spindly line-drawing of a young lady combing out her hair, in the style of Rossetti. Madame ffrench had given me that tip – a see-through mirror should always have some unobtrusive visual device on its surface, to hold the eye and distract it from whatever might lurk behind the glass. I then screwed the frame of this mirror to the panelling, completely covering the cavity for the spyhole

—so now I could spy through the mirror but none could spy on me!

And then it turned out that Miss Monteith truly did exist. Indeed, she was most upset to find her partner (in the sense only that she shared the rent) had departed. Miss Monteith was a rather pretty young woman, dark-haired and dark-eyed, with a trim waist and a full, voluptuous figure. I asked her if she actually enjoyed sharing the chambers. She said it was a matter of financial necessity.

'And, I suppose, your parents insist on it, too,' I went on.

She had no parents—and she considered her reputation so much beyond reproach that she hardly needed the likes of Miss Campbell to buttress it!' Why d'you ask?' she concluded.

'Oh, it's just that I'm looking for an overflow room — merely for storing things in, you understand. I'd happily pay Miss Campbell's share of the rent, just for the use of her room.'

Her face fell. 'I was rather thinking of moving into her room, myself,' she said.

I replied that that was even better, since her present room was immediately opposite the door. It would mean I could use it without traipsing through the rest of her apartment.

And so it was agreed. When I watched her undress that night — lifting her bubbies out of the coarse cradle of her moral underthings and caressing them and running her hands all over her body and diddling her finger in her cleft, I knew I had to have her. In the meantime, to keep my hand in – or, rather, to keep my hand *out* of the business – I dashed off to Lazy Daisy's to renew my acquaintance with Miriam, Sarah, Yvette, Virginie, Kiddy, Gazelle, Tendresse . . . and all the other girls there.

Little did I guess the bizarre means by which I was finally to have my way with the splendid Miss Monteith.

One evening, shortly after Miss Campbell's wedding cake arrived, I was roused from the form book by a most peculiar noise in the passage outside my room. I approached the door cautiously for I anticipated some kind of revenge attack from Tooley for the triple blow I had dealt him. My suspicions deepened when I heard a girlish giggle out there, followed by a hesitant knock, so I planted my foot six inches from the jamb and opened the door against it. The sight that greeted my eyes – or which I imagined greeted my eyes – was baffling indeed: a laughing woman with a naked torso yet completely dressed in her street clothes, both at her neck and from her thighs down. Behind her on the floor was a mass of torn brown paper and string.

A moment later I recognized the face as that of Gabriele Wharton, grinning her head off; the torso was familiar, too, but it took a moment longer for me to recognize it as Kitten's – and then, of course, the whole scene fell into place. This was the artist's wife delivering the picture I had commissioned and paid for before the Paris jaunt, when I was sniffing around Gabriele in the hope of taking her inside measurement. She was holding the painting in front of her as if the torso were her own.

'We Whartons keep our promises,' she said. 'Aren't you going to ask me in?'

I peeped down the corridor. 'Is, er . . .'

'Alfred?' she asked scornfully. 'What do you think! Do ask me in! Or are you already entertaining . . . someone?'

I grinned and stepped aside. 'Come in and set your mind at rest.'

'I've come here for exercise,' she said, 'not rest – and I'm not talking about my mind, either!'

I took the painting from her and led the way down to my bedroom. When we reached the door I threw it open with a flourish and turned to usher her in. To my astonishment she had shed most of her clothes on the trot between my front door and there. 'We haven't got long,' she said.

'In that case . . .' I put down the painting, scooped her up, and bore her to the bed.

'No more than three hours,' she added with an impish smile.

'In *that* case . . .' I lay beside her and stretched luxuriously. 'This is your night for unwrapping things of beauty.'

There was no finesse about her. In fact, my general experience of women has been that whores are far more delicate and refined than the amateuses I have known. Think of Rachel, flashing her bubbies at me from her sickroom window; no whore of her social class would dream of doing such a thing. And Nannette, teaching me the joys of copulation via Miss Brown, her bumhole. And Calamity, who was an amateuse until I helped elevate her to professional status. And Miss Campbell – my God,

Miss Campbell! Not to mention Miss Monteith . . . but I'm forgetting – I haven't yet described the episodes with Miss Monteith. They were the most lickerish of all – as you'll shortly discover.

Gabriele Wharton unparcelled me as if I were the finest present anyone ever gave her. Iron Jack was, of course, waging the old Worsted War in a plethoric fury. A good whore would have undressed me subtly, tantalizingly, leaving Iron Jack until he was whimpering, begging, screaming for one touch of her elegant fingers. Gabriele burst the buttons off him so rapidly that he sprang out at her like a jack-in-a-box. Then she uttered one crude cry of delight and grabbed him with both hands as if he were a cricket-bat handle – waggling him round like a rogue joystick, crying, 'Wheee! Wheee!' all the while.

Then, before I could insist on a little order and decorum, she fell upon him with her generous mouth . . . and, a few seconds later, I no longer cared to interrupt her for any reason whatever. I was still almost fully dressed when, a minute or so later, she wriggled her fork up near my head and raised one thigh so that I could see the erotic equivalent of an eight-course banquet, half concealed among the lacy frills that garnished the open crotch of her drawers.

However else the amateuse may suffer in comparisons with her professional sister, there is one department where she cannot lose – her quim. High-class whores take wonderful care of their quims, massaging them with oils and lotions and washing them sweet and clean several times a day. But the fact remains that something like half a dozen ugly great spermspouters thrust themselves hungrily in and out of those delicate portals each and every day, giving them between two and three *thousand* thrusts – or anything up to twenty thousand thrusts a week. Madame Amateuse would count herself happy to receive that much attention from M'sieu in an entire year. And the difference shows.

I would not say that if you mingled half a dozen whores and an equal number of amateuses and laid them on their backs, thighs spread and quims open (oh, what a picture – pardon me while I calm my pulse!) – I could claim to distinguish them infallibly. But let me poke each of them, a dozen or two thrusts per quim, one after the other (oh! O-o-oh!), and I'd soon tell you t'other from which. The amateuse quim has a trembling, vibrant quality, an eagerness to experience each tiny sensation – a gluttony for sensation – that would soon kill off any whore who possessed it in equal measure.

So Gabriele did not merely *permit* me to explore her innermost mysteries, her quim fell upon my lips and tongue like a wolf on the fold. She fed my passion as I fed hers. Her lithe and living vagina quivered in dizzy rapture at each sly advance I made into her. And I knew it – not because she threshed about and gasped and sweated like a brood filly – not because she strained her pouting quim for more, more, more – but because her holey of holeys itself *shared* that tingle directly with my questing tongue.

What Miss Campbell and I had achieved in twenty-four hours I somehow condensed into Gabriele's allotted three – with a little bonus at the end.

'D'you remember what you did with Kitten that evening

in Arthur's studio?' she asked.

I did, of course – and I needed no direct request to repeat it there and then with Gabriele. We had been rogering away for two and a half blissful hours by then; she had seen the Great God Pan more times than she could count – indeed, she was on that enviable plateau, available only to women, where life is one long stupor of carnal ecstasy. So when I withdrew for the few seconds it took to roll on a lamb's bung, and then slipped my spermspouter back inside, the mere act of settling myself for that long, motionless vigil made her flutter and tremble as she fell straight back into her limitless orgasm. And there was another difference. Kitten fought it every inch of the way – out of some kind of twisted loyalty for Tooley and the bargain she thought she had with him, but Gabriele just lay there and let joy pour over her, through her, around her.

I had my thumb in her bumhole when I finally shot my bolt. The hydraulic shocks in there, as the semen surged, surged, surged in its eagerness to fill her, felt like the blows of a hammer. It was the first orgasm of my life in which I actually lost consciousness for a time – only a few seconds but it was like the sleep of the just, deep and refreshing.

We rose and splashed around in the bath for a while – and there I noticed one final difference between whore and amateuse. If I'd paid a whore for three hours, there'd be a strong impulse to *use* her until the very last. But with Gabriele it was wonderful to relax, to soap her body, pamper her bubbies, finger-soap her cleft, kiss her, scratch her back with the loofah – and for each of these delightful acts to be perfect and complete in itself, not a prelude to one last, desperate sticky.

When she was dressed again we enjoyed a wee dram together in my drawing room. I asked her when she could get away again and she said, casually, that she'd be coming to see me every night for the next three weeks! And on some of those occasions she'd be able to stay all night. Privately I thought her ambitions a little excessive but Iron Jack disagreed on the spot – very publicly.

When I asked how she could be sure it was safe she explained that Alfred was away for at least three weeks, painting family portraits at Heatherington Hall.

I gasped. 'Where? D'you mean Sir Charles Bossom's place?'

She nodded. 'D'you know him, then? Well, I suppose – being the sex-fiend you are – you would, of course.'

I assured her I'd never set eyes on the man in my life. 'But,' I added, 'didn't you know that Kitten is his daughter? Her real name is Kitty Bossom. He flung her out when he caught her doing an upright knee-trembler with one of the footmen in a darkened doorway.'

Gabriele dissolved in hysterical mirth and it was several minutes before I could get any sense out of her. 'The joke, Smiler dear, is that Sir Charles is the man who's been buying all the paintings Alfred's been doing of Kitten. And all my photographs too! His own daughter! Oh, my God!' and she dissolved into laughter again.

I saw nothing funny in it whatsoever. 'But he's a religious maniac practically,' I objected. 'He's set up all these charities but they won't give a penny to women who *sin* – and 'sin' means only one thing to him.'

'But aren't they *always* the worst?' she asked, staring at me as if she was amazed I could be so naïve as to think otherwise.

'I suppose they are,' I admitted, thinking ruefully of Miss Campbell.

People talk a lot of nonsense about how sexually repressed we all were in the Victorian age. Actually it was the golden age of sex. I know. I was there. We thought about sex incessantly, men and women, day and night. What else was there to do? We didn't have the motion pictures, the wireless, the youth club, motor cycles, and all these other modern distractions to get in the way of the Primal Pursuit of humankind. But, you may ask, what about the ever-present chaperon? Well, all she did was remind young men and women of what they *might* be doing if she weren't there. Also there was the constant covering-up of any bare flesh except the face – what was that but a standing reminder of all the *naughty bits* we dared not show? Even hands had to be decently sheathed in gloves because, ho-ho, we all knew where hands had been! Parents thought about sex all the time – in particular, how to stop their offspring from doing it – especially the daughters. The result was inevitable: their offspring thought about it all the time, too – but from the opposing point of view. Especially the daughters.

I'll give you one trivial example of the sort of thing that happened a thousand times a week. When I was fifteen I was interested in butterflies. At a church picnic one summer afternoon I chased a butterfly toward the corner of the field. I hadn't gone a hundred yards from the group when I met Crissie Kelly coming back from a call of nature, so I turned about and strolled back with her, chatting merrily about *Lepidoptera* all the way. End of 'escapade.' But the looks I got from the vicar, his wife, Crissie's mother, my mother . . .! Of course, my mind – which had been a hundred miles away from such well-known places as Hairyfordshire, Bushey Arches, Much Hadham, Feltham-in-the-Groyne, and Maidenhead – was suddenly filled with a vision of Crissie's crack, two miles high and smiling wide. Multiply that sort of incident a thousand times and what have you got? An obsession! The only result of all this prohibition was that boys aired their tools and girls dropped their knickers at every chance they got. I once rogered a young woman, an utter stranger, in a crowded carriage during the evening rush hour on the London Underground between Liverpool Street and Shepherd's Bush; could such a thing happen today? The only man I ever met who *never* thought about sex (in a personal context) was the stage manager of a pornographic theatre in Port Said. When will people ever learn?

Anyway, the foregoing is by way of preamble to my experience with Miss Monteith, which will otherwise seem incredible to those who believe the current myths about Victorian 'repression.'

Gabriele Wharton's last words had reminded me of Miss Campbell, as I said. So, naturally, my first thought after Mrs W. had left me that night was to see what Miss Monteith might be up to. I sensed something was wrong even as I approached the spyhole. For a start, it was apparent that the 'Smiler' embroidery no longer masked the hole from my side; someone had stolen into my bedroom and tightened the string on the back so that it hung a little higher. I smiled indulgently. Obviously it was some little trick played by Miss Campbell before she left – for she still had my key.

Then my stomach fell. She did, indeed, *still* have my key – or had Miss Monteith found it since? Was this *her* work, then, rather than Miss Campbell's? The question was obliquely answered the moment I put my eye to the hole.

At first I thought I was staring at a reflection of my own eye in the back of the see-through mirror. Then I became aware that the mirror itself was no longer there; no thin lines in the style of Rossetti could I discern. Then the eye moved to one side when mine did not. I realized it was Miss Monteith, gazing coolly back at me and not caring that I knew she had tumbled to my treachery.

I cannot begin to describe the hot, hot, shame that came over me then – or, rather, before I could even begin to describe it I would have to add that it was immediately quenched by what Miss Monteith did next. She backed away from the space where my mirror no longer hung and allowed me to see that she was stark naked. She went to the bed, turned back the sheets, lay on it, and diddled herself in the most lecherous manner all the way to an orgasm. Then she smiled up at me and blew out her candle.

I was sweating all over with my letch but I was too spent from my three hours in that paradise between Gabriele's thighs to do anything about the equally delightful haven between Miss Monteith's that night. The following night, when she gave the same happy demonstration, I was even less capable, for Gabriele had come at six and stayed until ten. And the next two nights were no better. Much as I enjoyed feeling Gabriele's limbs twined around me and her juicy vagina milking my spermspouter of his last willing drop, I racked my brains for some way to get her to stop visiting me for a day or two; the wanton waste of Miss Monteith and her pouting quim was like a thorn in my side.

But none of my subtle blandishments worked. In desperation I took her out to dinner at the Café du Nord, thinking that I could at least curtail her demands on me and leave a good bit over for Miss Monteith. We returned at about ten, 'with an hour left for play,' as the cricketers say, and I was just praying that Miss Monteith had not chosen that night to go out, or to begin a new sales tour, which would be just my luck.

I need not have worried, for the first sight that greeted our eyes on entering my chambers was Miss Monteith herself, out cold – though she was wearing the hottest things in underwear I'd ever seen – on my sitting-room floor. I could hardly pretend that a near-naked woman, dressed in such provocative undies, was an innocent cousin up from the country. Indeed, the alcohol on her unconscious breath would alone have precluded that. I had no choice but to tell Gabriele the truth, or a heavily condensed version of it.

Unfortunately, Gabriele herself had also imbibed rather too freely over dinner that night, which had put her in a distinctly reckless mood. 'D'you know, Smiler,' she said,

'I've often wondered what it's like to be a man. D'you mind? I'll never get a chance like this again.'

And without waiting to see whether I approved or no, she slipped out of her dress and lay on the floor beside the comatose Miss Monteith and started to feel her up.

'Listen,' I said. 'That's not the way. Use a bit of finesse. First you kiss. Then you caress her shoulder . . . arms . . . the back of her neck. Then you slowly work down to her nipples . . .'

'Oh, damn all that, Smiler!' she cried. 'I don't have time.'

And she put a thigh over Miss Monteith's and slipped a finger straight down into her crevice. 'Ooh, it's not like mine at all,' she cried in delight. 'It's rather nice, actually.'

Miss Monteith obviously thought so, too, for she uttered a lascivious sigh and pouted her quim in a way that made me realize how horny I was, all of a sudden. To this day I'll swear she was conscious all along, though she always claimed she didn't wake up until much later, when she and Gabriele were in bed. Alert or not, she was most certainly alive to those nuzzling fingers in her crevice.

'What do I do next?' Gabriele asked.

'You lie on your tummy between her thighs. You caress them tenderly and push them apart. You gaze in stupefied adoration at her quim in all its alluring detail. You explore it with your lips and tongue . . .'

'All right, all right!' She crawled between Miss Monteith's thighs and began. However, the moment she gazed at that lusciously vulnerable quim she blushed deep red all over. I had not realized that the sight of a wide-open

206

crevice – which was like a shout at the fork of those welcoming thighs – can have as powerful an effect on another woman as it has on a man. Yet Gabriele was no ordinary woman in that respect. She had clandestinely photographed dozens of quims in that condition. Using her telescopic lens and a fine-grain plate, she was able to capture their images in every drooling detail, which she could then enlarge to many times life-size. So she was no stranger to the actual *sight* of the thing. The difference now lay in the nearness, the warmth, the aroma, the three-dimensional *reality* of it all . . . also the thought of all those amorous nerve-endings, tingling away in every hot little nook and cranny – singing out *touch me . . . lick me . . . fondle me . . . possess me!* And who would know their desire better than another woman?

The sight of her blushes caused me to change my plans for the remainder of the evening; all thoughts of partaking in Gabriele's make-believe vanished and I decided I would merely watch and assist – and learn. Gabriele would be gone in an hour, anyway, and then I could come into my own – or Miss Monteith's, if she had recovered her wits by then.

Still Gabriele hesitated, spellbound in fascination at a sight few women ever see.

'Press on,' I urged, 'or she'll go cold on you.'

She lowered her lips to Miss Monteith's labia. A woman's lips are exquisite enough in themselves, but to see them gently kissing and nudging and grazing among those divine and secret folds is a sight no man could ever forget.

Miss Monteith fluttered with excitement and lazily parted her thighs wider yet. And as Gabriele warmed to her pleasure she grew bolder in what she attempted. The unfamiliarity of the situation wore off and she began to think and feel like a woman – to feel on Miss Monteith's behalf, even though she was doing a man's work down there.

She kissed, she sucked, she buried her entire face in soft, juicy pussy and matted beaver. Her tongue darted in and out like a manic mouse or she spread it like a neat's tongue across the folds and fills. But not once in all that time did she actually touch Miss Monteith's *coquille*, which was swollen to the size of a walnut by now and must have been desperate for a little attention.

And at last she got it. Gabriele opened her mouth as wide as could be and clamped it down to cover everything, from Miss Monteith's Venus mound to the slender little opening into her vagina. What motions her tongue made inside that cave I cannot imagine, but they drove Miss Monteith to the borders of madness.

'And now?' Gabriele asked, panting furiously. 'What can I do now? Bring me a candle or a big dolly peg. She wants something up love lane – I can *feel* her wanting it.'

'I have something even better,' I said, for I had just remembered that Kitten had left a ladies' devil behind – so called, of course, because it has two wicked horns. She had brought it from Lazy Daisy's as a joke, to show me what some of the girls there got up to when half a dozen men had failed to light their fires. 'I'll carry her to the bedroom,' I said. 'You bring what you'll find in that top drawer there.'

Miss Monteith remained in a blissful stupor (as she later claimed), even though I dumped her onto the mattress from a foot or two above it. I pulled her legs down straight, just to see, but she gave a happy sigh and parted them again. What a glorious body she had, with her big, ripe bubbies peeping out under the frills of her naughty undies, quivering like jellies . . . and her round, voluptuous belly, sheathed in sinful, perfumed silks that concealed nothing . . . and the scarlet lips of her vertical smile, shimmering through the wet, black hairs of her beaver . . . I could have gloated over her for hours.

But Gabriele returned in high excitement, asking in delighted tones, 'What *is* it?' – though from the way she was pretending to masturbate it, she did not require me to tell her. In fact, it was not the rough, horny priap – what Kitten called the 'Ivory Beast' – that puzzled her so much as the smoother, delicately curved *other* horn of the ladies' devil. Kitten had called that the 'baby-rhino horn.'

'If you'll just lie down beside Miss Monteith,' I replied, 'I'll show you how to put it on. Open your legs wide . . . wider . . .'

She giggled. 'Why don't you poke both of us now, Smiler?'

'All in good time.' I smeared a little cocoa butter on the rhino end, which, of course, was for inserting into her. 'Besides, I would never roger an unconscious girl. I would be too distracted at the thought of all the fun she was missing.'

I held the ladies' devil by its Ivory Beast and gently ran the rhino horn up and down Gabriele's crack. Let me tell you – to push such an object into a living, receptive vagina, especially one you know and cherish in every detail, is a godlike act. Gabriele's eyes went wide with astonished pleasure as I felt for all those tiny zones where I knew her most luxurious sensations were hidden. She gasped. She forced her thighs wider and wider yet, reaching her spreadeagled crevice up and imploring me for more, more, more.

And Miss Monteith's eyelids, I'll swear, fluttered minutely open as she tried to peep at what I was doing.

This ladies' devil was a courtesan's special, a real deluxe model with tiny rubber fingers on a convex pad. This pad was so placed that when the two horny parts were deep in each vagina, rammed to the hilt, those soft little fingers helped the nearby clitoris out of the spectator's seat and into the heat of the fray; in fact, they did such devastating work on those exquisitely sensitive buttons of pleasure – reducing any woman to a state of carnal stupor within moments of their first thrilling touch – that I often wonder why we males are born without their living equivalent. Thinking it over rationally, however, I realize that if we had them, civilization would never have begun; we should all still be lying around in caves, screwing each other witless in one unending erotic binge.

And an erotic binge is precisely what Mrs Wharton and Miss Monteith enjoyed together as soon as I had laced the strings of the ladies' devil tight around Gabriele's hips and thighs. It was a binge of the first magnitude ... Force Nine on whatever that earthquake scale is called – the force they can measure all round the globe.

Of course, since the carved helmet of the Ivory Beast had no sensation in it (though it was swollen and horny-looking to a sensational degree!), Gabriele had to watch as she put it in. I helped her kneel between Miss Monteith's loosely opened thighs and push them apart; I also bent them at the knee and lifted her *derrière* to slip a cushion underneath.

The ladies' devil, in the U-shaped portion between the two horny bits, was made of some fibrous, springy material (I said it was deluxe). As a result Gabriele could push the Ivory Beast forward and back, or from side to side, just like the real thing; naturally, each of these movements produced a corresponding wiggle in the rhino horn, which was firmly lodged in her own vagina. That encouraged her to some very active, not to say passionate, wriggling at times.

She started it right from the moment she first inserted the brutal-looking knob of the Ivory Beast into the outer vestibule of Miss Monteith's vulva; she just caught the tip of it in that hole and then, using it as a lever, writhed like an Oriental dancer, bringing herself to the edge of the boil. It was a wonderful education to watch her as she inserted it deeper and deeper into Miss Monteith's belly. She knew precisely what wriggles, what side-to-side twitches, what sudden little thrusts and what lingering retreats, what teasing hesitations, and what masterful lunges would ambush the raptures that lurked deep in Miss Monteith's womb.

I reached forward a privileged hand and caressed the backs of Miss Monteith's thighs with the most delicate straying of my knuckles. It was too much for her. The pleasure that now gripped her made her cry out, a formless moan of ecstasy, and shudder, and twitch, and sweat, and grind her hips . . . all to the point where it was absurd for her to pretend to be unconscious any longer. (She, of course, claimed it was what revived her.) Her dilemma was that – being a decent, modest, demure, innocent young spinster – she could not possibly open her eyes, discover she was being rogered by another woman, and abandon herself in the way she now desperately desired. So, pretending to be only half-conscious still, she reached up her arms, mutely and blindly entreating Gabriele to lean forward and lie fully on top of her. Then, of course, she'd be able to fling her legs up over Gabriele's *derrière*, hug her tight, and stare at the ceiling in such euphoria she couldn't be blamed for not noticing all that long fair hair and those two ripe bubbies pressed against hers.

Hee hee! I was ready for it. The moment she reached her arms toward Gabriele I grasped her by the heels and lifted them, standing up so as to twine them together again around Gabriele's neck. This caused the Ivory Beast to plunge his full, wicked length deep into her vagina.

She opened her eyes, gasped with 'amazement' to see who was doing this to her – and then lost control completely as she shuddered and twitched in the grip of what I'm sure was the mightiest orgasm ever to make her its victim.

It started Gabriele off, too, and soon they were both twitching and shaking like drunken marionettes – to such an extent I feared they might do harm to each other with the ladies' devil locked so firmly into both their vaginas. I hastily unfurled Miss Monteith's legs and let them fall full length on the bed. In the same movement I pulled Gabriele's limbs flat between them so that she collapsed on Miss Monteith's quivering form.

For a while they did nothing but pant hot breath in each other's ears – until it became clear they were no longer breathless but merely prolonging it rather than having to acknowledge each other's existence.

'Forgive me,' I said. 'Mrs Wharton, allow me to present Miss Monteith. Miss Monteith, this is Mrs Wharton.'

They stared at each other, murmured a shy hallo, and then collapsed in hysterics. Then Miss Monteith said, 'May I have this next dance, please?' – and off they waltzed again.

The highlight for me was when I lay between their thighs, with Gabriele on top, pumping the Ivory Beast in and out of Miss Monteith's lusciously fleshy quim with a majestic slowness and power, squirming a little to keep the rhino horn tingling nicely inside her own. And I watched it all from less than twelve inches away! Those two delightful pussies were both throbbing with passion by then, pouring out their juices as if they would drown me where I lay. What a sight to blind one's eyes! And the perfumes of debauchery that choked my nostrils! And the sticky, squelchy, bubbly symphony that deafened my ears as their excitement rose and rose!

At last I could stand it no longer. I made a fist of each hand, leaving only the middle finger of each poking out – Long Lauder and the Earl of Almond, I called them in the nursery – and rammed them as hard as I could up inside each girl's bumhole, where I wriggled them like the tails of excited puppies.

The effect on the two girls was absolutely *electric*. They shrieked .. they twitched like coneys in a snare . . . they shivered and sweated like victims of fever . . . and at last they collapsed in utter exhaustion.

And then I untied the ladies' devil, kissed each horn of it reverently before laying it aside, arranged the two girls, still half-stupefied with ecstasy, on their bellies, and passed back and forth between them in perfect copulation for the next half-hour. Miss Monteith stayed on after Gabriele left and we made two more tours of paradise before, sometime in the small hours, she returned to her own apartment without waking me.

And that was our pattern for the rest of that week. The two girls took it in turns to wear the ladies' devil while I watched avidly and from close quarters, as before. I would never have believed there were as many variations to the simple act of pushing a hard, fat bar in and out of a soft, yielding cylinder as those two wanton young women showed me between them; and the privilege of watching and then copying was one I enjoyed *in full measure*, as the saying goes.

They never quite achieved the wild, orgiastic abandon of that first night but, wisely, I'm sure, they never set out to try. Instead they explored the subtler, deeper qualities of erotic bliss, enlisting my aid where possible. On the second night, for instance, instead of introducing Long Lauder and the Earl of Almond to the Misses Brown at the moment of crowning glory, Miss Monteith asked me to put

the round heads of two knitting needles in there instead.
I'm sure she expected me to twirl them delicately and pump
them minutely in and out – which would certainly have
been in keeping with the long, slow, profound orgasm she
and Gabriele were enjoying together. But I pushed them in
about three inches and then flicked them gently with my
fingernails, which sent indescribably spasms of pleasure
through their bodies.

These happy ceremonies, however, came to an abrupt
end when Miss Monteith had to go on another sales jaunt
and Arthur Wharton returned home from making the
Bossoms look as if they were the most respectable family
in England.

I took up the embroidered invitation from the girls of Lazy
Daisy's and spent several happy evenings there,
rediscovering the fact that copulation can, after all, be a
clean, uncomplicated affair as long as you don't try it with
modest, respectable, virtuous amateuses. On my second
evening there I saw a new girl – a shy young gazelle who
reminded me so much of Kitten. Nell was her name, a
slender whisper of a thing with a body perfectly poised
between girl and woman. I arrived at ten, the hour when
they stripped to their underthings – or nothing but stockings
– to sit in the salon. Nell was plainly embarrassed by the
whole proceeding so I sent for a negligée and got her to put
it on before she sat in my lap and leaned her head against
my shoulder.

We hit it off from the start. I asked her where she'd
worked before and she said she was only sixteen and this

was her first day in the Oldest Profession.

'And to how many gentlemen have you given a taste of paradise today?' I asked.

It was not the way *she* had viewed the business, I'm sure; she gave a surprised little laugh and said, 'Why – five so far, I suppose.'

I slipped a hand inside her negligée and gave her bubbies a good feel-over, ending up by squeezing and fondling her nipples, which soon began to harden in a most agreeable fashion. 'And I expect they enjoyed a touch of these two beauties?' I suggested.

'They were a bit hasty,' she admitted reluctantly.

I slipped my hand into her fork then and got the knuckle of my thumb into her vestibule, flexing it and making it quiver from side to side. 'And did they light any fires down here for you?' I asked.

'I forgot myself with the first one and came right off as soon as he got inside me,' she admitted.

'Let's try again,' I said. 'I make but one promise – we shall not be hasty.'

Her eyes boggled when I purchased two hours of her time, but I was thinking of all the things Obispo and Malakoff had done with Calamity at the *Maison ffrench* – things I had tried to do with Miss Campbell and Miss Monteith, and with Gabriele, only to be thwarted because they had minds and bodies of their own. I wanted to do them with a girl who had probably never done most of those things before, so the other girls at Lazy Daisy's would not have suited the plan at all.

In the beginning dear young Nell was more fascinated

than thrilled to have such close and scrupulous attentions paid to her body. She blushed with shame when I parted her thighs and started to feast on her delightfully untrammelled young fig. I believed her when she said my five predecessors had been a bit hasty for there was no sign of their traffic up that delicate gorge. And the feeling of shame was with her still when I bent her forward over the headrest of the chaise longue and slipped the full length of Iron Jack into her vagina from behind. It was only when we moved to the other end that she began to warm to our games, when I sat down, with my kneecaps pressing the backs of her thighs, and grasped her by the hips to draw her slowly toward me, parting her knees ever wider over my thighs.

There is no more beautiful sight on earth than the naked *derrière* of a sixteen-year-old girl, viewed from two feet away, backing towards you, and with your own two hands straying over those perfect curves in absolute and unchallengeable liberty. And if at the same time your thighs are forcing hers to part ever wider, so that your One-Eyed Jack down there is gazing up into the centre of bliss, trembling in the heat that's pouring out of her furrow . . . well then, you're on heaven's doorstep.

Young Nell must have been thinking somewhat along similar lines for I became aware of some subtle change in her during that voluptuous approach. Her muscles grew tense and there was a new vibrancy in them; I could feel it pulsating between my hands, wherever I caressed her alluring bottom. And when I let my thighs fall loosely apart, forcing hers so wide that Iron Jack buried his helmet between her fine, firm labia, she gave a weak little gasp and collapsed, engulfing him at once, right to the hilt, in a vagina that was distinctly more alive and juicy than it had been five minutes earlier. I raked my fingernails lightly up and down her spine and had the satisfaction of feeling her whole body flutter with the first intimations of orgasm.

I brought her to it then and there, moving back along the chaise longue until I could lean against the backrest and support the weight of her leaning against me. In this position my hands were free to play sensual havoc with her bubbies, her distended nipples, and her little detonator of pleasure, all puffed up with lust at the first dimple of her crevice. And she just lay there, reaching back and clutching my hips in desperation, digging in her nails for fear I might go away, grasping and trembling, with the sweat sprouting from every pore.

After such a beginning she realized – or perhaps she didn't but her body did – that she could trust her feelings to me with confidence. The wariness left her and she took up each new position with a laugh and spread herself for me with a girlish eagerness for novelty that was truly delightful.

I had brought a *Maison ffrench* bellystool back with me from Paris and left it at Lazy Daisy's for my own use whenever I visited there. Young Nell almost threw herself upon it and wriggled her lithe little bottom in her eagerness to feel me cover her. By then she was almost overdoing her orgasms, reaching for them long before they arose spontaneously and clinging onto them long after they should have subsided to make space for the next. I had known girls do that before and they had always ended in a profound melancholy – of short duration, it is true, but unpleasant enough to cancel out all the pleasure. So I decided to break into the Malakoff routine and apply a little Obispo.

I carried her over to the bed, lay her on her belly, raised her *derrière* with a couple of pillows, and then asked her please to lie *absolutely* still while I poked her. 'It's going to be rather tedious for you, I'm afraid,' I added 'because I'm just going to go on and on and on for about half an hour – and I don't want you to move or talk at all for all that time' . . . and lots more in that vein, telling her how *dull* it was going to be.

Of course, it had the desired effect. She stopped her frenetic grabbing at every little stray thrill that came along and concentrated the whole of her being on the only part of her where anything was happening: the four elastic walls of her vagina. I don't think she had ever before experienced those profound, deep-seated orgasms that begin somewhere near the innermost basin of a girl's love canal and swell in ever-widening circles until they possess her entire body, from the soles of her feet to the ends of her hair to the tips of her fingers; but she began to feel them then.

They were so delicious that I took fire from them, too, with the result that after poking her for only twenty minutes I felt my buttock muscles clenching tighter and tighter at the end of each slow, lascivious thrust and I knew I was on that long, sweet, unstoppable escalator to the stars. When at last I came it was so glorious – for her, too

– that we both passed out for a minute or so.

And then it was over for her – not in a fit of melancholia but in a burst of happiness and a zest to please that helped me to go on loving her for a further hour, until I shot her between wind and water for the second time. She was then the perfect whore to me – bright, merry, eager, attentive, cooperative, minutely responsive. She knew it, too. I could almost hear her making the comparison with her behaviour at that moment and the way she had been with her five earlier lovers that day. She must have felt all along that something was lacking in her earlier performance, but only now could she give it a shape.

And I, for my part, did everything to encourage her, by my admiration for her new-found skill and by my appreciation of all those charms to which she gave me such unstinted access – all of which was quite genuine. Before we returned to the salon she flung her arms around me, kissed me tenderly, and then just hugged herself tight to me for several minutes, shivering all the while.

I enjoyed her favours on many evenings after that and always did the same things with her in the same order. It was like a touchstone to her – or a well at which she could endlessly refresh what became in time one of the finest erotic skills – in the professional sense – at Lazy Daisy's.

I was right about Tooley; the triple insult I had delivered him was too much for his pride to suffer. I won't say that the idea of insulting him had been the last thing on my mind but I'll swear it did not rank very high in my intentions, either; I was far more interested in seeing those three gorgeous girls well launched in their careers. However, the fact that my insult was almost an accidental by-product of my main purpose only made it worse in his eyes. It also made him canny. That evil, scheming little brain of his must have told him that any revenge on his part that involved a person who went in where he and I stuck out would get him nowhere – or would get him from ankle-deep to knee-deep in the old proverbial. But what else was he to do?

We were not on social terms; the circles in which we moved overlapped only at placed like Lazy Daisy's, which I could pretty soon turn into tiger country for him, if I were so inclined. He could snub me and blackguard me all he liked and I should not even notice it. His friends would, though – and wonder why he protested so much. 'No smoke without fire,' they'd tell each other, and pretty soon the gossips would have cooked up a story ten times more wounding than the actual, sordid truth.

The only area left was the one that unites human beings the world over, whatever their circle or rank – money. And the only way he and I could meet in that sort of area was over the card table. They said he played a mean hand at poker, but I didn't mind; I was pretty confident I could play even meaner.

I had just worked all this out for myself when he approached me one night at Lazy Daisy's. I got the feeling that even his arsehole was wreathed in smiles as he walked toward me, hand outstretched. 'I think it's time we buwied the hatchet, young S.,' he said. 'No hard feelin's, eh? Water under the bwidge, what!'

'Bridge?' I replied as I shook his hand. 'Surely you mean poker? You're shit-hot, I hear. Fancy a chance to make it honours-even?'

He was like a man with two pricks; obviously he'd devised some elaborate little playlets in his mind whereby he'd slowly lead me, the unsuspecting victim, to a position where I could not refuse a game. To have me come out with the suggestion, just like that, made it seem that the gods were smiling on the venture already. Only after he'd returned from a careless hour upstairs with Nell did the doubts begin to assail him. Why had I been so swift with the suggestion? What sort of player was I? The only word he could get on that was from Maisie, who told him I'd played a group of the girls at strip-jack poker one day and ended up wearing four overcoats, myself – with five naked girls against me.

By the evening of our match, however – which was to take place at the Young Turks – all his confidence had returned. The entire club knew this was what they call 'a needle game,' so the card room was crowded and everyone was keen to take a hand. To test Tooley's resolve I laid a hundred pounds on the table and suggested he do the same – and that we should play until one of us had won the other's pot. 'After all, we're not out to ruin each other are we, old boy?' I added with a nervous giggle. But he would have none of it and jokingly accused me of running before I even heard the enemy's bugle. Of course, he was rich as Croesus; five thousand a year was his petty-cash allowance.

Our stakes were modest enough for the first hour or so – mostly fivers and tenners for the ante and single sovereigns for the raises. Blazes, tigers, Dutch straights, and round-the-corner hands were allowed, but not at their true mathematical values. I bluffed furiously on several hands and crowed like a child when I happened to win, rubbing their noses in the worthless hands that raked in the shekels. I bluffed in the manner of all rank amateurs – opening the bids limit-up, smiling breezily and much too broadly. By the time we broke for a light supper I was several hundred pounds down and Tooley a thousand or so up.

As so often happens with gambling men, when they make a few winnings they are consumed by lecherous desires. Tooley vanished upstairs for twenty minutes with a very pretty, auburn-haired waiter-girl with a glorious figure. I myself had cast a gladsome eye on her many times already that evening – frequently enough for even Tooley to have noticed. My glances were reciprocated, I may add. She was a bright girl – brighter than most around that table – and understood my purpose exactly. Tooley looked a bit of a scarecrow when he came back down. She gave me a surreptitious wink. I knew then that I had to have her. A girl who could wreak such havoc with an old veteran of the buttock-jig like Tooley was surely one I should get to know better.

I shan't go into every boring detail of the game that followed; only a stroke-by-stroke account of some golfing triumph could be worse. But I will say this: Poker is the queen of all card games because it combines the two most important elements of the human spirit – the ant and the grasshopper. The ant toils steadily away, calculating the odds on every deal and the odds against improving it by drawing one, two, three cards ... or a whole new hand. The grasshopper sits immobile for long periods, watching everyone, waiting for the moment to make that inspired leap to riches and security – the leap that lesser men call folly when it fails and genius when it doesn't.

Toward midnight, when the club would close and our game have to end, I had clawed my way back to a more or less neutral position, thanks to some plodding, unspectacular play; I was perhaps only twenty quid down. I had obviously learned my lesson and no longer tried to bluff on poor hands. Tooley, I could see, was getting desperate; an honours-even game would leave him back where he started, and he would have admitted me into his social circle for nothing!

My quandary was something different. I wanted to beat him without humiliating him, for then he would turn dangerous. I wanted to beat him in a way that would leave him able to laugh, a little ruefully, perhaps, but without bitterness. If I did it on a Royal Flush (the one unbeatable hand, for those who don't know these things), it would be satisfactory to neither of us. I wanted to beat him all on my ownio, while Dame Fortune slumbered. So it had to be on a bluff.

The pretty, auburn-haired girl must have been thinking along similar lines for she now tried to help me. Her job, in between being taken upstairs for a quick knee-trembler every now and then, was to pass out the drinks. But, with the tension mounting as our inconclusive game drew toward its close, the fellows often signalled to her to stop moving around when the play grew high. While moving round she contrived to see what hand Tooley (seventh from the dealer) had; when ordered to be still, she contrived to be at my side (fifth from the dealer), pressing herself tight against me. To be specific: pressing her Venus mound firmly against my elbow. What firm, plump, meaty promise was in that delightful swelling! And what information, too – for she rubbed it from side to side when she would say *no*, and up and down for an encouraging *yes!*

When we came to what would have to be the very last hand, I was – thanks to this intelligence – slightly up – a hundred pounds, perhaps, which also happened to be our limit.

A rather desperate Tooley suggested that for the final round the limit should be raised to the sky. I agreed and the other five did not dare demure. They knew what real game was afoot here and would fold pretty soon. I was dealt two pairs and threw in for a complete new hand of five. I remember it now – the sequence as I read the squeezer marks at the edges, one by one: ace of spades, eight of clubs, six of hearts, four of hearts . . .

I swallowed and held my breath, closing my eyes in silent prayer . . .

Two of spades!

I pressed my hand hard against the green baize to still its trembling. I had an utterly worthless hand and I was going to take him for everything he'd care to bet. I could feel the disappointment radiating from my pretty cheat and realized she was now my one Achilles heel. I turned to her, seeming to notice her for the first time, and said, 'Hallo, little angel, pray sit down at my elbow here. I feel you have brought me luck at last.'

It was a little unusual, but so were the circumstances. A young officer seated her in a chair and the game proceeded. Tooley was grinning with a confidence he had not shown for some time. The first man passed. The second fellow – God bless him! – pushed in his two fivers without saying a word. I pretended not to be looking, being too busy squeezing my cards once again past my incredulous eyes, just as I would if I had drawn a Royal. The rest passed until the bidding came to me.

I swallowed and said, 'I'll open for the limit.' In any previous game it would have meant an opening of a hundred pounds.

I was reminded from several quarters that the bidding had already opened and that there was no limit on this hand.

'Oh . . .' I stared around vaguely as if still in some kind of shock. 'I'll raise it to a hundred, then . . . er, I suppose. That's what I meant, anyway.'

It unsettled Tooley. I had not opened for the limit since supper. I had played an unspectacular game with cool intelligence since supper. Was I changing my spots entirely for this last, desperate round? Possibly, possibly – but could he risk it? Perhaps I really did hold the spectacular hand I was trying so hard to seem nonchalant about. He came in at a hundred where he ought to have raised to five – especially since (as I soon discovered) he had a full hand, fours on aces. I had an edge that I never lost. The betting was between the two of us. He'd raise me. I'd raise him – and I quietly sweated blood. He folded with the jackpot at twelve hundred. The cheers raised the rafters.

I did not show my worthless hand but I noticed the dealer palm it as he gathered in the cards and I knew the story would get about. To end it all with a flash of sportsmanship I gathered up the money and pushed it toward Tooley, dumping it exactly half-way between us. 'Cut you for it,' I suggested. 'If you draw high, you take it. If I draw high, I keep it and I'll take little Lady Luck here home with me for a couple of days and nights. She's surely worth twelve hundred!'

There were protests all around that Honour – the girl's name, as I now learned – was not Tooley's to give. A rule book was trundled out and an obscure rule discovered that a member could, indeed, commandeer the exclusive services of one of the pretty waiter-girls for a night but only if he treated twenty fellow members (drawn by lot) to a free ride at Lazy Daisy's. It was an outrageous condition, of course – designed to prevent any member from trying such a thing. But there it was in black and white.

Poor Tooley! Not only had he lost a couple of months' allowance, but to risk getting it back he'd have to fork out another hundred or so to buy me a dose of lifelong popularity among forty of his fellows! No wonder he fought long and hard with himself before he agreed.

The deck was shuffled and I drew first. There was a gasp when I showed a king. Tooley's trembling hand reached out, grasped the pile about half-way down, lifted, jiggled until one card fell back (that being a superstition of his, it seems) and turned over . . . a queen!

They cheered me to the echo. Honour grabbed my arm

with excitement. I turned over the card Tooley had let fall back.

It was, of course, an ace!

The secretary asked me to sign the visitors' book – something he had pointedly failed to do on my arrival. I wrote:

> *He offered me Honour.*
> *I honoured his offer.*
> *For the next two nights*
> *It's on 'er and off 'er!*

The old ones are best, you must agree.

In the cab on the way back to Headrow, Honour was hugging herself with glee. She confessed that when she saw my first deal of that final hand – two pairs – she felt bleak enough. But when she saw me draw a new hand of five worthless cards, she thought the bottom had dropped out of the world.

'And when did you realize it was exactly the hand I desired?' I asked.

'When you made me sit down by you,' she replied.

'I didn't *make* you do anything,' I said. 'And nor am I going to make you do anything now, Honour. If you don't want to get into bed with me, then . . .'

'I don't have much choice, do I,' she commented bleakly.

'Of course you do – that's what I'm telling you. If you don't want to open your legs to me, we'll spend a couple

of happy days at the races, or go walking up in the Dales
– whatever you like. And then I'll take you back.'

She received this in stunned silence. At length she
asked, 'And what about you – what'll you do?'

'Talk with you. Enjoy your company. I'm more interested
in *you*, I think, than in that secret smile between your
thighs.'

'Talk about what?' she asked.

'Your life. Life at the Young Turks, life away from
there. Your thoughts. Your hopes. I wanted to know these
things from the moment I saw you there tonight.'

It was a novel proposition to her and, despite the
lateness of the hour, she lingered long in her bath. The
water was tepid by the time I nipped in for a quick all-over.
When I came back to the bedroom she was in one of
Kitten's nighties, brushing out her lovely long auburn
hair, which she had worn in two coiled plaits until then.
She had obviously decided to test me. A man who risked
over a thousand quid on a worthless hand – and then risked
it again just to spend two nights with her – and then told
her she was free not to grant him her Favour . . . such a man
was so far outside her ken as to be worth investigating.

'Can we sleep in the same bed – with a big pillow
between us or something?' she asked. 'So's we can talk.'

Without a word I took a huge feather bolster out of the
cupboard and laid it down the midline of my bed. 'Madame!'
I said as I turned down the sheets on her side before
vaulting over the bed to my own.

'Penny for your thoughts,' She prompted as soon as I
quenched the lamp. We lay on our backs, unable to see

each other, staring at the random patterns cast on the ceiling by the street light outside.

'I was just thinking – watching you at the Young Turks this evening, one girl among all those officers. You seemed so cheerful and outgoing – yet you must have known that at any minute one of them might tap you on the arm and take you upstairs. And I couldn't imagine what you must be thinking. I couldn't imagine myself as a woman in that situation – or being a manservant, say, in some club of Amazon officers – wandering among a dozen comely young warrior maidens, knowing that most of them were going to want me to roger them that evening.'

She laughed. 'That's the point, though – a man couldn't possibly do it!'

'That makes you feel proud, does it? You feel superior?'

After hesitation she said, 'Yes.'

'D'you see them as people – all those officers – or just so many rampant cocks, waiting to have the starch taken out of them?'

'They don't see me as a woman,' she replied defensively. 'I'm just a warm, wet hole with hair round it to them. Most of them, anyway. There are one or two ...' Her voice trailed off.

'Yes?'

'But once your legs are open, they're *all* the same.'

'Do they give you any pleasure – in the way that you pleasure them?'

There was an even longer pause before she replied this time. 'They're all too hasty for anything like that.'

'I met a woman in Paris earlier this year, the madame

of a very high-class house of pleasure, and she told me she never went to the opera or a big military parade or anywhere where she'd see men dressed in all their glory without also seeing them in her mind's eye – seeing them as she knew them best. She'd meet a grand general with his plumed hat and spurs and medals, but in her mind's eye, there he was, trousers round his ankles – short, fat, bandy legs, covered in hair, and a stiff prick wagging at her like an unsteady yardarm, all veined and red and begging.'

Honour burst into laughter on the other side of the bolster.

'You recognize the feeling?' I prompted.

Reluctantly she admitted it was so; when any of the officers came into a room she always had a picture of him with his flies open and his belly ruffian thrusting up out of his linen, staring at her like a one-eyed Cyclops. 'Don't you men get the same thoughts about all the girls when you go to Lazy Daisy's?' she asked.

I had to agree with her. 'But the difference is,' I went on, 'that for me to imagine a frilly opening in a girl's drawers and the glimpses it affords my mind's eye of her vertical smile is almost too pleasant to bear. I don't think the same is true of you, though.'

'What do you think of me?' she asked. 'Have you pictures in your mind of *my* vertical smile, as you call it?'

'No,' I said – and it was true.

'Why not?' she whispered.

'I don't know,' I replied – and I didn't know, either. I didn't even understand where these words were coming from; I spoke them out of a kind of compulsion. 'I suppose it's because I don't want to *poke* you, or *roger* you, or *fuck* you – or anything like that. I don't want to lay you on your back and part your thighs and gaze my fill of your secret charms. I don't want to kiss you there, or lick you there, or explore you with my tongue. I don't want to *have* you in this position and that position . . . I don't want any of these things I've done with dozens of other girls. I just want this moment, when you're lying there and I'm lying here . . . I want it to flow – magically – into another moment where we're fused together. D'you think that's absurd. D'you think two people can be in love for just two nights?'

During this speech she began to squirm, trying to be surreptitious about it. I guessed she was taking off Kitten's nightie so I quickly shed my own pyjamas.

She did not answer.

'Eh?' I prompted.

Still I got no reply.

Gingerly I reached my hand over the bolster but could not feel her there at all. Then the bolster wriggled and a moment later her hot young body writhed out from underneath it, straight into my arms – and her passionate kisses were on my lips and her big, soft bubbies were against my chest, and her taut little belly was pressed against mine, and, without any conscious move on my part, Iron Jack was drowning in bliss in the hot, wet heart of her exquisite vagina.

Honour unsettled me. I believe I did fall in love with her for just two nights, but, as with all my love affairs, I took much longer to get over it. I *knew* the real trouble, of course

232

– I was missing Kitten and didn't want to admit it. It was absurd. I *knew* we could never live together in a faithful, monogamous affiliation – neither she nor I were fitted for it by temperament. Yet I knew we should be miserable apart. I used to stand at my window, which faced east, and crane my head out, looking south – toward Paris – and think of all the hundreds of miles that separated us . . . and of all the good reasons for returning to that queen of cities, especially now that I had a windfall of twelve-hundred quid to play with . . . and of all the good reasons for resisting those sirens in my mind.

Every now and then I'd see a girl who'd remind me of Kitten in one way or another and I'd have a little daydream in which I ran downstairs and opened the door and there she was – all radiant with beauty and just dying to rush upstairs to bed with me. And then came the day, about three months after we had said goodbye, when I saw one who was *so* like her – and who was actually walking up my little alley – that I had to run down and accost her, no matter who she might be.

I opened the door – *and there she was!* It truly was my own beloved Kitten, all the way from Paris!

She laughed at my consternation. 'Have you been waiting at that window all these weeks, Smiler?'

'Weeks?' I questioned. 'It's been months – and the answer is yes . . . practically.'

Her grin broadened. 'Then you must be as desperate for a poke as I am, eh!'

We raced to the bedroom – where all at once she became solemn. 'Smiler, dear,' she said, running a finger up and down my shirt-front, 'I want you to help me round off this year of my life. You realize it's almost a year since you took my virginity that afternoon at Lazy Daisy's?'

I nodded. 'What a lot has happened since then!'

'A lot in one way – not enough in another. But do you remember that afternoon?'

'Vividly.'

'Do you really, Smiler? You're not just saying that?'

'Why? Is it very important to you?'

'Very. I'd like to do it again. Exactly as we did it then. I want to start again. I really had no idea what was happening . . .'

'I didn't, either – not much. My cherry was broken by dear Maisie on the previous Sunday. I came back for more lessons on Monday, Tuesday, Wednesday, and Thursday. And on Friday – as a reward for faithful attendance, I suppose – I was ushered into a room where you were waiting.'

'. . . waiting to let a man get inside me for the first time in my life.'

I took her in my arms and kissed her – so happy I was almost in tears.

'We can't re-create that scene now, darling,' I murmured.

She shook her head. 'I agree. But that's not what I want, anyway. I want to remember it – not re-create it. Remember it. And this time I want to add *your* memories, too. It sounds ghastly, I know – and I'd never dream of asking anyone else such a favour. But *you* could do it. In fact, you're the *only* man I know who could.'

I eyed her askance. 'You mean do what we did that day

– but also tell you what I remember thinking while we did it?'

She nodded and blinked her eyes, which sparkled so beautifully in anticipation of my saying yes that I hadn't the heart to say no.

'Actually,' she said, 'you even blurted out how inexperienced you were. You said, 'This time last week I'd hardly even kissed a girl. So I hope you don't expect to find me a two-million-horsepower, gas-fired Casanova today!' D'you remember that?'

I did, though I'd forgotten it until then. It began to bring the rest of it back, too, in that same fine detail. 'And I felt so weak at the knees I had to sit on the bed. And you sat beside me and tried to kiss me on the cheek. But you were nervous, too, and made a hash of it, so you stood up and turned away from me so I couldn't see your blushes.'

She did each of these things as soon as I mentioned them, as if I were calling out stage directions. Then, when her back was turned, I whipped off my shirt and went and stood behind her. 'Yes!' she said. 'Your bare arms about me – that's right. And I was almost in tears. I said I didn't know anything.' She turned and put her arms around me and kissed me.

'That's not what you did last year,' I warned her.

'I know. But I've made the rules so I can break them. I want to tell you how you saved my life. No – *gave* me a life . . .'

'Gave you The Life!'

'Listen! You told me I was one of the most beautiful

235

girls you'd ever met. You said it was a privilege just to *talk* with me. You said if it was a horrid ordeal for me, we could just lie side by side and talk – and you wouldn't peach on me.'

I laughed. 'You say it in a soft, sentimental tone now, Kitten, but you were quite ratty at the time. "Don't I appeal to you in that way?" you asked.'

It was the truth but she was not to be shaken out of her sentimental mood. 'All I remember is turning round and seeing your naked torso and thinking you were the most stunningly beautiful creature I'd ever seen.'

She drew away from me and lifted her hand to touch my arms and chest – just as on that day. 'I still do,' she murmured.

'There's more of me,' I told her, and she smiled, remembering that those were my words then, too.

'But I took my own blouse off next?' She made a question of it.

I nodded.

When she touched her bottommost button an extraordinary thing happened to me. My *body* began to remember – that is, my body's memories took over from those of my mind. I would never have believed that a simple act – like watching her undo the bottom button of her blouse – could *still* make my knees tremble and put all my muscles in a flutter, as it had done on that magical afternoon a year ago. But it did. I felt the hollow craving in my belly that only the heat and sweetness of a girl can satisfy. She, too, had the same hunger on her by now.

'That first glimpse of your corset,' I whispered as she

continued to slip her buttons free. 'White satin. Then your fine, untouched skin rippling over your ribs in the dip at the side. Your sweet little stays – and how superfluous they were! And still are . . .'

'Never mind *now*!' she gasped. 'Just keep telling me about *then*.'

'O-o-h . . . that first peep at your pale bosoms! So voluptuous, so round, as they shimmered through that voile or whatever it was on the top of your corset. And how they shivered with the pounding of your heart!'

'All I remember is the adoration in your eyes, Smiler. You made me feel like a princess.'

'That was more lust than adoration, Kitten. The smell off your skin was driving me insane – musk and cinnamon . . .' I lifted her arms over her head – which raised her bubbies out of her corset. 'And your breasts are as perfect now as they were then – two superb miracles – to be as large as they are and as soft as they are and yet to remain so firm and provocative! And then the spicy reek that rose from your armpits, all around me, assailing my nostrils . . . oh, Kitten!'

She had her eyes closed by now, her face raised toward the ceiling, a dreamy smile on her lips. She had remembered what I did next. She was waiting for me to start doing it again.

I raised my hands to her elbows, level with the crown of her head, and started to run my fingernails down, down, slowly down over the taut, freckled skin of her arms, down into the musky red shrubbery of her armpits. That day she had been ticklish, today she was passionate and wanton.

We kissed – a long, lingering, voluptuous kiss. My fingernails strayed on down the sides of her breasts and quivered gently on the skin beside her nipples – which now, as then, were swollen and sultry.

When I took them between my fingers and squeezed them softly, she let out a gasp and flung her arms around my neck. She pressed her mouth to mine and writhed her head so violently that her fair fell about my face. Then, when she could bear my tormenting of her nipples no longer, she grasped my hands and pressed them against the delicious curves where the small of her back swelled out to form the ample moons of her *derrière*. I ran fervent hands over those exciting swellings, trying to imagine that the lips which smiled down there in secret, in her dark, feverish crevice, had never before been parted by the horny intruder . . .

It almost worked; I almost forgot the thousand and more gristly ruffians who, since that day, had gone barging up that sweet canyon and shot their wads of joy into its blind end; and so, I think, did she. She certainly behaved as if she had never before been so defencelessly unclothed, so close to a man – and that man in such a dangerously randy shape. Her breath came in gulps and shivers and she stared at me like a mouse hypnotized by a snake.

I watched in fascination as I lay back on the bed and let her do what she had done that day, too: open my flies and discover Iron Jack in all his rampant, febrile glory.

She giggled nervously as she knelt between my parted and still trousered thighs. When she leaned forward to start popping my fly buttons, her bubbies swung over me like ripe melons. 'Did I undo them or you?' she whispered. 'Wasn't I afraid to hurt it?'

I chuckled. 'You were. But I told you to pretend you were unwrapping a present – something warm and cuddly, just for you!'

'Oh, yes!' she murmured, and her hands closed gently round the top button again. Then, like an earnest little schoolgirl attempting some difficult variation of cat's-cradle for the first time – frowning, licking her lips abstractedly . . . her fingers plucked at my buttons until *abracadabra*, there he was: Iron Jack, free at last in the warm summer air, shivering nonetheless – but not with cold! – bloated with his craving and begging for her compassion.

A year ago she had asked if she might touch him; today she wanted to rearrange history. She grasped him gently and tucked him back in my underpants, hiding his knob under its belt so that just his pale, swollen underbelly showed through the parting of the garment. '*That's* what I ought to have seen first!' she said. 'The way he bursts out like a jack-in-the-box . . . I saw too much all at once. I didn't know what to do first.'

'What would you have done,' I asked, 'if this much was all you could see?'

She grinned her gamine grin. 'I'd have done this . . .' And she began to rake her fingernails gently back and forth across the shaft of him, giving his spermtube the extraordinary delusion that he was already shooting wild gobbets of milt. 'And this . . .' She lowered her head to my form and kissed and licked him, the full length of his shaft.

I swallowed hard and tried to think of cold baths. 'You'd have seen quite an eruption if you had,' I gasped.

She hauled the rest of Iron Jack back out into the blissful air and grasped him firmly in both hands, like a cricketer holding a bat. 'Oh!' she exclaimed in affectionate anger. 'These *things*! These *things* you men have! Will they ever give us peace?'

'That's not what you said next,' I told her.

'I know.' She pulled an embarrassed face. 'I said, 'D'you want to see my tra-la-la?' God, what a naïve question!'

'And I couldn't answer. I was too choked with . . . I feared I'd die of sheer pleasure. And you just lay down on your back, remember?'

'Like this.'

'And you let your thighs fall loosely apart . . .'

'. . . while you scuttled down the bed like a squirrel – and plunged your head underneath my petticoat, between my knees . . .'

'Like this!' I cried, being under her petticoat already by then.

'Yes. Yes!' Her voice was shivering. 'What did you think, then, Smiler? I tried to roll my petticoat back to see your face but you stopped me. What were you thinking then?'

'I felt as if I had poked my head inside the den of some dangerous female . . . animal or something – a wildcat, a civet, a vixen. I feel it again now, if you want to know – just as strongly as I did then. Oh, Kitten! This perfume that pours out of your "tra-la-la" is so . . . aromatic . . . so full of zest . . . and so erotically overpowering, all in the same moment, it stupefied my mind and it made my body a slave to you for life. There now! That's the truth – the real truth about that day. So now you know.'

She drew her petticoat up around her waist, so brusquely she almost tore it. 'No more!' she pleaded. 'I remember it. I remember it all.' She reached down and grasped Iron Jack in her hand and then leaned back again, tugging him toward her wide-open crevice. 'Just go in now and fill me, *stuff* me till I burst!'

It was probably the briefest engagement we ever enjoyed, and yet it is one I shall never forget. The moment Iron Jack touched the blind end of her love canal, she gave a mighty gasp and every muscle in her went absolutely rigid. Then, shivering and panting, she clawed at my body and clutched me tight against her, throwing her legs around my waist. The sweat was starting from every pore and she quivered like a filly at her first covering. And, as on that earlier occasion – also never-to-be-forgotten – I started squirt-squirt-squirting inside her, flushing her belly through with hot gouts of ecstasy.

It was late that evening and we were still lying in bed, having feasted on each other's bodies to the point of exhaustion. She had seen the picture of herself and laughed at the title I had given it: *Nude Rising* – especially when she heard the story behind it. Naturally I still made no mention of Wharton and her father.

'So tell me – what's wrong with the *Maison ffrench*?' I asked.

'Absolutely nothing,' she replied. 'It was heaven – the nearest to paradise that a girl could possibly get. And yet that is what is wrong with it – for me, anyway. I hope there isn't a life after death – and I certainly hope there's no heaven – because, after three months at a place like the *Maison ffrench*, you suddenly realize heaven is impossible. I mean you realize it would slowly-slowly, bit by bit, turn into hell. So I left before that could happen.'

'And the other two?' I asked in some alarm, fearing that my reputation with Madame ffrench would be in shreds.

'Oh, Calamity's absolutely in her element!' she replied. 'Dido, too, in her way. Dido hasn't got a lot of imagination. She doesn't realize how different things might be.'

'I still don't understand, though,' I ventured, relieved to hear that she was the only deserter.

'The spring floods were over,' she said, 'and some of us had to go. I asked Madame if I could be one of them. She was a little surprised, but I think she understood. In a way it was her fault.'

'How so?'

'She got to reminiscing one evening about her life as a harlot – that's what she calls a whore, you know. Because her name, Charlotte, encloses the word harlot – so she says she was destined to it from birth. Also because it's biblical. D'you know her father was a bishop!'

I almost blurted out what I had since learned about her own father but thought it best to let sleeping dogs lie. 'What did she tell you about the good old days?' I asked.

'Well, they were bad old days, really – except she didn't make them sound like it. She worked in a brothel in

Hamburg when she was about my age, where the girls had to do over a hundred men *each* – every day! Can you imagine it! And there are girls who sit in open windows there, chatting with the men going by. And girls just standing on the streets, of course . . .'

'And you were protected from all that. She was telling you how lucky you were.'

After a pause she said, 'I know it sounds mad, but it made me feel that real life was going on *out there*, while we were just . . . I don't know. In limbo.'

'In paradise!'

'Yes! You may laugh but I meant that. It *was* paradise. We lived in the lap of luxury . . .'

'Which is only fair,' I pointed out, 'since your laps are the most luxurious in . . .'

'Are you going to let me be serious – or d'you just want to lie there making childish jokes?'

'Sorry!'

'We lived in utter luxury, sleeping in silk sheets, all the hot baths we liked – friseurs and manicurists at our beck and call – our own gymnasium – food to put Escoffier to shame. And we were the centre of attraction for all the richest, most powerful, most important, most magnetic, most interesting men in France – in Europe, really. I've had kings, princes, prime ministers, archbishops, field marshalls – you wouldn't believe it, Smiler! All those men before whom millions tremble, I've had them kneel before me, trembling to get in! Some of them quite handsome, too.'

'It must have become an awful bore,' I suggested.

'I warned you!' she replied. 'Actually, it didn't. I

enjoyed most of them as much as they enjoyed me – one or two a day, anyway.'

Her voice trailed off and she relapsed into silence.

'What then?' I prompted.

'I was just thinking – it wasn't really what Madame ffrench said, it was Calamity – d'you remember that time? When she pointed out we'd have to fuck fifteen thousand men . . .'

'I don't like that word,' I complained.

'Nor do I. That's why it perfectly fits what I'm trying to say. I only wish you were trying to listen.'

'Sorry – I am! Go on.'

'To fuck fifteen *thousand* men between now and nineteen-oh-eight! This wonderful, unchanging paradise was going to go on and on, day after day, for the next fifteen thousand men. Whenever I'd get bored enough to scream, they'd change the city around me. Next year I'd sleep in *Roman* silken sheets, have a Roman friseur, fuck Roman generals and dukes – until I screamed again. And then I'd get Viennese silken sheets and fuck Viennese archdukes and Ottoman sultans . . . and on and on and on. Four a day for the next fifteen thousand men. Fifteen thousand stiff cocks. Fifteen thousand little stickies left behind inside me. And meanwhile the whole of life would have passed me by.'

'You'd be rich,' I pointed out.

'And I'd have forgotten what to do with it. I'd wait to be told. Go to sleep, pretty miss. Wake up, pretty miss. Dine, pretty miss. Undress, pretty miss. On your back and open your thighs, pretty miss. After ten years of that I'd have to hire a maid just to tell me when to breathe. Don't you see what I mean?'

I had to allow that I did. 'So what next?' I asked. 'Do I fit into your plans, somewhere?'

'*Somewhere*?' she echoed scornfully. 'You're at the centre of them, Smiler! We're going off around the world, you and I – each in our own chosen profession. I could be dropped off in any city in the world, penniless and without food and lodging. And by evening I'd have half a dozen stickies inside my tummy and a purse filled with gold. And it's the same with you – a deck of cards is all you need. So why are we wasting our time in marble imitations of paradise or this northern backwater? Everything out there is waiting for us – the *real* earthly paradise.'

I thought it over, long and hard – for several seconds, in fact – and I had to admit it stirred my blood more than somewhat. 'The great advantage of our *earthy* paradise . . . you did say 'earthy,' didn't you?'

She pinched me and said, with jovial menace, 'Go on.'

'It's chief advantage is that it has so many entrances – hundreds of thousands of them – and they all have hair round them.'

She laughed. 'If you're warning me that you could never be faithful, you may save your breath, Smiler. If I know nothing else about you, I at least know that! So – is it on? I'm going anyway, but it'd be much more fun if you were with me.'

I replied that we could start any time she liked. I wondered about marriage – just to make the travelling more convenient, but thought it best to leave that until later. It was lucky I did, too.

Her thoughts must have been running down the same track for, after a silence, she said, 'I'll tell you exactly what was so unsatisfactory about living and working in a place like the *Maison ffrench*. It'd be like sixty years of married life concentrated into ten – being pampered, petted, fucked, and enriched – all in a gilded cage. And what sort of life is *that* for a thoroughly modern, twentieth-century girl!'

More Erotic Fiction from Headline:

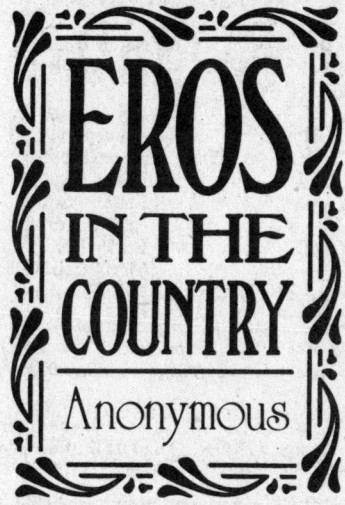

EROS IN THE COUNTRY

Anonymous

Being the saucy adventures of sweet, virginal Sophie,
her lusty brother Frank and young Andrew, the village
lad with a taste for pleasure – a youthful trio who
engage in some not-so-innocent bedplay.

Their enthusiastic experiments come to an abrupt halt
when they are discovered in flagrante and sent from
home in disgrace. And so begins an erotic odyssey
of sensual discovery to titillate even the most
jaded imagination . . .

Her tender flesh prey to lascivious lechers of both high
and low estate, Sophie seeks refuge in the arms of the
students of Cambridge, ever keen to enlarge on their
worldly knowledge. Meanwhile Andrew is bound by the
silken lash of desire, voluptuous ladies provoking him
to ever more unbearable heights of ecstasy.

EROS IN THE COUNTRY – where every excess of
lust and desire is encountered, experienced
and surpassed . . .

FICTION/EROTICA   0 7472 3145 1

A selection of Erotica from Headline